Waimea I Ka La'i
Photo Credit: Sarah Anderson

# Waimea I Ka La'i

RK LINDSEY, JR.

THE REGENCY PUBLISHERS

Copyright © 2022 RK Lindsey, Jr.

All rights reserved. No part of this book may be reproduced in any form or by any electronic or mechanical means, including information storage and retrieval systems, without permission in writing from the author and publisher, except by reviewers, who may quote brief passages in a review.

ISBN:   978-1-960113-24-5   (Paperback Edition)
ISBN:   978-1-960113-25-2   (Hardcover Edition)
ISBN:   978-1-960113-23-8   (E-book Edition)

Some characters and events in this book are fictitious and products of the author's imagination. Any similarity to real persons, living or dead, is coincidental and not intended by the author.

**Book Ordering Information**

**The Regency Publishers, US**
521 5th Ave 17th floor NY, NY10175

Phone Number: (315)537-3088 ext 1007
Email: info@theregencypublishers.com
www.theregencypublishers.com

Printed in the United States of America

Dedicated to my favorite cousin,
"Reginald Earl Lindsey, his beautiful wife,
Linda and family"

"WELCOME TO **WAMEA I KA LA'I**. COME IN, TAKE A CHAIR, SIT, STAY FOR A WHILE. HERE'S A CUP OF OUR BEST COWBOY COFFEE WITH A BISCUIT. LET'S 'TALK STORY'.....

Hawaiian Islands

"The loveliest fleet of islands that lies anchored in any ocean."

-Mark Twain=<u>Letters from The Sandwich Islands</u>, 1866

<u>Hawaiian Archipelago</u>

| | |
|---|---|
| Kure Atoll | 36.0 million years |
| Midway Atoll | 28.0 million years |
| Necker | 11.3 million years |
| Nihoa | 7.5 million years |
| Niihau | 6.0 million years |
| Kauai | 5.8 million years |
| Oahu | 3.4 million years |
| Molokai | 1.9 million years |
| Lanai | 1.3 million years |
| Maui | 1.3 million years |
| Kahoolawe | 1.0 million years |
| Hawaii | 500,000 years |
| Loihi | In Progress |

<u>Planet Earth</u>          4.6 billion years

"We do not inherit the earth from our ancestors, we borrow it from our children."

<u>Native American saying</u>

.....AND WHEN YOU LEAVE, TAKE SOME OF OUR ALOHA AND **WAIMEA I KA LA'I** HOME WITH YOU."

# 1

We all have our happy places to escape to:
-<u>to meditate, reflect on life, escape</u> the noise and chitter-<u>chatter of the world</u>. My feet usually land on the same place every time. I like who I am. I don't need to change anything although the industrial guru I've been forced to see, says, I should. Why? Because the world has changed, and I must change with it. I tell him, what he considers 'common sense' is 'nonsense,' that the clock on the wall must be reset. Turned back. The world has and is going in the wrong direction. It's swung too far left. It needs to swing back to center. He gives me a dumb look. I tell him he needs therapy, not me and walk out the door, never to return to hear more of his nonsense. I'm in a comfort zone that does not need fiddling. A space that helps me run from the noise, chatter and drama of the world. Recently, I sought refuge in it to muse over how best to resolve a human relations issue. You see, I fired a worker with an attitude issue. I intentionally 'forgot' to consult our HR Director. The employee I let go is a millennial, who didn't like my 'command and control' management approach. So, I showed her the door, wished her well, blew her a kiss and made darn sure the door didn't touch her butt on the way out. Now HR is afraid, we will be facing a lawsuit. Ce sara sara.

-<u>to deal with a defiant family member</u>. I want to choke his neck. Mama wants me to use word gymnastics, my 'quiet voice,' for the umpteenth time. To speak softly and clearly. When you're dealing with stupid, you're dealing with stupid! In my bird brain, one must 'fight fire with fire.' To be consistent, one must fight 'stupid with stupid.' What can you do? I give up.

   -to just have space and time, to be still, to be by myself. Buddha had his Bodhi tree under whose canopy he sat and in time attained, Enlightenment. Jesus, the Garden of Gethsemane, where he went to reboot his troubled soul, before his treacherous journey to Golgotha only to be falsely accused by the Sanhedrin, insulted by Caesar, mocked by an angry mob, nailed to a cross, take a spear to the side, forced to wear a crown of thorns then dying between two thieves for the 'sins of the world.' The Psalmist, a grass carpet on which he meandered barefoot beside a bubbling stream through the 'Valley of the Shadow of Death.' Henry David Thoreau, his lanai overlooking Walden Pond and the woods surrounding it, where he watched the sun rise in the morning and disappear at dusk. Thoreau went to the woods because he "... wished to live deliberately, to front only the essential facts of life and see if I could not learn what it had to teach and not, when I came to die, discover that I had not lived." Grandpa Lindsey, sitting in his big wood rocker on the front porch of the house he built for our grandma on Waimea's dry side. The chair, where he spent the 'winter' of his years, waving at every car passing by on Mamalahoa Highway. The chair from which he held court. Often, an old friend would pull over to 'chew the fat' with him. They would chat and laugh the hours away. Recalling old times at Makahalau or Minukeole or some other *wahi pana* (storied place) on Parker Ranch. When he got tired of flapping his gums or weary of his guest, he'd turn off his cumbersome hearing aid powered by two big batteries that looked like miniature sticks of dynamite. I'm sure, there were many moments while rocking, tons of memories flashed through his mind about his half a century working cattle for the Parker's. Moments when he wished he was on his horse again. Driving, cutting, roping, and branding cattle. Mending fences. Taking out wild dogs. Capturing wild bullocks on the slopes of Mauna Kea. Our Tutu-man (Grandpa) was no rhinestone cowboy. Our dad, the spacious lawn fronting our Pu'ukapu house or the cornfield out back, where he'd lay down to rest, after work, crushing rock at the quarry with his three dogs, Monty, Muffy and Skippy, three mutts fighting for his sole affection. Monty always won. He was the fairest of the trio.

Our mom, the kitchen table where she would sip tea from the same old teacup, munch on a saloon pilot cracker, read her tattered Bible or the latest Reader's Digest and from time to time, peek out the window to see what progress we were making with our chores. She had this phobia, you see, about hands. 'Idle hands were the devil's work.' So, she kept me and my brother, known as Benjamin in his formative years, Ben Duke after he came out of the Marine Corps, busy. She kept our hands, very, very busy. Who she inherited that neurosis from, we will never know.

I have several special places where I go to to get away from the insanity, malarkey and messiness of my world. Today, it's the summit of Pu'u Hoku'ula. Hoku'ula Hill. Two of our grandsons want to meet to 'talk story.' To have a 'heart to heart' conversation. I agreed reluctantly, with this proviso. At a place and time of my choosing.

"Talk Story' about what, Elliot?" I ask.

"As I said in my text, Papa. Kui and I want to talk with you about you."

"Me! That's the last thing I want to talk about, Elliot. You need to know, I'm a recovering narcissist. I'm tired of going to these Narcissist Anonymous meetings every Thursday night. Tired of standing up and saying, 'Hi Bud!' You're not helping Me, get away from Me!" Next thing I know, Kui is tweeting me. Pouring on the pressure.

How do you say, 'No' to two precious grandsons. I cave in. So here we sit atop Hoku'ula (a *wahi pana*) on a glorious, 'see forever' Waimea morning. On high, sacred, special ground looking over our beautiful town. *Waimea i ka La' i*. (Waimea in the calm). All of us sitting comfortably in lightweight portable beach chairs. I say to them before we launch into their 'cross examination.' Let's just put ourselves on mute for a moment. Be still for a few minutes and absorb, soak in, breath in, enjoy, delight in all this beauty, wrapped around us.

The lime green hills. The Angus and Hereford cattle in 'stroll' mode, foraging happily and filling their bellies with soft grass. The horses galloping up and down the slopes of Pauahi, playing their version of 'chase master.' Kicking up their hooves as they frolic about. There's a blanket of thick, fresh snow shimmering in the morning sun on two of our *mauna* (mountains). Snow left behind by a storm that passed through during the night. The summits of Mauna Kea & Mauna Loa are dressed, adorned in neon white. We suck in the clean, fresh, chilly air and allow the rising sun's rays to take the edge off the morning chill. Rays that have traveled ninety-three million miles to warm our faces, spirits and hearts. We watch a *kolea* (golden plover) land at its favorite spot. A few seconds later, its 'honey' shows up and the pair disappear into a thick bed of rat tail grass. Something's up. Clearly, they don't want us to see what they are up to with our wandering eyes and curious minds. A *pueo* (owl) glides to and fro several hundred feet below us. Taunting, teasing us. Adjusting its flaps, as it cruises and bounces about on a light thermal. On the hunt for its morning meal. Suddenly it plunges downward, talons extended but comes up empty. It circles round and round, finally surrenders and flies way. It's target, probably a field mouse, gets to live another day. The *pueo* is my family's land *aumakua* (guardian) on my mama's side of our DNA chart.

I finally hit the mute button to return us to our purpose for being on Hoku'ula's summit.

"Isn't this a beautiful sight, Elliot, Kui?"

"It sure is, Papa."

"Waimea I Ka La'i. We are sure lucky to live here in this beautiful place."

"We sure are," is the instant feedback I get from grandsons 3 and 4. And, with it comes a question. "Who made all this possible, Papa?"

I'm quiet for a minute. Finally, I say, "*Akua*. God did. God made all this for us to enjoy."

"You don't believe there was a 'Big Bang, Papa.'"

"I'm familiar with 'The Big Bang' and it's 'Goldilocks Conditions.' No, I'll stick with Genesis 1:1. So guys, tell me, why are we here?"

Kui chimes in. "Papa, as Elliot explained in his text to you, we are doing an oral history project. We're interviewing *kupuna* (elders) about their memories."

"Memories of..."

"Memories of Waimea. About growing up here. About your life. About whatever you want to talk about. But first, we want to hear a story. And, following that, to talk about you, Papa. We have some questions about you that only you can answer. We want to document your answers, your memories. You are a respected 'thought leader.'"

"Whoa, Kui. We need to stop there. My head is starting to expand. It's extra-large already. 'Please, enough of the patronizing.' I reiterate that I'm doing them, a favor. 'Remember, guys I really don't want to talk about myself. I'm doing this for you. Not me. You really do want to hear one of my dull, boring stories at 9 in the morning? Are you serious? Aren't you too old for fairy tales, magic wands, Prince Charming, Sleeping Beauty, Cinderella, pixie dust, Jolly Ole St. Nicky Nicky stuff?'"

"Papa, we want to hear a tale. And, no, we are not too old to hear your stories. Tell us the version of your Creation Story that you told us on my tenth birthday for the very first time."

"Which one? My memory is not what it used to be, Elliot. I told you a bunch of stories. Help me."

"The creation of The Hawaiian Archipelago. Your version."

"Aren't you tired of that story, Elliot?"

"No! Absolutely not."

"How about you, Kui?"

"*A'ole* (no), Papa. I love it."

"Well, okay. Let's see. Give me a minute to clear my throat and gather my thoughts. How old are you now, Elliot?"

"Eighteen"

"And you Kui?"

"I just turned eighteen, Papa. Remember, my party was two days ago. You toasted me with three 'banzais' and pissed my mom off when you gave me my own glass of champagne."

"Gees, *e kala mai* (sorry), my mind is in the 'twilight zone.' It's out there on the range. I'm sorry, Kui. I think I'm trying to suppress, erase that part of the day from memory. Vaguely. you're nineteen?"

"Nineteen minus one."

"Eighteen. I can bring you with me to Waimea Grill now."

"Ah. Ah."

"Why not?"

"Tutu, won't allow it."

"Heck, she doesn't have to know."

"She'll find out somehow."

"Nah, she won't."

"She found out about you driving when you were not supposed to be driving."

"What are you talking about?"

"She was in LA at a teacher's conference. One evening after dinner she and three colleagues went to watch a Laker's game at the Colosseum. Somebody saw you driving into town. You weren't supposed to be driving. Called her and told on you. And she called you. Remember that?"

"Was Colby Bryant still playing for the Laker's?"

"I don't think so. I think he was retired already. Papa, you are trying to distract me. Remember, she called you? And remember what you told her?"

"I, in fact do. I said, 'Why, badah you.' I'm still trying to figure out who saw me. And, ratted on me. I was tired of eating sandwiches. I wanted to eat a nice steak dusted with rock salt and black pepper, frosted with ketchup. With a big bowl of white rice covered with mayo and mac salad on the side. A real *paniolo* (cowboy) meal. So, yes, I drove into town. Just three miles. No big deal. On Sunday evening, traffic is always light. The worst that could have happened is, I would have run into a utility pole or a eucalyptus tree. Had my dinner. Talked with Dan over a cold beer. I was having a great time. Until she rudely interrupted us."

"Mr. Pereira, the owner?"

"Yep. He overheard me on the phone."

"Talking with Tutu."

"Yes. He knew I was 'busted.' I told him I just could not believe somebody tattled on me. Whoever it was who saw me, phoned Tutu."

"Who was at a basketball game 2400 miles away. Papa, you were, one driving when you were not supposed to be driving. And two, eating what your doctor said you were not supposed to be eating. You just had a hemorrhagic stroke like a month before. Plus, drinking a beer. Oh my gosh!"

"Guys, look at it this way. Life is a risk. You only live once. Life is short. You must live in the present. The past is *pau* (done). The future. Who knows what's around the bend? I was enjoying the present moment. Okay. You gotta cut me some slack."

"Tutu, called you. Then what?"

"It was not, a breathy, sexy, pleasant voice, 'How are you, honey. Oh, I miss you. I wish you were here with me. Do you miss me?' It was, the voice of a Drill Sargent, 'Are you driving? Why are you driving? You know you are not supposed to be driving!" Needless to say. It was a very short call. After we hung up. I cussed my cell phone. I was ANGRY. My plan to have a nice, quiet, relaxing meal was disrupted by a phone call from the LA Mausoleum. My adrenaline is pumping hard. My steak is sitting in front of me. I grab the ketchup bottle. It's a new bottle. Never been opened. With my good hand, I open the white plastic cap, pull the silver foil off the spout. And dump half the bottle of red stuff on my rib-eye steak. Spread it out over my rib-eye like I was frosting a cake. I ate every grain of rice and chewed the meat off the rig eye with gusto. I ate every mac noodle. Even had apple pie ala mode. Plus, I drank two more beers."

"You did not?"

"Oh hell, yes. And, had a glass of red wine. Compliments of wise ass Nancy, the waitress. You must have red wine with meat. An hour turned into a two and a half stay at the restaurant. So, I missed American Idol that night. Driving home there was a DUI roadblock by church row. A bunch of veteran cops were strutting around with their *opu's* (bellies) drooping over their belts. The old cops were mentoring, showing some young punk rookies how to manage a DUI stop."

"Did the cops stop you?"

"Oh yes. I was the first one in line. I put my caution blinkers on, watched them finish setting up their cones and signs. One cop comes over with his flashlight. Shines it around on the back seat. I had three packages on the seat. He wanted to know what was in it. I told him fresh 'weed' I had just bought from a farmer in Lalamilo. He asked if he could have permission to look in the bags. I said, 'Heck, of course. Go ahead. Be my guest. Look under the seats. In the compartment. Under the hood if you want. I got nothing to hide. I believe in transparency.'"

"'Weed' as in marijuana. Did he ask for your license and stuff?"

"Yes."

"Why did you say you had 'weed' with you?"

"I wanted to have some fun. Ask a stupid question. Get a stupid answer."

"Did he?"

"Look in the bags?"

"Yes."

"What did he find?"

"Dirty clothes and more dirty clothes."

"So, what did he say?"

"He called me a 'wise ass.'"

"He did. Then he stuck his flashlight in my face."

"Why'd he shines his flashlight in your face?"

"He wanted to see if I was ugly, I guess."

"Papa. Let's be serious!"

"Nah! He was checking to see if my eyes were red, blood shot."

"Were they?"

"They were red earlier. When I was leaving the restaurant, I heard someone who just walked in, announce the cops were setting up a roadblock. So I put a few drops of Opcon A in my eyes. They were clear as a freshly polished wine glass when he scanned my eyes. And, I had a clump of gum in my mouth. I could have kissed him. Guess, he realized I was handsome. He wished me a good night and waved me on. I gave him a shaka sign, turned off my caution flashers and drove home. Now that I think of it. I could have drove around the island that night and made it home okay."

"How long a drive would that have been?"

"Two hundred eighty-two miles. About a six-hour drive."

"You were driving against your doctor's instructions."

"It was more of a suggestion. A suggestion. Not a directive."

"Waimea is a small town, Papa. It's impossible to keep a secret here. You know that!"

"Of course. I sure miss the 'ole Waimea days.'"

"Why? What was so good about them?"

"Kui, Elliot. In the 'ole days,' if we were driving inebriated on Mamalahoa Highway."

"Inebriated?"

"'Under the Influence.'"

"Driving drunk!"

"Elliot, you sure have a need to be clear, exact, precise. That's a good trait to have. The cops would pull us over. Take our car keys away. Drive us home. And they lived right here. Now, they drive in from Kohala, Honoka'a, Hilo or Kona. They're not part of our community. Drive drunk these days. They dump you in jail. They don't fuss around."

"And they shouldn't fuss around, Papa. There are too many cars on the road these days. Driving drunk or drugged out on the road is inconsiderate, irresponsible and downright dangerous."

"You're right about that, Kui. I can't argue with you. Waimea is a Peyton Place.

But it's still a beautiful small town even though the population has quadrupled since I was a kid. It's Waimea I Ka La'i. I will never live anywhere else. Never! Well, let's get to my story. Since you're both older, I'll give you an advanced iteration. An upgraded version. I needed to contemporize it. I've really improved it since I last read it to you. That must have been five years now?"

"About two, almost two years ago. Contemporize! Is that a real word?"

"It is now. I made it up. I think it's rather 'hip.' Please remember it's my story. And, at my age, you need to cut me some slack. Okay!"

"Yes, it's okay. And it's okay if you use a few bad words, Papa. We won't tell. Elliot and I have narrowed, boiled the focus of our conversation with you to three main topics. Your Creation Story, how it was formed and along with it some local Pele, Fire Goddess stories. A few things about you. Traditional stuff and your specific views on Hawaiian sovereignty and astronomy. And, what you think we should become?"

"Like a job? A vocation you should pursue?"

"Yes."

"I don't know about that one. I may have to pass on that one."

"Well, think about it. We know you like to meander and that's okay. Because in your wandering you reveal a lot about who you are. We'll use the position of the sun to track the time. Lala and Samuel may interrupt us, if the surf is up at Paniau. How does that sound, Papa?""

"Sounds perfect. If the surf is up, you will be heading for the beach?"

"Yes."

"Sounds perfect. Here we go. I must warn you in advance. Don't tell my creation story to the folks at the University?"

"Why not?"

"Them frolicking liberals..."

"Papa, you can say what you really want to say, however, you want to say it? It's okay. It's just us. So, no need to mince words."

"I'm working on improving my French, guys. City French not Country French. 'Lead me not into temptation.' Please! They're going to send your frolicking butts down the road. So, keep your noses clean. Do good work. Stay away from controversy. Just go with the flow. Pay attention. Focus on getting your *opala* (rubbish). Stuff your heads full of liberal propaganda. With that *opala* in hand you're going to make more money than those who don't have an *opala*. The experts say along with more earning power you will live longer. Be healthier. Happier. You will meet smarter, better looking *wahines* (girls)."

"I think you mean *palapala* (degree), Papa!"

"Sorry, yes, *palapala*. *Opala*. Same thing. What the hell."

"There is a difference, Papa. A big difference."

"Really?"

"Yes. Like you just said. *Palapala* is worth something. *Opala* is rubbish. You have a *palapala* don't you?"

"Got my *opala*, a B.A. in Sociology from UH-Manoa. That was supposed to be followed by a PhD but that didn't pan out. Even my economics profs were getting in the way. They wanted me to get a PhD in Economics. It was called the 'dismal science' then. Over time, another option popped up. My mind was a mindful mess. A cluttered mess."

"What was that option?"

"I could have gone to law school."

"Why didn't you?"

"I was sick of school. Law school was on the other side of the world. East coast. And, then I met Tutu. So a PhD in Sociology or Economics or a JD became low priorities."

"Really! I thought you liked school?"

"I did. But I needed a break. And, during all that noise, another door opened."

"And that was?"

"A PhD at another university. UCS. I went to UCS instead."

"We never heard of UCS. You must mean USC? University of Southern Cal. 'The Trojans.'"

"I do mean UCS. It's the acronym for the University of Common Sense. Obviously, you've never heard of it."

"No. So what was your major, Papa?"

"Imiola. Working on a PhD in Imiola."

"Imiola? Why, that's my dad's name!"

"That's right, Kui. Imiola, 'to seek life.' I wrote the degree description myself for my PhD."

"You designed your own degree?"

"Sure did. All by my lonesome."

"How'd you do that?"

"Argued my case before a panel of professors. Sold them a barrel of goods."

"They agreed?"

"I argued long and hard. They couldn't penetrate my arguments. I used 'Chinese torture' on them. They gave up. Just wore them down. Wore them down. At the end of all the scholarly, back and forth. I told them I wanted a contract to memorialize our verbal agreement. With a special clause."

"Which was?"

"Along with designing the course. I could take as long as I wanted to complete it. Got it at home. I'll show it to you one of these days. Signed by President Harlan Cleveland himself."

"You're still working on your PhD?"

"I am. Got a couple more years before I complete my dissertation."

"Gosh, you've been on this quite long. When did you start?"

"Let's see. 1970. Fall of 1970. This is 2020. Thirty plus twenty. What's that?"

"Fifty years. Half a century ago. And, you still don't have your PhD in hand?"

"No, not yet."

"Why so long?"

"I'm in no rush. Been on cruise control. A 'slow boat' to Cancun. It's a 'work in progress.' I liken getting my PhD to a rose bud."

"Rose bud?"

"When it's ready to burst open and reveal its beauty. It will. Until then it's an exercise in *ho'omanawanui* (patience)."

"Papa! I thought credits expire after so many years. Then you need to start over."

"Kui. Elliot. That's the beauty about getting an *opala* from UCS."

"Papa, it's *palapala*."

"*Palapala*. At UCS, learning is a 'lifetime' process. The 'rain check' I have is forever. There's no expiration date. My 'rain check' is good until I 'enter the forest.'"

"'Enter the forest?'"

"I'll receive my PhD on the day I die. When 'I bite the dust.' 'Enter the forest' is a native American saying. The inscription on my urn will read: 'Bobby Lindsey, PhD, in Seeking Life. He pursued his dream and found it 'At the Rainbow's End.' Yes. I'm doing my practicum right here. Right here in Waimea I ka La'i. Right here on the Waimea plains, in my dreams, cowboying on the Parker Ranch. On the slopes of Mauna Kea roping wild cattle. In the shadow of the Kohala mountains, riding my horse, Rippah. Oh, he was a fine *ho'ololio* (horse). God bless his soul. Together we weathered *kipu'upu'u'u* (slanting rain), *makani* (wind), *wela kala* (hot sun). Driving cattle from Holoholuku to Pu'u Pa beneath a big blue sky by day. Sometimes at night under the Pleiades, the Big Dipper, Orion. My birth constellation, Taurus, the Bully.

And *mahina* (moon). Yes, this is my campus where I learned and continue to learn how to *malama* (steward) the *'aina* (land), animals, horses, cattle, sheep, goats, dogs. To care for people. To be a veterinarian, good enough mathematician, decent meteorologist, astronomer, agronomist, horseman, roper. How to *malama* stuff and much else. Well gents, I'm ready to start my story. I'm going to take you on my 'Merry Go Round' ride around the *pae'aina* (archipelago). Welcome to Waimea I ka La'i, our little slice of Heaven on Earth. This is my story of how our archipelago came to be thirty-six million years ago. Rising from the Earth's mantle to the top of the Pacific Ocean. But the real story is in the Book of Genesis. Genesis 1."

"And Papa, at the end of the story, we want to hear a few Pele stories."

I pull a carefully folded paper out of my shirt pocket. "I thought you wanted me to respond to this list of questions. We should get to this list first."

"No, Papa. Your Creation Story. Then a few Pele pieces. Then, as time allows. A few controversial questions. Astronomy on the Mauna. Federal recognition. Hawaiian sovereignty. A few others. But the real focus is you."

I sneer at the thought.

"Well gentlemen, I'm ready to start my story. So, let's get going before your brothers show up."

"Papa, they may. They may not."

"Once upon a time, a long, long, long time ago, before the sun rose and peeped over the eastern horizon, to begin its daily stroll across the Pacific sky over the world's biggest Ocean."

"Around the time the asteroid you told us about crashed in the Gulf of Mexico and punched a great big hole on its floor. The impact caused a huge, violent tsunami with the water it displaced. Water that rolled over the Earth and destroyed the dinosaurs and life on the entire planet!"

"No, this was later. Forty million years later! Way, way later, Elliot. The ocean was having a major tantrum. Why, it was in a funk? No one dared ask. Just minutes before, it was calm. Fast asleep. In a coma, snoring. It was a sparkling mirror. Suddenly, gale winds came from out of nowhere and howled across its surface. Things got gnarly. Really gnarly."

"It was raging mad."

"Yep, like a scorned wahine."

"Scorned wahine?"

"Mad lady. Like when Tutu (grandma) is mad with me about nothing."

"It was 'pissed off.'"

"'Pissed off,' describes the scene perfectly. It sure was."

"Papa, there's a saying. 'Happy wife. Happy life.'"

"Yea, I've heard it several times from a couple of my wimpy friends."

"Is it true?"

"It's for want of a better word. A 'myth.' At best an overused cliche that should be retired. Scrubbed off every romance novel ever written since the beginning of time."

"Really?"

"Really. You'll both find out soon enough. Don't drink the kool aid from the milk can. It's one big…"

"Lie."

"Yea. That's a good word, Kui. 'Lie.' It's a descriptor with a nice punch to it. Like how a jack hammer sounds."

"Why, Papa?"

"I like 'Lie' because it packs a punch. 'Myth.' Eh, it doesn't have piazza. Doesn't have sizzle. I think you know what I mean. Best we move on, otherwise I'm going to get really distracted. And get my 'foot stuck in my big mouth.' It's an election year so I need all the votes I can get. I need to be careful now with iPhones and social media."

"You, barely survived your last election."

"Didn't expect the libtards to turn out in force. But whether you win by one vote or ten thousand. A win is a win."

"You get to stand on the platform and solemnly swear to defend the Constitution."

"You both know me. I don't like to lose."

"Why not? It's a humbling experience some say."

"I'm not ready for the 'some club.' It's bad for the ego. I plan to win another election. Kui, I'm beginning to make a left turn when we should be going straight ahead. We might end up in the 'drink.' Let's see, where were we? Right here. 'The sky, the sky not wanting to be left out, crashed the party, thus amplifying the drama. I like amplifying. I considered amped, teased up, strengthened. I like amplifying.'"

"The sky stirred the pot up."

"Revved up the engine. Punched the gear shift into third gear, 'peeled rubber' out of the parking lot. and left in its wake, a lot of smoke and the stink of burnt rubber. Crying and screaming, like a dehydrated baby, needing a tit. I mean a pacifier to suck on. The firmament accompanied by lightning and thunder, dove headfirst into the tempest. Lightning lit up the heavens from Chile to Tasmania, Vladivostok to Seattle, Manila to Juneau."

"You could have said 'illuminated the heavens.'"

"I could have. Maybe I will. Only problem is some of my buddies at morning coffee are going to think I'm showing off."

"Yea, that wouldn't be good."

"It might hurt my olu'olu (humble) image. But I'll think about it. At my age, heck I really shouldn't be worrying about what people think.... that! I've got all these AARP privileges piling up. Got to start using a few of them before they expire. 'Thunder rumbled across the Pacific from Mongolia to the west edge of the Americas, the high Sierras to Mount Fuji southward to the Cook Islands, jumping over Antarctica to Cape Horn at the south tip of Africa.'"

"Papa, South America."

"Africa."

"Papa, Cape of Good Hope, is on Africa's south tip."

"Are you sure, Elliot?"

"Yes, I am."

"Well okay. I'll accept your word. For the time being!"

"I'm sure glad we weren't around when that storm was happening."

"Me too. 'Rocking and rolling, everyone and everything beneath it. Not wanting any part in the hostility, the full moon, quietly danced its way unnoticed to the other side of the world.'"

"I always knew the 'man in the moon' was a smart dude."

"He's a scared-y cat, a woose, but he sure knows how 'to get lip stick on his collar.' How to romance the ladies."

"Never heard you use that phrase before, Papa."

"I'll take some time to explain it later. While all this kabuki was taking place on top of the Pacific, a powerful magma plume blew a hole through the Earth's crust, thirty-five miles below."

"Below the surface."

"Yep. 'Millions of cubic yards of molten magma, sulfur, noxious gases and volcanic debris poured out of the hole at the bottom of the sea.'"

"Wow. I'm sure scientists who study and chase volcanoes would have loved to document the event!"

"Absolutely. They could have engendered a few more research papers. They would have been ecstatic."

"'Engendered.' What does that mean?"

"Means 'to produce *opala*.' Research papers. Doctoral theses."

"Oh, okay. Thanks, Papa. I just learned a new word."

"Humm. Don't you folks learn vocabulary in school these days?"

"Sometimes. Yes! Sometimes."

"Don't you walk around with a dictionary or thesaurus in your pocket?"

"No, Papa. We just pull up stuff on our computer or our iPhone. Well, when we need to. I could have done that, but I knew you had the answer. And again it's *palapala* not *opala*."

"*Palapala*. I loathe 'New Age,' 'black hole,' 'black box' approach to learning. I really want to elaborate but I won't. Now where was I?"

"...at the bottom of the sea."

"...at the bottom of the sea. Eve with the help of two conspirators, had patiently probed, pecked and chipped away at the crust searching for a soft spot to wiggle, slither through for months."

"Who's Eve?"

"The leading lady in my story."

"Humm. Papa, every time you tell this story, the lady's name is never the same."

"Really!"

"Yes."

"Ah, what the hell. It's a lady in the lead role. So, it's common sense that it must be a lady's name. That's the main thing. You remember what the lady's name the last time was?"

"Neenaokole. The time before that it was Dolly. There was Babe. Hanoi Jane. Missy Poo. Tokyo Rose. Melaneeah. But yes, Neenaokole."

"Neenaokole, the lady with the 'cho cho' lips."

"You sure had no use for her. You called her a snitch."

"No, Elliot. Papa said she was a I went home and told my mom what you said about Neenaokole, Papa."

"You did! Oh boy, oh boy."

"It was inadvertent, Papa."

"'Inadvertent.' What does that mean?"

"It was an 'accident.' By 'accident.' It just slipped out of my mouth."

"Why, did you tell her?"

"She asked me what my favorite part of the story was? So, I told her."

"Of the entire story, that was it? That one piece. Ah man."

"It sure was."

"She must have been impressed?"

"No, she was not."

"Can you tell me, why you chose to tell her that particular part of the story?"

"Because I was impressed. That's the part of the story I liked. I really liked that part. It was the most memorable part for me of the story. Papa, to see you excited and worked up. It was funny. I liked seeing the glare in your eyes. The muscles on your face and forehead got tight. The veins on your neck looked like they were going to pop. You stood up. You got out of your chair. You started pounding the table. You looked like a pug. A pug dog. Your eyes became fiery red. You began to perspire. You were really animated. I'd like to meet this Neenaokole lady. She must be a 'trip.'"

"She is a ...c c. So, what did your mom say?"

"She said the next time she saw you. She was going to tell you to open your mouth real wide. And, she was going to scrub your mouth, Papa. With chili pepper water, Clorox and lots of soap. You won't get the corona virus. Plus, she wanted to cut your tongue in half."

"I won't get any kind of virus. That's for sure. Now that explains why she's been making excuses as to why you couldn't 'hang' with me for a long time. There was always some excuse. You guys were always doing family stuff. Picnicking at Beach 69. Surfing at Paniau or A Bay. Hiking into Waipi'o or Pololu Valley or Awini. Something was going on at school. A play or a performance of some kind. Now I know why you haven't been able to 'hang' with me!"

"The word we use Papa is 'chill.'"

"'Chill.' I'll file that in my pea brain. 'Chill.' Did she say anything else?"

"She also said she was disappointed."

"With whom?"

"With you."

"Listen up guys. There's some stuff we must keep to ourselves. You gotta help me out. I've been missing you guys. I must 'course correct' this matter. This is a Civil Defense issue. Geez, you need to know. I'm an old troubadour. I need advocates. Both of you and your brothers are my only champions left in the world. Most of my advocates are pushing daisies. Staring up at the bottom of their tombstones or flowerpots in the boneyard."

"What's a 'boneyard,' Papa?"

"A cemetery. What did your dad have to say? Anything!"

"He did."

"So, what did he say? I hope he stuck up for me."

"He supports our mom."

"Really!"

"Oh! Okay, guys. Look here. I need your help. This is my 'go forward' plan to get me and us out of this dilemma! We got a problem. It needs fixing. We need to snag it. 'Nip it in the bud.' Turn it into an opportunity. Okay!"

"Yes, Papa."

"Please, from today on, stuff we discuss here on Hoku'ula must never leave Hoku'ula Hill. When we leave here. All the 'privileged and confidential' stuff we talk about. Stays right here! Right here on this hill! What we talk about is, top secret. It must remain classified for a hundred years. I repeat. What we talk about on Hoku'ula Hill must stay right here. Okay!"

"Okay, Papa. Just name, rank, serial number?"

"Your mom's and dad's get overly sensitive at times. They have so much else to worry about. Don't add me to their 'worry wart' list."

"My mom's going to ask, so I have to tell her something."

"Make something up. Just make something up."

"But I'm not good at making stuff up. At lying."

"Hey Kui, if our President can bull shit. You can. He's our Commander in Chief. This is the Papa of our Country. At last count this orangutan has told twenty thousand lies in less than four years. It's like anything else, Kui. It takes practice. And I'm sure you've heard the saying. 'Practice...'"

"'Practice makes perfect.'"

"Amen. I try to live by this saying every day. 'Happy Life makes Happy Wife.' So, I'm applying the standard to you."

"You said earlier that's a myth, Papa. I'm confused."

"I'm confused as well, Papa."

"Let me un-confuse you. I'm giving things just a little twist in the opposite direction. In my favor. 'Happy Life. Makes Happy Papa.' Keep that tucked away in your head. You know guys. I'm so proud to be your Papa. All four of you. The two of you and your brothers are my life. And Tutu's of course. You are my and our reason for living. You are all smart dudes. So, when your moms ask you. 'What did Papa talk with you about today?' Just tell them, he told us his Creation Story. He gave us a science lesson on the planets and the heliocentric theory. He dumped some statistics on us. The moon is 240,000 miles from earth. The sun, 93 million miles. Mars, 140 million miles. Our brain weighs about three pounds. It's got eighty billion to a hundred neurons. Tell them stuff like that. Good stuff. Stuff that will fiddle their 'heart strings.' You know what I mean? What I'm getting at."

"Of course. Stuff that makes you look good. What about Jupiter? How far is it from us?"

"490 million miles."

"And. Venus?"

"162 million miles."

"Are you sure Papa?"

"Hell, yes! Of course! I'm damn sure. Look it up on your iPhone. And, if this doesn't satisfy them. Tell them I gave you some other statistics. Sound travels 1,100 feet per second. Light 186,000 feet per second. From the sea bottom to the ocean surface. It's about 35 miles. Tell them I talked about how the Hawaiian Archipelago was formed. It's not bullshit. They will be impressed. Our island is 500,000 years old like that. The CIA uses that tactic a lot. Create a distraction. I bet they don't know any of this stuff that I just shared with you. Impress them. Talk about good stuff that makes me shine. Make me look like a choir boy. Not Tom Sawyer or Huck Finn stuff. Not rascal stuff. Intelligent stuff. Earth is the third closest planet to the sun. Venus and Mercury are closer. I'm not making this up."

"Did my mom ever talk to you, Papa?"

"About my French?"

"Yes?"

"No, she didn't and I'm glad she didn't."

"Why?"

"I would have given her my rank, name, serial number. Like my hero, one of my heroes, John McCain. So, remember! If you get stuck and can't think of anything. Get caught with your panty around your ankles. Name, rank, serial number. Nothing else. That's all. Now where were we?"

"'They found a soft spot to wiggle through like a snake.'"

"Thanks, Kui. 'Once through, their plan was to build a ladder.

An escalator to the top of the sea. To the sunlight 35,800 fathoms above. Drop a statistic like this on them. Impress your moms, guys. I need you to be my champions. Otherwise, they're going to think the worst of me. They won't let you 'chill' with me. That I'm taking the two of you in the wrong direction. You know what I mean? I don't mean to be redundant. But, at my age, I ain't got many champions left. Most of my champs are dead. They're no good to me anymore. Their ashes are in expensive cans or bones in a casket six feet under the ground in a graveyard somewhere in Waimea. The few who are still alive are limping around with titanium knees or rebuilt hips or ventilators stuck up their noses. We're making the pharmaceutical companies rich with all these pills we must take. Now with this Covid pandemic, we must wear Halloween masks when we go to the supermarket or the bank or post office."

"Don't you get together with your buddies every day except Sunday, Papa?"

"We do. For coffee. Those of us who can. Who can walk around but our numbers keep dwindling."

"What do you talk about?"

"The same old boring BS every day. It's really no fun. The new pill the doctor prescribed. Our latest ailment ta few of us wear like a 'badge of honor.' The obituary column in the newspaper. Which we really shouldn't talk about, but we do. We grumble about our mayor. About potholes on the highway. How spoiled today's kids are. We talk about legislation. Articles we need to read in the latest AARP newspaper. Another congressional effort to eliminate Social Security, Medicare, Medicaid. The President wanting to get rid of the US Postal Service. How we wish we can undo or retract today something stupid we did or said years ago. Marty Hess. He's eighty-nine. He grumbles constantly about Annabelle."

"Annabelle?"

"Yea. He cussed her out again the other morning."

"About what?"

"She overcooked his eggs and burned his bacon. And his toast was not toasted the way he wanted it. Nothing intellectual ever comes out of his mouth. Just grumble, grumble, grumble. He's really demented, and he doesn't even know it. His dementia just keeps getting worse. He's a zombie. And he's got dyslexia as well."

"It sounds like he had something to complain about."

"No, he didn't."

"I'm surprised you're defending old man, Marty."

"I'm not. You see, Annabelle dumped him thirty years ago and married Paul Douglas for his money. She's dead. She died twelve years ago. That's what I put up with every day."

"By choice."

"By choice. I got a name for our club. It's a good one."

"We have no doubt, Papa. What is it?"

"The Walking Dead Club."

"How can that be, if you're alive?"

"There's eight of us left in the club. We all have our ailments. We're all hanging on for dear life. We started with twenty members. Six of our eight members are 'brain dead.' Walking around but have no sense of what day it is. Sometimes, some of us don't know what our wife's name is. We forget to take our meds. Often, if we do remember, it's too much or too little. Four days ago, I had to take Mr. Luce to the ER to get his stomach pumped out. He overdosed on his high blood pressure medication. He overdosed again yesterday. Back we went to the ER."

"Why, do you have to worry about him?"

"I'm on his emergency call list. Plus, he lives close by. Two houses down from us. I told him the next time I'm calling 'Roto Rooter.'"

"Papa, you're funny."

"Two other members had to renew their pacemakers. One member got a vasectomy yesterday. I asked why, at his age? He wears a yellow band on his wrist because he's a 'fall risk.' He needs help getting up on his feet. And, when he's on his feet, he falls on his butt."

"What he say? How old is he?"

"Seventy-four. He wants me to be best man. He's getting married to a young lady two weeks from today. He's done with raising kids."

"How young is she?"

"Sixty-nine. They're going to Bermuda for their honeymoon. He doesn't want to get her pregnant. We laughed and told him the next time he goes to the hospital; he's going to need a pacemaker. This is my long way to let you know, Elliot. You did right. You did right but you and Kui need to keep this in mind. I don't have much gas left in my tank. Right now, I'm operating on fumes. My needle is touching the bottom of the E on my gas gauge. So, the time I get to spend with you, in the time I have left, is precious. It's limited. Get my drift?"

"I get it, Papa. I meant no harm."

"I know you didn't. You did right. You just need a quick truth management lesson. And I got the primer for that. You must learn how to doctor, manipulate, embellish, massage, tweak what you say to your folks to keep me in their good graces. You see, you both got this thing called influence. Influence on your parents. You must employ that influence with prudence and care. Should I elaborate?"

"No! No, Papa! We get it. Be like a politician? Answer a question without answering it."

"Like a politician. Exactly. Dance three times around the rose or cactus bush without getting thorns stuck in your butt. 'Name. Rank. Serial Number.' That's a safe one to use."

"What number shall we use?"

"1 8 4 7 for you Elliot. That's the year Parker Ranch was established. For you Kui. 1 9 4 8. That's the year I was born. Got it?"

"Got it."

"What about rank?"

"Elliot, Air Force General. Kui, Navy Admiral."

"Why, Air Force? Why, General?"

"Your dad could have gone to the Air Force Academy. That's why Air Force. General is the highest rank you can achieve. Both ranks are easy to remember. Any more questions? What about you, Kui?"

"Papa. I'm curious. When you and your friends meet what else do you really want to talk about?"

"We avoid what we really want to talk about."

"Which is?"

"The inevitable."

"The inevitable?"

"Yes, I know we're sitting there, knowing our numbers are shrinking and wondering who's going to 'enter the forest' next.' It's like playing musical chairs but it's something we don't have any control over which chair we will fall into. The inevitable is out of our control. For me, I just live in the 'present moment.' So I have to make every moment count."

"That's scary and it's sad."

"We've all lived long lives. If we didn't make use of the time God has given us. I don't know what to say."

"Papa, we're ready to get back to your story."

"Very well. Enough on that topic. We've 'beat that old horse to death.' Poor horse needs a transfusion. Moving on. Let's see now. Where were we? Here we go. 'Upon reaching the light, they would construct a string of islands in the most isolated corner of the earth's biggest ocean. Build a tropical Paradise of Never-Ending Summers. Islands, the First People from Hawaiki to discover would call, The Hawaiian Archipelago. And, years later, Mark Twain in his 1866 *Letters from the Sandwich Islands* would describe as 'The loveliest fleet of islands that lies anchored in any ocean.' Drop a note like this on your parents this evening when you're having dinner. A note like this will surely shock the daylights out of your mom's. Your dad's also. I'm positively sure. Be sure to tell them, Papa, quoted Mark Twain, word for word. In fact, before you drop the quote. Ask them if they know what Twain said? I'm willing to bet you a hundred bucks, they have never heard it. They'll want you to spend more time with me. Later, I'll quote stuff from Samuel Kamakau, John Papa I'i, Viktor Frankl, David Malo and Henry Thoreau for both of you to put in your quiver. I want to fill your quiver with arrows you can use when cornered. When barraged with questions about me. Did you know all this stuff before?"

"No, Papa."

"What have you been learning in school anyway?"

"Process stuff. Critical thinking. Problem solving. We don't learn facts. We're taught ways to find the facts we need to know. To determine their relevance, application, usefulness to everyday life. How to apply what we learn in the classroom to everyday life. Our teachers always remind us that our heads are not empty water bottles waiting to be filled with water, with facts that have little or no use to everyday life."

"This modern pedagogy drives me nuts."

"Why?"

"It's a waste of precious time and good tax money to me, is why."

"My dad says it makes sense."

"Well, truth be told. I've had this debate with him."

"What was the outcome?"

"I lost! He creamed me with his 'the world has changed' premise and therefor education pedagogy must change to prepare your generation for the future. But I still believe we need to return to the 'command and control' approach to education. I'm old fashioned. We need to get back to basics. Read in. Ritin. Rithmetic. I don't like this liberal crap. This laissez faire, 'let them do as you please,' 'spoil brat,' montyisorry approach doesn't work with me. Reward kids, give them a ribbon or trophy even when we know they don't deserve one because we don't want to hurt their feelings, pop their self-esteem. That's BS. I think we'd better get back to my fairy tale. My blood is beginning to bubble. The thought of all this useless 'new age' …. that's being spewed in classrooms across America today. Millennial and Generation Z kids graduating today are ill prepared. When they enter the workplace, employers must get them up to par. Invest in remedial education. Align their liberal education with the 'command & control' requirements of the workplace."

"My dad says it's an alignment issue. And the solution is very simple."

"What's his solution."

"Educators and employers need to come to the table. Have conversations, cooperate and collaborate. Develop a workout. Not be 'ships passing in the night,' he says. Alignment, working together needs to happen. And the sooner, the better."

"Oh Lordy, I'm starting to get a migraine. Lord, cursed Lord, help me. Now where were we?"

"Eve was tired of being held…"

"Eve was tired of being held prisoner on the dark side of this boiling cauldron. Her home, the only home she'd known since she was born.

Then Eureka! With the help of two likeminded friends sharing a similar plight, they found the chink they were looking for. Do you know what a 'chink' is?"

"Yes, a crack. A weak spot."

"Very good, Kui. It's not a racial term as some say it is. 'Wasting not a moment, the trio bullied their way through the opening. Liberated at last from the wretched crock pot that was supposed to be their 'happy place' forever.'"

"Papa, I don't remember you being so animated when telling this story before."

"This was a teachable moment I just could not avoid. 'In life Kui, if you can make something better. Do so! Seize the moment! Go ahead and do so.' The plume looked forward to being free of the family who took her in when her under aged, drugged out, homeless, dysfunctional, narcissistic, desperate mother gave her up twenty years before to an equally desperate couple who promised her messed up mama that they would give her the moon and all the stars in the galaxy on a silver platter. Even the sun. They would give her newborn a better life than she ever could. Provide her five-pound five-ounce shivering baby a warm, decent, safe, loving home. They even tossed in an ivy league education and Christian values. Help her infant, mature into an 'industrious and virtuous' woman. Splatter, shower her baby with unconditional love."

"Sounds like a great deal to me."

"In life 'if something sounds too good to be true, it probably is.' Sadly, it was all a ruse. An empty promise. They were two malcontents with evil intentions. What they committed to was not worth the trust her mother agreed to in 'good faith' when giving Eve up."

"'Good faith.' As in how you do business?"

"Exactly! It was a transaction made in 'good faith.' On words alone."

"You have a smirk on you face, Papa."

"Folks like this incense me."

"Why?"

"They were cons. As it says in the Desiderata. 'The world is full of trickery' so be careful. They said they didn't need a piece of paper. A contract. Just a warm, honest handshake. And Eve's mom was stupid enough to trust them."

"Papa, she was in a desperate situation."

"She no doubt was but she had an option."

"She did?""

"I'm getting to that piece. She should have gone to her mom and dad. They would have taken in the baby. But she was just too proud. She let her pride get in the way."

"She trusted these strangers?"

"More than her parents, unfortunately. Strangers who had an ulterior motive laced with 'bad intent,' Elliot."

"I see."

"They took her in because they had a household of boys. Ten rascals, spoiled, rambunctious brats. The couple so wanted a girl. Every baby after the first was supposed to be a girl. The girl who never came. They were one short of populating a football team and concluded adoption was their best and only option.

"I'm sure glad I never had a sister."

"Why not, Elliot? She would have been the 'love of your life.' The 'apple of your baby blue eyes.'"

"Very doubtful, Papa."

"Why are you so skeptical?"

"I've known a lot of girls and they are a pain in the ass to deal with."

"She would have made your life interesting."

"I don't think so."

"Well, we'll never know now, will we?"

"Thank God. Did you have sisters, Papa?"

"No. It was just me and Uncle Ben."

"How was that? Did you get along?"

"We had our moments, but Uncle Ben was and continues to be a great brother. The best brother I could have ever had. May I continue?"

"Sorry. Please, Papa."

"Where was I?"

"Eve was..."

"Eve was the girl they were looking for. This infant, cradled in this haggard woman's arms whose warm tear drops were falling on the baby's pink face. Wrapped in a thin blanket, shivering from the cold. Screaming at the top of her fragile lungs. Both huddled a few away from a flaming fifty-gallon iron drum. Their life's possessions nearby. Stuffed carelessly in doubled up plastic trash bags piled high in two rusty shopping carts about to tip over under all the weight they were carrying. Eve and her mom were homeless and penniless, with no one to turn to on this dismal night. Eve, an innocent child. Sharing, bearing the sins of her reckless mother."

"Eve's mother had run out of lifelines. Even the church which was always open to her was shuttered tight on this stormy night. She pounded on the rector's door, crying desperately for help. But her cries for mercy went unanswered. It was raining hard, raindrops the size of golf balls falling on her and her poor baby out of a stormy, dark sky. To add to her agony. She was in pain as she had just broke water three hours before and managed by a miracle to deliver Eve all by her lonesome. She was forced to use a rusty scissors to cut the umbilical cord which had been the bridge for eight months between her and her little one. This miracle 'rainbow of life' who just popped out of her womb."

"One of God's miracles."

"One of God's miracles, yes. Tired and broken, she took cover at her usual spot. Her newborn was hungry and dehydrated. She put Eve to her withered breasts. Both were bone dry. They looked like dried up prunes. She was too tired and in too much pain to panhandle at the street corner the last few days. Thus, she had no money in her pocket to buy food. To buy anything. And Eve had arrived prematurely. A month early. So that made her already complicated situation even more complicated."

"She didn't have any milk?"

"Nope. No milk and no contingency plan. The baby's crying and screaming was getting worse. The noise was driving her crazy. Nuts! Out of the darkness a voice shouted out. 'Can we help? Do you need help?'"

"My baby. My baby is cold. And it's hungry. Please, please! Please, help my baby. Please!"

"The couple was curious. 'Is it a boy? Is it a girl?'"

"It's a girl. I gave birth to her a few hours ago." The couple got excited when they heard, 'It's a girl.' Really excited."

"Oh my. What are you doing out here with this little one on this wet, cold night. You should be indoors. You should not be out here on the street in this dreadful weather. This baby. This poor baby."

"On that gloomy night, Eve's mom poured her guts out to this seemingly warm, Godly, caring couple. In a fit of desperation, she gave Eve up for two crisp one hundred dollar bills, a crap-load of shallow promises and a navy blue pea-coat."

"Her mom dumped her?"

"She did. Little did her mama know these were folks who could violin with the best in the Hampton's and outwit the Lucifer in Gotham City."

"They were bs'ing her?"

"They were but to their credit they did keep one promise on a short list of promises. Her inoa (name). Her mother had named her Eve and pleaded with them not to change Eve to Beyonce, Chastity, Honey Girl or something else. 'I beg of you. Eve. Her name is Eve. Please keep her name.' It was an easy request. They liked the name as they were evangelicals, born and bred, in the cauldron's 'Bible belt' and observed the Sabbath faithfully. Who partook in the Eucharist faithfully on Sunday morning at early mass and exhibited hypocrisy shamelessly from midnight Sunday to midnight Saturday. Eve, after the first woman God embedded in the Garden, from a rib God stole from Adam so he could have company. A playmate."

"I like the name, Eve. And I like the Bible version of creation that you're touching on."

"I'm glad you do but mine is comparable. At least I like to think so."

"You think so, Papa?"

"It's possible one day, my iteration of how the Hawaiian Archipelago came to will be published in science journals around the globe. That it will be taught in general science classes. It might even end up as a book in the Bible."

"Papa."

"I'm serious. Genesis II, possibly. Like Second Chronicles or Second Timothy. Or in some journal with the likes of Charlie Darwin and the Galapagos Islands. Who knows what the future may bring?"

"That would be really cool."

"It would be. Ah, to dream. 'Miracles. Miracles. Isn't that what dreams are made of?' Getting back to business. 'When her mom pawned Eve off that night. That was the last Eve saw of her.'"

"How sad. They only had a few hours together."

"It was sad. Makes me want to cry. What about her dad?"

"Her mom was a 'freelancer.'"

"A 'freelancer?'"

"She played around. And, got herself pregnant. By whom? She didn't know. Her parents warned her she was toying with 'fire.' But she didn't listen. And unfortunately, the ……. who 'knocked her up' ran for the hills instead of sticking around to help. Lend a hand. To accept his *kuleana* (responsibility). Help her raise this baby. What did her stupid parents know anyways? They were 'freaks.' They didn't know anything."

"She called them 'freaks.'"

"Yes. What they told Eve was going to happen happened."

"She got pregnant?"

"She had fun. Boy, did she have fun while it lasted. Giving Eve up was a good decision. Who she gave Eve up to be a bad idea."

"This makes me want to cry. It really does. Have you ever cried in your life, Papa? We've never seen you cry. Or drop a tear. And, in telling this part of the story. There is a harshness in your tone, Papa. In your voice. You sound, you look angry."

"You sense that, Kui?"

"I do. It's obvious."

"Good. How about you, Elliot?"

"I do as well. I'm seeing a side of you I've never seen before, Papa."

"To answer your question, Kui. No! I don't cry."

"Why not?"

"For one. Crying is a waste of time. Two, it's a waste of precious water. Three, never had reason to. Four, real men don't cry. Remember that. Real men do not cry. Real men are tough as nails. Lindsey men do not cry. Paniolo, do not cry. We just 'grin and bear' our way through any storm that blows our way."

"Have any?"

"Have we had any crybabies?

"Yes."

"A handful."

"What happened to them?"

"They were shipped off to Antarctica in zodiacs and told never to return to Waimea. They were turned into different ice forms. Penguins. Seals, Dolphins. Mostly penguins. A couple whales."

"You're kidding, Papa!"

"I am. I am. I saw my dad cry once. He tried to hide it. He thought I didn't see him cry. But I did. He was quietly crying. Crying tears of sadness. It was in church."

"What was he crying about?"

"It was his last visit home from the hospital. He knew this was his last visit home to Waimea. His last time to be with all the folks and the place he loved. That he didn't have much time left. Now where were we?"

"Papa, how old was he?"

"Forty-one."

"He wasn't old!"

"No, our dad was in the prime of his life. He was healthy. He was strong. Then he wasn't. Help me, Kui. I lost my place. Where were we?"

"The couples real..."

"Thanks. 'The couple's real intentions for Eve surfaced when she turned seven. They began treating Eve like 'The Ugly Duckling' in Hans Andersen's fairy tale. Giving her at first, little than no access to peers to nurture lifelong friendships with. No trips to the playground. No stuffed animals to cuddle. No more bedtime stories, warm hugs, good night kisses. The older she got. The uglier things got. All her learning opportunities came to a screeching halt. There was no more sitting behind a desk in the 'red schoolhouse' where she was at the top of her class, voted 'most likely to succeed.' The kudos stretched on and on. She was blessed with so many gifts. An analytical mind. A curious mind. A good heart. She made friends readily. She had a fantastic memory. She was on her way to a tremendous future."

"She was a nerd.'"

"She was. Yes! She had a gift for both music and languages. One of her teachers claimed she was clairvoyant. She never had piano lessons. Just came home one day from school, sat down at the piano and started to play Fur Elise and a week later, Mozart and Beethoven. On a grand piano which had sat silent for years just gathering dust. Sitting quietly in the living room waiting for someone to gently slide his or her fingers over the keys. I see kids like this on television now and then. Some of them are four, five years old. They are blessed to have these special gifts. Where it's from? Their parents have no clue. Eve was denied access to books and a computer. Her ten brothers each had their own. She asked for one. The answer was, 'No.'"

"Why?"

"Her 'parents' gave her no reason but I'm sure they were afraid a computer would open an even bigger world to Eve. And they did not want her to have access to that world. It would make it hard for them to keep her imprisoned. Applying to Harvard or Radcliffe, even the local community college melted away into a 'pipe dream.' She was denied training in the 'best practices' of 'virtuous and industrious' womanhood. It was all part of a diabolical scheme to keep her under 'house arrest.' From realizing her full potential. To turn her into a fully certified spinster."

"Diabolical. What does that mean?"

"'Diabolical' means evil, Elliot."

"Now that's a word I don't think I'll hear again."

"Hopefully not but if you do. You'll know what it means. And don't be shy. Tell folks it was not from Webster. You got it from your, Papa. Let's see. 'Disappointments! Eve had more than her fair share. There were just too damn many. Eve was tough but like most of us. In time, things got old. What started as a pimple festered into a boil, a boil into a tumor. It finally burst open. Eve had reached her 'breaking point.' She was tired of being a slave to this ungrateful family. Tired of standing over a hot stove cooking three meals a day, day after day after day, week after week after week. Of washing load upon load of dirty clothes, bed sheets, towels, stinky sweaty athletic uniforms, whatever else. She was tired of all the 'picking up after,' folding, ironing. Scrubbing floors, pots, pans, mountains of dishes. Polishing windows, water and wine glasses, silver candelabras. Feeding and cleaning after the family dogs. Though they were her only friends, in both the best and worst of times. The love and joy they gave her were momentary and simply not enough.

She needed and wanted more. Eve was yearning for human warmth, human touch. Thus, she colluded with two older companions. Bertha and Bessie, twin sisters, from across the street. The unhappy trio had worked up several schemes to rid themselves of their collective misery. At their last clandestine planning session. They were in full agreement. It was time to act. Enough talk. They had run out of ideas and were spinning in a circle. They were like a car whose wheels were bogged down, sinking in a mud bog. They needed to move on to that happy place they dreamt of night after night.

"Eve had just been bequeathed an asset. It was her birthday; a beautiful sunny morning and she was enjoying her twentieth year with her pals sitting under a tree in the local cemetery huddled over the latest and what she hoped would be the final iteration of their flight plan to a new life for all of them. The community graveyard was a haven where they could meet and talk freely over without fear of being discovered. She told them, she now had access to fire. And lots of it, to add to their ever evolving but now complete plan.

Bessie and Bertha told her they had made several attempts to break out of the cauldron. They had almost made it to 'freedom land' on one occasion. They reached the sunlight far above but ran out of fuel, fell short with about a mile to go to breach the Pacific ocean's surface and break into the sunlight. The light they had heard about from others. It was there. Right there. They were close. So very close. Am I putting you to sleep? You haven't been interrupting me."

"We're awake, Papa. Wide awake. I haven't been interrupting you because the story is getting interesting, Papa."

"Okay. Good. I'm glad to hear that. Eve was curious. 'So why'd you stop? Turn back? Return to this evil place if you were so close?'"

"Sheepishly, they admitted it was a dream. Just a beautiful, wondrous dream. Their 'flights of fancy' took them many a night to this fantasy place filled with all the stuff they longed, had wished for for so long. A place of endless summers. Skies full of rainbows. Flocks of birds floating on a spring breeze, chirping beautiful *mele* (songs). And, happy people gathering on tree lined streets, old friends sharing gifts of time and memories soon to be lost.

"Eve disclosed she too, had had similar dreams. In her dreams, she unabashedly shared, 'I'm flying high into the sky, right into the blinding sun with my eyes shut tight. Oh, it feels so good to be caressed by the sun. My hair pulled back behind me by a soft trade wind. I feel like Super Woman. At times I get to float through a patch of fluffy clouds straight into a sky so clear and blue. It's a summer place for me as well. A summer place draped with a lei of tropical islands strung across the sea. Hidden in a lonely corner of the ocean. Islands bathed in sunshine with lush valleys chiseled into their windward edges, laden with granite cliffs, steep cliffs show casing curtains of cascading waterfalls after a storm. The leeward edges are sprinkled with sandy beaches, tide pools, coconut, pandanus and breadfruit groves. At dusk as the sun is setting in the west, I witness the most beautiful, glorious sunsets imaginable.'

A true romantic, she sees also a portrait straight out of a Hollywood romance movie. As the sun fades away, darkness grips the land. A warm, soft breeze rustles the palm fronds. A gentle thermal brushes over her. She inhales the fragrance of jasmine wafting through the seaside bar of the boutique pink colored Waikiki hotel she checked into at noon. She's sitting all alone on a sofa overlooking a neon blue lagoon. The whisper of the ocean and the hush of the waves, rippling, rolling softly over Waikiki beach are music to her ears. A quarter moon dangles over the south rim of Leahi (Diamond Head). It is a scene so sensuous, ethereal, alluring. A well-dressed couple show up. She can tell they are newlyweds on honeymoon. Still drowning in the romance phase of their relationship. The hostess seats them at a table for two in a dark corner. They ask her not to light the candle on their table. She does one better. Takes it away and replaces it with a bowl of plumeria flowers. Eve watches them clutch hands. Their sweaty fingers tightly intertwined. The twang of a steel guitar disrupts the quiet of the evening. She sips on her mai tai and observes the couple French kissing shamelessly under the light of the quarter moon which now is sitting directly over them. Their giggling begins to irritate her. And envy is beginning to get the best of her. She wishes Kamapu'a'a would quit playing his stupid game. Quit playing hard to get with her. Her four dinner invites have gone unanswered. She summons the waitress over, orders a bowl of sauteed Hamakua mushrooms, a thick slab of seared mahimahi lightly dusted with lemon basil and mashed sweet potatoes from Molokai. 'Dynamite choice,' the waitress remarks. And a double martini. She focuses again on the young couple. They continue to…"

"Yuck Papa, can you skip over this part?"

"Why Kui? This is the best part of the entire story."

"Nah. We're not into 'sucking face' stuff, Papa."

"Man alive. You sure don't know what you're missing. Okay. I'll skip over the next four pages but Kui and Elliot. This is the best part of the story. It's the build up to what's coming. The foundation. The core. The *puuwai* (heart) of my story. Guys, this is the best part. Come on. If you go home and tell your moms this part of the story. They are going to send me a quick text and ask me to read it to them in my raspy voice. In fact they're going to ask me to read it a second, maybe a third time. I'm serious."

"Thanks. Maybe some other time, Papa! Before you move on. Who's Kamapu'a'a?"

"Kamapu'a'a is a guy she's been pursuing for a while, but he's been stiff arming her. Putting her off. Ignoring her. Tell me. Why would you guys turn a girl away?"

"A bunch of reasons. She might be ugly. She could be bossy. She could be dumb. An air head. A big gossip. A big flirt. She can't keep secrets. Has bad breath. All the above. Why was Kamapua'a 'stiff arming' her?"

"Kamapua'a was interested in Bertha. He was after Bertha."

"Why?"

"Eve was just too smart for him. He couldn't stand smart *wahines* (ladies). Most smart men are like that you know, Elliot."

"But you're not like that, Papa?"

"No, that's why I chased after Tutu. She was smart and she was beautiful. Beautiful, inside and out. She was the combination, everything I was looking for in a woman. I saw her sitting against the wall all by her lonesome at a party. I liked what I saw. My eyeballs were like a heat sinking missile on an F-35 fighter plane. They locked in on her. She was my target. I launched the missile. Hit the target. Dead Center. 'Bull's Eye!' And Tutu was mine. All mine."

"Sounds like it happened right away."

"Like anything worthwhile. Worth pursuing. It took some work. It did."

"Now that's a story we can handle, Papa but none of this 'sucking face'"

"There's more to that story which we can talk about later. So, let's see. Where was I? 'Now the moon…'"

"Papa, please. Please stop. You agreed to skip four pages of the 'suck face' part."

"I forgot. Let's see, you're both eighteen now. You'll be begging me to complete this part of the story in two years. Just wait and see. You both are going to come home with a girl, maybe two girls, one in each hand and you're going to beg me to read this chapter. I'll make note of the page. Page 26 of Chapter 1. I'll fold it over now. I'll skip over let's see. These four pages. I'll be waiting for that day and when it comes. I'm going to rub it in."

"No, we won't. That's a day that will never come."

"Want to bet on it?"

"Nope. Our moms don't want us to ever gamble, Papa."

# 3

"Guys, life's a gamble. Don't hide under your mom's skirt. You're too old for that. You don't know what you're missing. You boys got to get off your hoss every now and then. Dust off your jeans. Blow the dirt out of your nose. And 'slap some leather.' Stand up on your own feet. See what the real world is like. You got to get out of that lala land bubble you're being kept in. You got to get some dirt under your fingernails. And some mud and manure on your chaps. You got to open your kimono. Bring balance to your life. Good grief. You're shortchanging yourselves on some real life stuff."

"Papa, my mom said when I'm around you I need to be careful."

"She did!"

"Yes, she did. This is exactly what she said. That you can be a 'heap of trouble.' A troublemaker."

"I knew it. Now why would she say such a dastardly thing?"

"Because you have a reputation that precedes you is what she claims."

"Ahh, that's ancient history. I abandoned my 'childish ways' centuries ago. When Columbus worked out his contract with Queen Isabella and King Ferdinand. I became a man when I was sixteen. And you're eighteen now. You got some catching up to do."

"We just heard something like that recently."

"What I just shared with you comes straight out of the good cookbook."

"What cookbook is that? Sam Choy's?"

"It's got a black cover. Usually, a black cover with a bunch of books tucked between the covers. An Old and New Testament. The B-I-B-L-E."

"We heard it in Sunday School. That's where it was."
"You still go to Sunday School?"
"Yes. Every Sunday."
"Oh my. Oh my! Aren't you too old for that?"
"No, Papa. There's a class for adults too. You should come."
"Hell no."
"Why not?"
"Your mom would drop dead if I did. We should get back to my story. Let's see now, where were we? Where did I leave off?"
"Eve winds..."
"Ah yes. 'Eve winds the clock back to an earlier time. She sees high mountains carved by glaciers into the 'aina (land). Two of the mountain's summits on the largest and youngest of the islands are draped from time to time with snow. The sea teems with life. Honu (turtles), corals, mano (sharks), puffer fish, yellow tang, eels, shells, spinner dolphins. Colorful fish adorn the fringing reefs, carpeted with coral beds of many colors. The uplands are clothed in lime green hills often shrouded in uhiwai (floating mists) pummeled by kipu'upu'u (slanting rain). Meadows once empty are now home to four legged animals imported from far away as gifts to the chief; cattle, horses, sheep, goats. She's describing Waimea I Ka La'i. The forests are thick with trees whose limbs are habitat for forest birds found nowhere else in the world and blossoms that provide all the nectar they need to survive. She's describing Kilauea Forest. Golden plovers from the far north and humpback whales from the Bering Sea arrive in November and leave in April. She's describing the channel off west Maui and east Molokai. This is an abundant land populated by golden skinned people from Hawaiki. Our people. Polynesians, bringing with them in double hulled canoes the political, social, cultural, economic and spiritual tools necessary to exist in this place of plenty.

"Papa, Eve is sure a smart lady for someone who was not allowed to remain in school."
"She was like President Lincoln."
"How so?"
"She taught herself next to a stone bowl fired by kukui nuts. Lincoln, a kerosene lamp."

"Just like our 16th President."

"Yep. She sees a young chief. He is ambitious. Fierce looking, the kind of guy you don't want to meet in a dark alley. Take on in a street fight. He's practical, full of common sense. He's progressive. And achieves what no other chief was been able to accomplish. Kamehameha is his name. Kamehameha, the 'Lonely One.' With cunning, the help of battle experienced warriors, the counsel of pale faced strategists using muskets, cannons and battleships. Kamehameha kicks butt and becomes 'Lord of All.' Eve does not stop. She dreams on. She's on a roll. She also has a Summer Place. In Nuuanu Valley. She's living in a place and time where summer never ends. The first people to discover this archipelago, our people, were able to live for centuries in complete isolation from the rest of humanity and built for themselves a self-determining civilization. Eventually Europeans and Americans began arriving in tall ships. Interlopers, coming to our pae'aina (archipelago) for diverse reasons at different times. Came into our 'comfort zone,' invaded our bubble and turned our 'cart' upside down. They brought with them, 'Life's one and only Constant.' CHANGE. In some ways, for better. In some ways, for worse."

"The Americans imported Asians to slave on their sugar and pineapple plantations. And coaxed our *kane* (men) to work cattle on their fields of green. They replaced our economy with theirs. With Capitalism, an economy built on sand. *Kala* (money, markets, profits first, people last). Ours, was built on *pohaku* (rock). Our ancestors were from a time when the perspective was that we are all connected. People and *'Aina* (Land) working in harmony. With the *'Aina* as Chief and us, it's Servant. All family, one big family. Sky, sea, the fish of the sea, the birds of the forest, the clouds, the stream waters flowing from the mountains to the sea with oversight provided by 40,000 gods peeking over our shoulders. Checking up to be sure we were taking our roles seriously. 'Take care of all who feed you and they will take care of you.' We knew when enough was enough. Save some for tomorrow. Give back, sustain the resource so that it will keep giving. Take only what you need and no more. Share your bounty with others."

"That's terrible Papa, don't you think?"

"In some ways, yes. In others, no. Not really."

"How do you mean?"

"Man is a curious animal. He has this need to see what lies beyond the horizon. He has a need to explore. To fulfill his curiosity. Until he does. He will not stop. It was going to happen at some point in time. Our ancestors found Hawaii first and settled in. Then Captain James Cook and his crew stumbled upon us. It was the same with North America as we learned in American history. The native Indian, native American, settled America first. Columbus fell a little short on the deal he worked out with Queen Isabella. The pilgrims landed at Plymouth Rock in 1620. I'm sure you've heard the story of Captain James Smith and Pocahontas. The establishment of the thirteen colonies. The Louisiana Purchase. The Trail of Tears. The Alamo. The Louis & Clark Expedition. Seward's Folly. And, on and on and on. Change affected the native Indian as it did us. Their 'cart' got turned over as well. Europeans settled on the East coast of North America. Looking west, they could not see where the land ended so they packed up their belongings and kids in covered wagons and moved west. As sad as our history is, we had it good compared to native Americans."

"How so?"

"Their 'cart' was trashed. Their villages were burned. Men killed scalped. Women abused. They were forced to move off their ancestral lands."

"That was terrible."

"It was. But Kui and Elliot, as Hawaiians, we had it so much better."

"You make it sound, Papa. Like it was not a big deal. You know there are going to be folks who will disagree with you. Who will be angry with you? They brought their diseases with them that decimated our population. Almost wiped us out. Cholera. Measles. Typhus. Leprosy. Rodents. Brought their rodents and bugs. We are known as the Endangered Species Capitol of the World."

"Like what?"

"Rats, cats, mongoose, coqui frogs, white flies which are destroying our native forest birds and other species. They brought us a brand of economy which destroyed our subsistence economy. We are consumers now. We once were able to sustain ourselves. We once were a self-sufficient, self-determining Nation. But no longer. Eighty per cent of our food is imported. Ninety per cent of our energy. Washington DC is telling us what we can and cannot do. Capitalism has not served us well. You made that point a few minutes ago. Here's a question?"

"What's your question?"

"Do you think capitalism and globalism are good for us?"

"In some ways, 'yes.' In others, 'no.' Along with 'good,' comes bad. That's the duality of Life. That's how it always was. That's how it always will be. I know for sure. Boy, do I know for sure that the critics are going to jump out of the woodwork, jump right on top of me. That I'm going to be 'tarred and feathered.' Even by family. I have a right to express my opinion. It was a big deal. A big deal. But guys, we need to be practical. Life has got to go on. Today, folks are tearing down statutes of historical figures. Figures who played a major role, for better or worse, in the history of our Country. Stonewall Jackson. Robert E. Lee. Jefferson Davis. Even Columbus. This stuff happened. It's embedded in our Nation's history. A sad, tragic blemish on our Country that cannot be denied nor erased. The change that has to be made is inside us. The bigotry. The hate. The prejudice. Until we clean our insides of these gremlins and replace them with the 'fruits of the Spirit.' The change we want to see will never happen. We will never fully be that 'sweet land of liberty' and 'beacon on the hill' so many have sacrificed their lives for. What's happening in America has found its way here. Captain Cook's few monuments are threatened with removal as well. It's ridiculous. Cook is, for better or worse, a significant player in our archipelago's history. Who's next? William McKinley? What about churches? Are all our Christian churches going to be torched next? The names of streets, roads, freeways, buildings are going to be changed. This can get out of hand. Let's get real here. Let's focus on things that really need changing. There are two sides to every story. Like my friend, Dr. Wayne Dwyer says, we need to have minds 'open to everything and closed to nothing.' We must preserve our humanity. What needs to change is the human heart, the mind, the human spirit. So, what if someone disagrees with my views. It's okay. It's not the end of the world. This emotion called respect sure is in short supply nowadays. Just look at the evangelicals on the evening news and how ignorant they sound. It's totally disgusting. Totally bizarre."

"We hear you, Papa. Yes, we do. Before you have a heart attack, we should move on."

"I'm almost done. When it comes to the Overthrow. Our Queen did the right thing in 1893. We cannot wallow over what happened in January 1893. It's a waste of time to prolong the debate and bicker as to how she should have handled things with the US. She was there in real time. So, she did what she felt in her heart, was best to do under the circumstances. For her Country. For us."

"Why not give reconciliation one last try?"

"I got my view. And my view is if we do, we will be wasting time grinding on the same old, tired bone. We need to move on otherwise we will die in the past. Shortchange ourselves of all the good things life has to offer us. Life is precious. Life is too short. Our time on earth limited. We are here. Then we are gone. We need to look forward to better times, better days. We need to live in the present moment. As I mentioned previously. Our people found Hawaii first. This special place, twelve hundred years ago. Then Cook stumbled upon us in 1778. Now, we're part of the United States of America."

"The Nation that stole our Country."

"A tragic fact. Yes! America, the world's beacon of democracy, stole our Country. But my simplistic reasoning is this. We can't keep crying over spilled milk. Wiping the tears off our faces on the same old rag."

"Why not?"

"We are going to drown in our tears. In our anger. While we are sobbing and sinking in our tears, the thief is doing mischief somewhere else and laughing all the way to the bank. So much has happened since 1893. How will we untangle a past that has become so complicated and messy. So much has happened since the Overthrow. So much has changed in all that time. And, what's sad is! The route towards reconciliation with the US has divided us rather than united us as a people. And who do you think is the cause of the disunity?"

"I don't know."

"It's us. We, as a people. Ourselves. How we can bring our people together, to heal this divide which exists, is the billion-dollar question? I've always been an optimist but have come to realize in my waning years, this is an impossible mission. Our mom had the right idea.

Sovereignty starts here, within oneself. One needs a strong inner spirit. Start there, first. Start small. Then build, grow your seed and nurture it. Do for yourself and *malama* (care for) your family."

"A 'bottom's up' scenario."

"Yeah, you can call it that. We don't have a Nelson Mandela. Someone who can bring us together as a people. I'm saddened to say this, but we don't. So, let's just look forward to better times and better days ahead. America stole our Country from overthrew our Queen. The Country that put a man on the moon in 1968. A country that is governed by 'The Rule of Law,' not by a chief's emotions, moods, feelings. A Country where 'freedom rings.' That has a Bill of Rights. Free elections. A free press. Now, we can say whatever we want without fear of being clubbed to death on the *heiau* or killed in a battle fought exclusively to resolve a disagreement."

"So, where is your mind now?"

"In this moment, the present moment. There are new worlds to discover. New galaxies to explore. I'm excited about the plan to send a manned space craft to Mars. Who knows, we might find a planet way out there with life on it."

"How far is Mars?"

"225 million kilometers from Earth."

"Papa, in miles?"

"140. 140 million miles."

"You're sure we're going to see a Mars landing? 140 million miles, that's so far away. How can you fuel a spacecraft to travel that distance? If something breaks, who will fix it? Food, where will all the meals, water be stored? If someone gets seriously sick or claustrophobic. How are those issues going to be handled?"

"They are great minds working on those practical issues and questions already. It's going to happen. I know it is. Not in my lifetime but yours for sure. Hey, time is passing. That swell you guys have been waiting for at Paniau has just arrived?"

"How do you know, Papa?"

"Watching the clouds. That's how. So, we should be getting back to my story. Samuel and Lala will be popping in soon. Where were we?"

"Eve could not…"

"Eve could not suppress her excitement. 'I want to find that place.' Inspired by her excitement, her colleagues agreed. 'Let's go find that place. Let's go now! We have everything to gain. Nothing to lose.' They had no idea that the three of them would be the architects and builders of this archipelago of Never-Ending Summers just above the equator. It would take them millions of years and hundreds of change orders to construct but they had the time, patience and perseverance needed to construct it. Little did the three of them know, they would soon be taking the first step of a very, very long journey."

"They spent what little free time they were allowed, quietly looking for a soft spot in the cauldron's interior. And, eureka, they found it. For the first time ever, Eve used her newly acquired gift of Fire. A heritage passed on to her by her maternal grandfather. A gift denied her mom because of the dishonor and disgrace she brought upon her family because of all her poor, obtuse, reckless choices. She was defiant, rude, self-absorbed, narcissistic. But the twig that broke their spine was her refusal not to give her baby up to them when it was born. Not forever. Just until she could get her act together. Hoping on hope, they begged and pleaded with her for months. It was an exercise in utter futility. Bullheadedness was a family trait. It was payback time and a father scorned sometimes does what a father scorned does."

"Which was?"

"He gave Eve the gift that was originally destined for her mom instead. Unwittingly."

"Unwittingly? What does that mean?"

"Unknowingly? She wasn't expecting it?"

"It was a total surprise. For her, mom. And for Eve. Yes! It was what they needed to implement their plan."

"It's just too bad they could not work things out."

"It was unfortunate but that's life. Many attempts were made by her mom and dad to steer her. Put her on a path so she could have a good life. They did their very best to help her become a responsible and contributing community person. A decent human being. They gave her their best."

"She didn't appreciate it."

"Sadly, she didn't. She didn't appreciate the rules they placed on her. That's what good parents do. Give their kids structure. A box to live in. Parameters. She called them 'freaks.' Said they were 'old fashioned.' Suggested they read Dr. Benjamin Spock and catch up with the times. She had the audacity to give them a copy of Spock's book. Her dad looked at the cover and threw it in the trash. She told them that they needed to modernize. Contemporize their thinking. She was going to do things her way. Show them the way. And she did."

"So that was it!"

"That was it. Her defiance was outrageous. It reached the point where it was best to let her go. To let her fly. As much as they didn't want to let her go. They did. Her dad packed up her things and threw her out of the house. Showed her the door."

"Did they think she was going to 'crash and burn?'"

"I think they were like most parents."

"Which is?"

"They were praying and hoping she would come to her senses. But pride! Her own selfish pride made things difficult. She remained unapologetic. She refused to grow up."

"That's very sad."

"So, let's get back to our story."

"Papa, I can't see you doing what Eve's dad did to her mom. You're such a softie."

"I would never put up with that kind of c..p either, Kui. A softie I am not. There are certain things I will not put up with as a dad. Being disgraced. Disrespected. Dishonored. These are three of a long list. I will never put up with a punk kid. Never. Especially my own. Her mom deserved what she got."

"But Eve, she didn't deserve to be shunned. She had nothing to do with her mom's bad attitude."

"She did not. Unfortunately, she was 'guilty' by association. That's how the ball bounces sometimes guys. The innocent is hurt as well."

"Which is not fair."

"Life sometimes is not fair. But in the end, redemption showed up in a gift box plopped by a stranger on her doorstep."

"Papa, you have to give us the details about the gift."

"I didn't tell you that part before?"

"No, you did not."

"Well, I'm right at that part of the story."

"Great."

"Well okay. Got my bearings. Here we go. 'She was busy polishing the living room floor when there was a loud knock on the front door. It only took her half a minute to respond but by the time she opened the door to see who it was. Whoever it was, was by the mailbox, heading down the sidewalk of their tree lined street. A tall muscular man with a long gait, salt and pepper ponytail wearing a blue baseball cap, dressed in a navy-blue shirt. His sleeves were rolled up. Tattoos plastered his bulging arms. He was in a big hurry. In leaving, he left a trail of cigar smoke in his wake. Eve called out, 'Please stop. Who are you? Who is this for?' He took the cigar out of his mouth and without looking back replied in a loud, clear, friendly, baritone voice, 'Enjoy your gift from your grandparents. It's going to help you and your friends achieve your dream to 'reach the light.' To reach eternity. Enjoy it but be very careful. Be sure, be very sure to read the instructions, forwards and backwards. Very carefully.'"

"She chased after the stranger. Her curiosity was getting the best of her. She wanted to find out who he was. '...gift...Happy Birthday... achieve your dream...Very carefully.' She was hoping he would stop even if only for a moment to open a window into her past."

"Please, please stop."

"Another day. I got to run. He was there then he was gone. Vanished Evaporated into the air."

"Like Caspar, the ghost?"

"Like Caspar. He had accomplished his mission and clearly was in no mood to linger and make 'small talk.'"

"Eve was disappointed. She stood in place for a minute with jaw wide open. Then did the only thing she could do. Hurried back to the house, picked up the rectangular box leaning against the outer edge of the door frame. She was pleasantly surprised. It was indeed definitely for her. She was taken aback as she had never received a package before. She took it to her bedroom and placed it on the nightstand. There were no other markings on the nicely wrapped box. Just her name inscribed in beautiful calligraphy. EVE ANN FAY. She shook the box. It didn't rattle. And it was heavy. At least twenty pounds. Whatever it was, it was something solid. She slowly and carefully unwrapped the mysterious pink box and lifted the cover off. Beneath it lay a beautiful card signed by the maternal grandparents she had never met. And would never meet. James and Mary Kaala Fay. The card was accompanied by a five-page letter."

"Papa, can you read us the letter?"

"Another time. It's all mushy stuff. But one of the pages laid out the process on how she was to use what was in the box. You want to take a guess what it was?"

"Something for a girl. Something heavy. Got no idea, Papa. Just tell us!"

"A sawed-off double barrel shotgun."

"A shotgun. What an odd gift to give a girl."

"A shotgun that spit fire. It will make sense in a minute."

"Just tell us Papa. Don't stretch us out."

"She read the instructions repeatedly, with all the cautions it came with as she had been told to do, until it was all firmly committed to memory. She was able to connect what the stranger had told her as he walked away with the card's contents. 'Use it wisely.' She looked at the gun. Pulled it out of the box and tucked it firmly into the crook of her right shoulder. She liked how it felt and liked most especially the way she looked in the mirror."

"She must have looked like Super Woman."

"Oh, better than. Better than. She looked like Wonder Woman. The only guns her brothers had were pellet guns. But nothing the equal of hers. She was tempted to fiddle with its trigger but the card's message said clearly that she should squeeze it ONLY when necessary."

"Why?"

"Because it was going to spit fire. Fire she had never seen before. It would demolish, melt, incinerate, cauterize anything and everything in its way. It was going to spit fire like the mythical fire dragon in the movies."

"Like Drogon, Viserion or Rhaegal?"

"Never heard of them."

"Characters in Game of Thrones."

"Nope, don't know that game. Eve was the proud owner of this ominous shotgun that the letter that lay on her nightstand said its dual barrels would shoot real fire. Her grandpa's letter emphasized, the shotgun when used, would implode the Capitol Building in the mid-section of town in seconds. And it would decimate an entire city block in minutes. She was astounded."

"Wow, I can use a gun like this in several ways. Many ways." Eve said to herself.

"Ideas quickly filled her head."

"Her mind was racing but she had to get back to her chores. She had been distracted long enough and needed to get the dining floor polished and a bunch of other assignments done. She carefully put her gift back in the box in which it came along with the wrapping paper, ribbons, card, hiding it all in her closet. Eve quickly completed her scrubbing and cleaning. The gift gave her the 'pick up' she needed to make it through what otherwise would have been just another day. All the while thinking about the visitor who refused to give her some face time. Was it her grandpa? Or someone representing him? Her curiosity was beginning to get the best of her."

"It was her special day but her 'family' treated it as just another day. No one wished her 'Happy Birthday' at breakfast or before they left the house that morning. There would be no gifts she knew from any of them. Just a slew of grumbles, complaints and bitching when they got home. The usual."

"She needed to hurry as she was running late. It was the one day during the week when she could meet with Bertha and Bessie at the cemetery. They were at a place where their plan could not be refined further. It was done. It just needed to be operationalized. Put into action."

"Now it's back to where we were with the story. Here. Here we go. 'She met with Bertha and Bessie at their secret spot. The cemetery where the town's people came only when they had to send someone off to the boneyard. Where they simply went through the required motions that made them feel holy and spiritually competent on 'end of life' rituals. Reading a few passages from the Gospel or the Book of Common Prayer. Singing Amazing Grace and Rock of Ages or How Great Thou

Art. Dropping a few tears along the way. And, ending with 'Hail Mary, full of grace. Four balls take your base' if it was a guy. The base being a hole in the ground six feet deep over which eventually a stone was placed to identify who the lucky resident was. So, they didn't suspect the three spinsters were up to anything much. If anything, Eve and her buddies were affirming the town folk's belief. That they were three weirdos, just three old maids, three harmless nut cases, congregating with the spirits of the dead on a lazy, sun shiny day."

"Though a bit late, Eve proudly brought her sawed off, double barrel shotgun along with her and put it gently in front of Bertha and Bessie. Right there under the shade of the banyan where they always huddled. 'A weapon for a birthday gift!' Initially, both were appalled just as she anticipated they would be. She passed around her birthday card and explained the power of her gift. Immediately, Bertha and Bessie, had a change of heart. They were as excited as Eve about the possibilities the ominous gift added to their plan. Directed and unlimited fire power. Whoa! She, well they, would be fighting, Fire with Fire. Bertha and Bessie, encouraged Eve to use her gift."

"When?"

"Now! This very moment."

"Are you serious?"

"'Of course, we are! Of course, we are!' both chanted in unison. All of them had no idea, they were playing with real fire. They did not know this was their pivotal moment."

"Eve, cradled the shotgun's butt in her right shoulder, took aim at the 'chink' in the cauldron's ceiling and gently squeezed the trigger. Powerful volcanic jets of fire penetrated what was supposed to be an impenetrable ceiling. It took a few seconds for her to manage the shotgun's recoil but once she had that figured out, she declared full scale war on the cauldron. The cauldron which had been for them, not a warm, loving, safe home but a living hell, a prison."

"They looked in awe, watched with glee as the cauldron's roof collapsed and chunks of shattered mantle piled up all around them. Fire that seconds ago kept them in bondage and now in Eve's possession, was their Emancipator. A wide *puka* (hole) for them to flee through had just opened. Eve got carried away with her new toy. She kept squeezing the trigger."

"They stood frozen stiff for a moment looking at their *alanui* (pathway) to freedom. Like Moses had done for the Israelite's when he parted the waters of the Red Sea with his staff to help his people flee the wicked Egyptian Pharaoh to Canaan. Eve had done for them with her new toy in a minute. The time had come for them to execute the plan they had quietly and meticulously worked on forever to move them finally to this fairy tale 'Land of Never-Ending Summers.' The time had come for them to take their dream and make it real."

"After recovering from their moonstruck moment, Eve broke the silence. 'We cannot! We must not turn back to the pain we want to leave behind us.' Her companions in crime assured her they would make it to the top of the sea. To the sunlight. With her Fire and their collective counsel, she would build for them through this alanui, a series of ladders to the top of the Pacific Ocean. An escalator to freedom. An elevator to 'eternity.' Yes, the road would be long, filled with obstacles, disappointments and potholes for sure but at road's end, a spectacular place would be there to meet them. A place lathered in sunshine and draped in rainbows. An utopia of poppy fields, birds bubbling with song, a sky filled with rainbows."

"Even with all the confidence Bertha and Bessie showered on her, Eve was still a wee bit skeptical, unsure of herself. She had a question. 'How could they be so certain they would make it?' Bertha and Bessie smiled and laughed, not at her but at her incredulity. Both told Eve, clearly and emphatically, that she possessed in her DNA what they did not have. Two special chromosomes. One, called Fire. The other, Perseverance. The Fire she just used to puncture a hole for them to sneak through, created a hot spot on the ocean floor which has never been capped in 34 million years and scientists in 2020 forecast will be spewing magma for another 500,000 years. The Perseverance that had brought them this far. To this fiery point. To the 'tipping point' they needed to fly into a future which would be of their creation and only theirs."

"This is stuff we can share with our moms."

"Absolutely. And your dads. Ah, my future is assured. You got my message. I've made a breakthrough. You got my back. Whew! Impress them. Let them know your Papa is not the Huck Finn or Tommy Sawyer, they think I am. I'm a good guy. Tell them, their fears are baseless. Tell them, I'm truly one of Jesus' disciples. I've been reborn. I'm now a choir boy. Emphasize I'm a 'fisher of men' put on the Earth with a rod and reel to serve God and be a blessing to others. Including, you Elliot and you Kui, as well as Samuel and Lala.

"With her Fire power and all the strategic and tactical lessons learned from their dreams at escape. They had no fear and no doubt that they would prevail. 'We will succeed. Besides! We are *wahine* (women) with nothing to lose.' As *wahine* they would be creating a brave new world. A Woman's world. A world where 'We will have a voice.' This was their fleeting moment. A moment to revel in. They would not turn back. There was too much to look forward to. They were confident they had all the assets necessary to secure their freedom and build a ladder to this 'brave new world.' A world they would be the architects of. Their world."

"They repeatedly emphasized that they trusted and believed in her. Yes! She was stubborn. Stubborn as an ox but not reckless. And, for as long as they had known her, she was patient, smart, thoughtful, mindful and strategic in all she did. They had total faith in her judgment. And they anticipated because they were of the 'weaker sex' they would not be taken seriously. Which they believed would give them an advantage, competitive advantage. Eve sat silently for a time gathering her thoughts as well as her emotions."

"I will lead on one condition."

"And what might that be?"

"We must continue to work as a team."

"Of course! Teamwork is the only way our plan will work. Can work."

With that understanding anchored in stone, the trio was ready to journey to their 'new world.' Onward. Upward. Skyward. To the light, the sunlight far above. They stepped across the point of no return and swore on their sacred honor they would never, no matter what, forsake, abandon their plan. They would never regret leaving their families who had used and abused them, treated them like scum, denied them the quality of life they were sorely deserving of. Families who allowed them to develop their hands but not their heads. They would never miss this place governed for centuries by patriarchs. Men, silver bearded men, infested with archaic traditions and handcuffed to old ways. Who insisted women were the lesser of the sexes. If they remained in place, like scores of women before them had chosen to do, the status quo would continue to prevail. Nothing would 'Change' for them. They would be powerless, voiceless. Forced to live unfulfilled lives. And, when death came knocking, die miserable. A small wee voice kept egging them on! Kept telling them: "You deserve better. Get out of here. Now!'"

"The breach in the cauldron was indeed their *kahea* (call to action). The inspiration they needed to move on. No one, no circumstance was going to put them back in the 'crock pot,' Eve had just busted them out of. Unfortunately, time was not on their side. The train was pulling quickly away. It all happened so abruptly. So unexpectedly. There was no time to say goodbye to their pets and rag dolls. Who provided them shoulders to cry on in bad times. Who gave them a reason to continue to live when they were ready to throw up their hands and call it quits. Eve had no time to retrieve three special books. <u>Little Women</u> by Louisa May Alcott, <u>The Ladies of Seneca Falls</u> by Miriam Gurd and Nathaniel Hawthorne's <u>The Scarlet Letter</u>. They took a last look at the hell hole which had been home for almost three decades.

As they stepped into their portal to freedom. Eve stopped them. 'Wait! Hold up a second. I should widen the hot spot so it can never be closed.'"

"Why? Let's just get out of here before a posse comes after us," Bertha exclaimed.

"Eve laughed. 'My flame thrower is bigger than any weapon they must throw at us. I'm suggesting this so other who want to escape will be able to.'"

"They watched as she unleashed her powerful inheritance for a second time, torching the edges of the hole to extend the quarter mile hot spot five miles out in a perfect circle. When she was done, they took their first step through the portal towards the light."

"Isn't there more to the story."

"Yes, there is."

"Then why are you stopping?"

"My superego is interrupting me."

"Superego. Who's that?"
"Kimo, he's part of my psychic apparatus."
"Psychic apparatus? Don't think we ever met this friend, Papa."
"No, you haven't. Sorry. I need to take this call."
"Where is he?"
"In my head. I'll be a few minutes. Let's take a ten-minute break. Grab a drink and a spam musubi from the cooler. There's fruit. Chips. Cookies. Help yourselves. Enjoy the beauty of Waimea. Sorry! I failed to mute my phone. Failing to do so was one huge mistake.

ΩΩΩΩΩΩΩ

"Kimo, what's up?"
"Wow, your creation story gets better and better, Kimo sabe."
"You think so, Kimo?"
"I'm impressed. You are getting to be quite the storyteller. But if you want some constructive criticism, I am more than happy to offer you a few helpful ideas. I would…"
"Kimo, your offer is timely, in fact I do! I'd appreciate your feedback. I really would."
"Ah, Kimo sabe, you must not be feeling well."
"What do you mean?"
"I'm pleasantly surprised, as you've never ever wanted my constructive criticism so readily."
"Well, I do today. I'm practicing my talk on my grandsons for a special audience…"
"I'm honored."
"So yes, I need to be really on top of my game. I want this to be a signature presentation with all the 'bells and whistles.' I think you know what I mean. So, yes! I really do want to hear what you have to say. The stage is yours, Kimo. Go for it. Let me have it! Pull no punches. I'm looking forward to your side bar critique! Help me make the 'best better.'"

"Let's start with the good stuff. First, I like your characters. You know how to ride the edge between reality and fantasy in developing them. You really make me feel sorry for Eve. Poor girl, she sure needed to get out of her horrific, loveless situation. Her mother sounds like my mother. Two, I love your hook. How you lured me in. That 'once upon a time, long, long ago' fairy tale, Goldilocks, Sleeping Beauty intro line still works. And, the stormy morning piece, your description of all that's happening on top of the water and on the bottom of the sea is top notch..."

"Kimo stop. Stop! Stop! Let's cut to the 'chase.' I got my grandsons on hold. I want to hear the..."

"The constructive stuff."

"The bad stuff."

"Constructive stuff. Bad stuff."

"Same. Same. Is there a difference?" Kimo was beginning to irritate me.

"Not really. Well okay. Here it is. Once upon a time five of my *kupuna* (elders), wisdom keepers, thought leaders had this to say about the *mana* (power) that comes with just getting to the point. Here is the first, 'Brevity is the soul of wit.'"

"What wise ass was that?"

"It's a line from Shakespeare's Hamlet. Willy Shakespeare is the *kupuna*, Thought Leader of those six words. You want to hear the next one or shall I quit while I'm ahead, Kimo sabe? My *na'au* (gut) tells me your blood is beginning to heat up."

"Please go on with the final four! And, be quick about it, Kimo." I struggle to say, "Please."

"'Be sincere. Be brief. Be seated.' The 32nd President."

"Eisenhower? General Dwight Eisenhower."

"Close. FDR."

"Are you sure?"

"I am. Here's the third quote from George Burns."

"I remember him."

"'The secret of a good sermon is to have a good beginning and a good ending; and to have the two as close as possible.'"

"You may quit there, Kimo. I don't need to hear the rest."

"Why not?"

"I know what your criticism is without you saying it!"

"You do?"

"Yes. You think my introduction is too long."

"It's good as it is but it will be perfect if you trim it some. A wee bit. Just a squish. Tighten things up a little. Otherwise, your audience is going to fall asleep. A few folks might walk out on you. Even shoot spit balls at you."

"Well, I'm not done, Kimo. I like my opening the way it is. I have a few more paragraphs to go."

"*You're* not done! Oh, my goodness. You're going to put your audience to sleep for sure. You are going to kill your audience. Good grief, boss! If you want to be an effective storyteller, a master storyteller, you must think about your audience."

"I don't want to hear whatever you have left to say, Kimo. I don't need to hear it. I've heard enough out of you. Go back in your cave and stay there. Just get out of my face."

"Just trying to be helpful, boss. Call me when the coast is clear. I'll be in my cave doing my meditation and mind stretching exercises."

"Good idea. Go be 'still' in your Zen Garden. Go be 'zenful.' Go be 'mindful.' And 'soulful.' I have a story to tell. A story to finish. An audience that's patiently waiting for me."

"I did my good turn for the day. Remember Kimo sabe. Brevity. Get to the point. 'Cut to the chase.'"

"Kimo, you sure know how to get on my nerves. Getout of here."

ΩΩΩΩΩΩΩ

# 5

"Who was that, Papa?"
"Kimo."
"A new friend of yours?"
"He's an old friend."
"He lives here in Waimea?"
"No."
"Where does Kimo live?"
"In my head."
"In your head?"
"Yes."
"We'd sure like to meet him."

"Nah. You don't need to meet him. As I mentioned, he's part of my psychic apparatus. Kimo, is my superego. There's Kai, my ego. Malia, my id. Kimo is the CEO of my corporation. CEO of my internal Board of Directors. Kai, Treasurer. Malia, secretary."

"Why don't you want us to meet him?"
"He's a jerk. Let me finish the story. Where was I?"
"He sounded like he was trying to be helpful, Papa."
"There's times when he really tries to be helpful."
"But not today."
"Not today. So where was I?"
"But alas..."

"But alas an obstacle appeared from out of nowhere to disrupt their meticulously designed plan. The troublemaker who stood in their way was the Pacific Ocean. The mighty ocean was there to greet them with tidings of 'little joy.' Like a power lifter in a strong man contest, Eve's powerful plume pushed up with all her flaming might against the weight of the massive body of water pressing down on them with deadly intent. Eve kept directing, blasting an incessant barrage of powerful volcanic fountains into the ocean's belly. Used her ominous gift to create a protective shield and an air space around them to help move them towards the light far above. To what would be in due time would be their 'eternity.' Her two cohorts playing the role of battlefield commanders kept constant watch for pockets of weakness in the enemy's front line. When finding a vulnerable pouch, they directed Eve to hose it with Fire. Fire whose heat was intense as the sun's epicenter. Fire, always ascending skywards, building a lava ladder to the sunlight, constructing platform after platform of lava steppes. They were relentless, focused, unforgiving. Determined to reach 'eternity.'

Employing gravity, the ocean pressed down as hard as it could on the threesome. Did it's darnest to force them back into the 'hot spot.' Intent on capping the wide gap. Then soldering it's seams shut tight. Never to be opened again. It tried to wear them down, dampen their spirits, doubt themselves. Suffocate them, using water boarding tactics, pouring water launched from big artillery cannons and forcing depth charges down their throats. It even mined their route with sophisticated improvised explosive devices. But no matter what the Pacific tried; nothing was working against the three. Eve's spirit, her grit bolstered by Fire, 'standing on the shoulders of her ancestors,' the confidence of two loyal friends and a flourishing belief in herself.

Their joint strategy could not be decoded. Their communications hacked. Thus, their battle plan was working, working better than anticipated. The signs were evident, the end, 'eternity' was near. They were in control, winning. That 'light' once so dim and so distant, glowed brighter, drew nearer each day. A collection of many little wins was leading to a big victory. Water had underestimated their passion to flee their tragic circumstances, their sense of purpose and commitment to trample over anyone who got in the way. The big question in Water's moronic mind along with his field commanders was, 'What did these three dumb spinsters from the dark side of the cauldron know about fighting a war? Nothing!' They did not have access to resources. They did not have battlefield experience. They laughingly and confidently predicted, 'This war is going to be over quickly. We are going to win 'hands down.' They, of course, assumed badly. And, in assuming badly, paid the price for their arrogance.

"They got their asses kicked."

"Hold on Elliot. Remember it's my story."

"Okay, read on. Sorry, I won't interrupt you, Papa."

"Thank you, Elliot. That would really help my train of thought. My ability to focus. 'Two of nature's most powerful forces declared war on each other eons ago. Fire versus Water. The Pacific Ocean continues to lose a war it could have avoided had it simply minded its own business and allowed Fire easy entry into the sunlight. In 2020, Fire is erecting a new island to attach to what British Explorer James Cook called the Sandwich Islands while looking for the Northwest passage."

"Papa, this is two hundred years later."

"It sure is."

"And magma continues to pour from that hot spot."

"And it will do so for a very long time."

"I'm sorry. I keep interrupting but I can't help it, Papa. I like your creation story even if it's fiction."

"It's okay. An occasional interruption is okay. It gives me inspiration. Purpose. Good energy. Some new ideas. Things to add. Things to delete. The Bible was written by humans. So was the Torah and the Koran. By folks trying to make sense of things. Answers to some of these great questions. How did the world come to be? What is our place is in it? Why are we here? What is our purpose on this beautiful planet? Who put us here? As a Christian, I have my view which is all the result of my upbringing. My dear friend Walter is Buddhist. He has his view. And Ahmad. He's got his. We all have our view. Our Story 'to tell the Nations?'"

"Ahmad. The dude who faces mecca several times a day on his mat. In his white sheet. Who wears a turban. And sticks his butt in the air."

"Yes. That's the dude. We had an aunt who was an atheist."

"Atheist? What's an atheist?"

"Someone who doesn't believe in God at all. And there are the agnostics. Those who are not sure. The 'fence riders' I call them.

Who are fighting within themselves. We had a doctor friend who was Unitarian. For those who believe in a divine, it's 'different strokes for different folks.' We all have our pathway to the Gold Gate. And that's okay. St. Peter will be waiting at my Gate. When I get to the Gate, I hope he lets me through."

"Back to the story, Papa."

"Loihi (long island) is a 'work in progress' and will make its grand debut in ten thousand years. When it sticks its head above the Pacific, Loihi will replace our very Big Island as the southern bookend of The Hawaiian Archipelago."

"Three courageous women battling the myth that they were the weakest of the sexes won the day. Won the war. Using feminine intelligence, they prevailed and built a staircase to the top of the Pacific. A ladder made of stone. When they ruptured the Earth's mantle, they found themselves in 'no woman's' land. Once the hot magma pouring out of the hot spot collided and merged with the ocean's cold water, viscous fluid was transformed into lava, starting a 'layering' process. A 'cake layering' process. Layer upon layer of lava sheets piled over each other and created over time our pae'aina, The Hawaiian Archipelago. A fifteen-hundred-mile-long lei of atolls, seamounts, islets, sandpits and islands. Some large, some small. All born of fire. All reaching for the sky. All originating from this hot spot, geologists and volcanologists forecast will be vomiting magma for another five hundred thousand years."

"Wow. Five hundred thousand years."

"Yep. Five hundred thousand years. Now that's a factoid you can share with your mama's when they 'cross examine' you at dinner tonight. A few layers were able to pierce the ocean's surface, but many remain submerged, preserved forever in watery darkness. Those that breached the surface became atolls and islands. Kure Atoll is the pae'aina's (archipelago's) northern anchor. Hawai'i Island, our island, it's southern anchor."

"That you mentioned a little while ago, Papa."

"You're paying close attention, Kui!"

"Yes, I am. I hope there's more to your story."

"Sorry, I'm getting close to the end. 'As Fire, Eve accepted the challenge to 'pick up the sword.' To do battle. And fight she did with the help of her two friends! In this unsigned, informal declaration of war. Their first casualty was Earth's mantle. The Pacific Ocean was next. Both had armies, strategists, technicians, battle plans, armaments of their own. But as Fire, Eve had an advantage. A competitive advantage. She possessed Fire but more than that, she and her 'partners' possessed passion. They had a purpose. They were 'fired up.' Their opponents from the 'get go' had underestimated them. Took them 'cheap.' Did their planning on napkins on the 19th hole at the Country Club over champagne. Just assumed they were dealing with naive ladies trying to trespass into a man's world who would tire quickly, long for home and give up. So, they under planned and ended up paying dearly for assuming wrong."

"They should have known better."

"Yes, so you would think. But that's what arrogance does. Well, to some not all of us. Eve and her cohorts had a clear purpose. Were tough as nails in spirit. They were focused and fearless. Together, they pressed forward and upward. Up towards the light! They kept adjusting their plan, strategy and tactics based on real time circumstances. Moving upward and always towards 'eternity.' Always toward the sun, the sunlight that grew closer, bigger, brighter and warmer with each passing day. Their instincts and sixth sense told them they were closing in on their target. They knew their foes would never admit they were losing the war and losing badly. They would never wave a surrender flag or send out a white dove. But that was the least of their concerns. They knew what they knew. They were going to reach the light. And that for them was all that mattered!"

"They closed in on their objective two hours before dawn rippled across the eastern horizon. Something surprising was occurring. The water cannons went silent. The depth charges no longer fell. There were no mine fields to clear. The forces of Water had lost their will to fight. Had run out of assets. But then the deafening silence of the long war they thought would never end, was replaced by the turbulence of an angry, raging sea and a dark, hostile sky. The sea was furious, choppy, ticked off. Mad about what! They had no idea. But they didn't waiver."

"They stayed with their plan and pressed on."

"Yes. The old saying is, 'If it ain't broke. Don't fix it.' And that's what they did. They stayed true to their plan. The setting moon looked like an aircraft carrier tossing, turning and bouncing about like a tennis ball adrift on an angry sea. Was it coincidence that this morning was much like the morning when Eve blew a hole in the earth's crust eons ago to open a door to their fantasy 'Land of Never-Ending Summers?'"

"The ocean was irate. It was salivating, foaming white with waves five miles long. Waves tumbling violently upon, crashing haphazardly over each other. Frothing white waves with faces, long faces fifty story's high. When the faces curled into barrels, the barrels were fifty feet in diameter. Barrels, surfers dream about. The lightning rods shooting from the heavens were intense. The sky was an inferno. Ablaze in every direction. The claps of thunder, simply deafening. Rocking, rolling, rumbling, roaring at will from one end of the firmament to the other. The rain poured down in vats with raindrops the size of golf balls. When the drops pelted the sea, the impact hurt. Though it was 'not the end times,' it looked, felt, sounded like it was. The ghastly scenes produced by the storm replicated images from Revelations 22, Armageddon, The Apocalypse."

"At the very second dawn broke across the horizon, the volcanic plume punctured the ocean's surface and fired an expansive mushroom crown of Fire, ash and debris high up into the twilit sky. At its zenith, the huge umbrella shaped crown splintered, shattered, broke into smaller crowns. Hundreds of them that looked like ballerinas, dancing about in the predawn sky. Mini parasols that scattered, loitered, dangled above the horizon. The point where sky meets ocean. And, after a time the miniature chutes fell earthwards and vanished into the sea. It was dazzling pyrotechnics show of 'shock and awe.' Brilliant colors splashed across the skyline, exceeding anything Van Gogh, Monet or Picasso could put to canvas.

"It was their way of celebrating a long, epic and hard-fought journey. Traveling from the bottom of the ocean to its crest (49,300 fathoms), from captivity to freedom, from darkness to light. They were toasting their victory. First, over Earth. Then Water. The trio had reached their destination. They knew what they were up against and to triumph, they had to use everything in their arsenal to achieve the freedom, the result they wanted. On one side of the spectrum, the fiery drama was stunning, stunningly beautiful and glorious. On the other, beastly, terrifying, and frightful. The sun rose in the east and started its daily trek across the dawning sky as it had done since the beginning of time."

"Eve and her companions had reached the 'Promise Land.' Not Abraham and Isaac's Canaan 'flowing with milk and honey' but a big, bright, cobalt blue sky drenched in sunshine and lathered in sunlight. With the Patience of Job. The Faith of Mother Teresa. The Stubbornness of a Mule. They defeated their antagonists. And, as they popped their fiery heads above the ocean's surface, the trio gleefully bellowed in sweet unison, "Good Morning World. We're here. It took us awhile to get here. Now that we're here. We're staying." They were, finally, finally able to rendezvous with First Light (*Kukui Wanao*). Wrap their arms around the Sun (*Kahikina*) and hug the Sky (*Lani*). It was their WOW moment. Eve would in time be crowned Pele, Fire Goddess of The Archipelago by the first people of these islands. The *kanaka maoli*, our people. Guys, that's my fairy tale."

"What happened to Bessie and Bertha?"

"They ventured off to live fulfilled lives of their own in a place filled with rainbows and night skies raining stars."

"So, they lived happily forever after, Papa?"

"Yes, they did. Did you like the story, Kui?"

"I sure did! You changed it a lot from what I remember. Thank you."

"How about you, Elliot?"

"Yes, I did. I wish there was more."

"I'm sure we'll be able to do this again."

"Papa, have you read the *Kumulipo*?"

"Yes, I have Kui."

"That's a good story also."

"Yes, it is. It truly is. It's the Hawaiian story of creation."

"There's the Bible story about creation and the Kumulipo Story. We've studied the Big Bang in science class. Which story do you like best, Papa?"

"All of them. I like all of them but to answer your question truthfully and directly. I like the Genesis Story best."

"Can you tell us why?"

"Of course. But later on. It's one of the questions I believe is on the list of questions you sent me which got me really thinking about my connection to God."

"Yes, it is on our list of twenty questions."

"Can we talk about it when we go down the list of questions?"

"Of course. Let's see, it's question three. Can you tell us some Pele stories before we get to the questions that Elliot and I have for you, Papa?"

"Are you sure. Most kids these days think Pele stories are a waste of time because it's mumbo jumbo stuff. Tall tales. Fairy tales. Made up stuff."

"Not us. We still like to hear fairy tales."

"Well then. Buckle up. Here we go."

"Papa."

"Yes."

"Will you reconsider?"

"Reconsider what?"

"Telling us about Kimo."

"You boys sure want to meet him, don't you?"

"Yes. And his brother and sister."

"Maybe at a time when he's not being a total jerk and smart ass. Okay."

"Promise?"

"Promise."

"Papa, we promise we will not interrupt you at all from here. Well on one condition."

"You're negotiating with me. I must say Kui, you are persistent. You got my mom's gene for persistence."

"Is that a good thing?"

"Well, it depends. Depends on how and when you use it. So, what's the condition? Tell me."

"You promise to tell us about Kimo at some point?"

"Fair enough. Fair enough. I accept. What's that look on your face about, Elliot?"

"I'm going to remind you, Papa. Sometimes you like to pretend, 'forget.'"

"Nah! I'm not like that at all. I'm very transparent. You know that. My face is a wide 'open book.' I've known the truth. For a long time, I might add. I've been set free."

"Papa, you still must finish the story about the car accident on Kawaihae Road. You said it was a black dog that ran in front of the car. You didn't want to hit the dog, so you ran off the road. But other folks who were in the back and front of you didn't see a dog. There's the story about who really put the thumb tacks and chewing gum under your second-grade teacher's chair. A kid named Bernaldo took the blame. Later, he said you bribed him. There are a few others."

"Don't you worry. Before this day is over, you'll meet Kimo. He tends to talk too much so I'm going to limit your time with him to five minutes. Five minutes and then he's back in the closet. Back in his Zen

Garden. So here are some of my Pele stories. I think two of these are repeats. You've heard them before."

"We don't care. Replays are okay, Papa. Right Kui?"

"Yea, repeats are fine. Plus, we know, Papa. Your repeats are never the same. We know you've done some editing."

Some of us have been fortunate to meet Pele in one of her manifestations and lived to 'show and tell' family and friends about these surprise, serendipitous encounters. There will always be the 'Doubting Thomas's, the skeptics, the non believers but that's okay. It takes all segments of humanity to 'make the world go round.' Some of the stories are difficult to believe about Pele as she is so mercurial.

A) There's Pele the tee toller manifesting herself as a beautiful, slender, tall, head turning young lady ready for a night on the town dressed in red walking down Kalakaua Avenue on a balmy Waikiki evening to take in a show in The Crown Room of The Royal Hawaiian Hotel. No, she's not looking for conversation, for company or even for love. She insists to the greeter at the door she just wants to sit alone in a dimly lit corner, away from everyone. Why wear a red dress that glows in the dark if one wants to be anonymous, persona non grata? That was what the gentleman who told me this story wondered. He was the one who waited on her. We both took Hawaiian 101 from Ms. Maukele at UH-Manoa in 1969. He said this *'wahine'* was gorgeous. She looked like a Brazilian model and was for the most 'pleasant.' But, but there was something ghostly, scary, strange, paranormal about her. Her eyes glowed red, red like the dress she was wearing. She had a lisp, spoke in English and Hawaiian, poetic Hawaiian. The woman gave him an 'eerie feeling.' She wanted scotch and asked him to set a fresh bottle on her table. Her own bottle of scotch. It was a law violation, but the bar tender said it was okay.

"The liquor commissioner was not going to be paying us a visit that night, Kai the bartender told me. The commissioner was going to be on the other side of the avenue. She pulled out a crystal glass from her purse and filled it herself. She then asked me to take two chairs away but to leave one. One, for Kamapua'a. She was sure he would show up. The only company she needed for the time being was her own. She took her 'scotch on the rocks' and downed her drinks like a stevedore on steroids. After drinking a whole bottle she requested another. He suggested she call it a night. To his surprise the sweet woman's arrogant, nasty side' surfaced. "She snapped at me. 'The night is young. I'll decide when I've had enough you little squirt.' She stood up, put her heels back on to show me she could walk a straight line in heels without wobbling."

"What did you do?"

"Got her another bottle. I honored her request. We let her break all the liquor rules. She finished that bottle. She asked for one more. Near the end of the show, she requested her tab. I got it from the bar tender. It was a size-able tab. She looked it over, smiled, thanked me. When I returned about a half hour later to announce, 'last call.' She was gone. I looked at the bottle. It was 'bone dry.' I could not..."

"It was empty is what your friend means. Right, Papa?"

"Yes, she drank every drop of it."

"She must have been drunk."

"Let me continue with their meeting and how it ended."

"...I could not believe she drank three bottles by herself and was not drunk at all. Her crystal glass was still on the table. It was turned upside down."

"What were her last words to you before she left?"

"Nothing. I didn't see her leave. None of my fellow workers saw her leave. From where she sat in her secluded corner, she would have had to walk past all of us. We would have seen her walk by, walk by in her bright red dress. There was no other way out. No other way. She simply disappeared, vanished into the night. Her tab lay on the table. A pile of fuzzy stuff over it."

"Fuzzy stuff. Like what?"

"Hair. I thought to myself. Oh no! She skipped out on me! Stiffed me. I'm going to have to eat her tab. I started to clear the table. Under the tab and the fuzz lay four one-hundred-dollar bills. It was more than her tab. She left too much. On the tab was a note. 'You're invited to see my show this coming weekend on the Big Island. *Mahalo* (thanks) for your *ho'okipa* (hospitality). Keep the change. Until we meet again.' The following weekend Kilauea Iki erupted. Our Hawaiian bartender said the hair was Pele's hair and the lady in the red dress was Madame Pele.

I asked him how he could be so sure. He said she'd been by a couple of times before and he had the kuleana (responsibility) of serving her. She was just checking up on her house."

"What house?"

"Leahi."

"Leahi?"

"Yeah. You know, Diamond Head. He said we were so lucky Pele paid us a visit and that I gave her a good time."

"Why didn't the regular bartender serve her?"

"This is what he told me."

"'She wanted me to take care of her for the evening! He was so happy she asked for me. He didn't feel comfortable around her either.'"

"He didn't have a choice."

"Got to make the patron happy. He then says to me."

"You know I'm Japanese."

"That's quite obvious," I say to him.

"I never believed in this kind of stuff before but that night. I served Pele. Our bar tender said I did. So, I know I did. That wahine sure gave me the 'hee-bee-gee-bees.' Sent chills up my back. I served her once and once was enough for me."

B) There's Pele the hitch hiker. A local pastor and his wife had no doubt they gave Pele a ride. She was hitch hiking on Red Road in Puna. They stopped and picked her up. "The frail, scrawny, smelly old woman said she was going to Kumukahi Lighthouse." They were happy about that as it was a short ride and she was smelling up the car. When they reached the four way intersection which was where she wanted to be dropped off the pastor looked in the rear view mirror to let the old woman know he was pulling over to let her out. The back seat was empty. She was gone. He looks in the mirror again and sees her walking back in the direction they had just came from. He jumps out and calls out to the woman to ask her what was going on. She was gone. They never saw her again. Other Puna residents have had a similar experience.

"So, how'd you like that story? Why are you so quiet?"

"Because Papa, it's hard to believe."

"If it was not for a pastor and his wife telling it. I would question it too. But coming from Servants of God it is credible."

C) There's Pele the *kupuna*, senior citizen, potential AARP member, elderly, hungry woman wanting something to eat and drink, walking up to two homes in Kaupulehu, North Kona at dinner time. She's turned away, has the door slammed in her face, at the first house. She's welcomed in at the second and is given the royal treatment. Served breadfruit, kalo, pipi kaula and fish on a kou platter. Her favorite foods. She asks for a jigger of bourbon. The man of the house pours her one. The family offers to put her up for the night, but she tells them she needs to get on home as it's past her bedtime. They offer her a *kukui* (candle nut) lantern to light her way. She graciously turns down the offer. As the woman gets up to leave, she thanks them profusely. She begins to trek into the night then turns around and, in a husky, voice tells them she'll see them again very soon. They're puzzled by her remark. The patriarch of the house assures the strange woman she is now family and that their door will always be open to her. She instructs him to place four kukui lanterns at the corners of his property. He asks her why? She replies, "You shall soon see. Just do as I say." She thanks them once more for their *ho'okipa* (hospitality) and bids them farewell. They watch the old woman trudge slowly up the steep slope into the moonless night. In the distance, they hear the surf pounding on the rocky shore. The man does as instructed. He's baffled but something tells him to trim the lamps. With the help of his oldest son, they put a lamp at each corner. A few hours later as the family lay sleeping, the ground beneath them starts to shake, roll and rumble. A series of tremors rousts them from their sleep. Fearing their *hale* (hut) might collapse, they run out of the thatched hut and observe a bright red glow on Hualalai's southeast flank. Hualalai is erupting. A wide ribbon of orange magma is racing towards them. The man tells his bewildered family to stay in place. They have nothing to be afraid of. The house whose occupants shooed the old woman away is gobbled up by lava. Their house is untouched.

"I wish I was there to witness the eruption coming down the mountain. It must have been a beautiful sight?"

"An eruption is a beautiful sight, Kui, Elliot."

"Have you seen one, Papa?"

"Seen several."

"Really?"

"Saw the 1960 Kapoho eruption before it covered the town. Saw the 1959 Kilauea Iki eruption. It was an awesome eruption. Seen several eruptions in Halemaumau Crater. Kilauea Iki was the most spectacular. The fountain was shooting 1900 feet into the sky."

"Really. And you saw it?"

"Yep. Sure did. My family had a front row seat on the edge of the crater from half a mile away. It was beautiful. Just spectacular and we saw it at the best times. In early evening and into the night. Seeing an eruption against a dark sky takes your breath away. We felt the heat. Heard the gasses hissing. Saw the lava bombs exploding in. We saw the ribbons of lava flowing down the side of the crater. We saw the lava splatters. Hot mud is what it was. The colors of the lava fountains were just brilliant. Everything just sparkles at night. That is the best time to see an eruption. The best time. We could hear the roar of the lava jets. And, to see this never-ending lava fountain shooting 1900 feet into the night sky. It's a scene I will never forget. We could see it driving into Hilo from Pepeekeo that afternoon. Pepeekeo to the eruption site in a straight line is thirty miles. A spiritual experience I will never forget."

"Why do you say for you it was a 'spiritual experience.'"

"Because it's part of the Creation Story. It's etched in my memory forever. New land is being created when we have an eruption."

"So the year was?"

"1959 was the year. In March 1959, Hawaii became the 50th State. Pele, celebrated Hawai'i's admission into the union with her own fireworks show at Kilauea Iki."

"Do you have pictures, Papa?"

"No. Unfortunately, we didn't own a camera. The only pictures I have of it are in my mind's eye. The park service has it all on film. On you-tube. Go look."

"I hope we get to see an eruption."

"You both will. I'll guarantee you that."

"Kilauea Iki was in 1959?"

"Yes. And the Kapoho eruption that covered Kapoho town was in early 1960. When Kilauea Iki stopped erupting the lava in the lava pool in Kilauea Iki had to go somewhere. The lava in the pool moved down slope along the east rift zone and popped out in Kapoho."

"As happened recently with the Pu'u O'o eruption!"

"You sure are smart, Elliot. That's it exactly. The lava pool needed a place to escape to. Kapoho was that place. 1960 was a bad year for our island."

"Why do you say that, Papa?"

"Kapoho town was destroyed by lava. Hilo town was destroyed by a tidal wave."

"Did you see the tidal wave?"

"No, but we saw the aftermath. All the destruction it caused"

"Really."

"We stayed in Hilo a few days before the tidal wave struck. We saw the town three weeks after the wave hit. The entire waterfront was gone. Well, a tiny portion of the west end where Koehnen's is was still standing. But most homes and businesses were decimated. Our favorite restaurant, Sun Sun Lau, was gone. All that was left of it was the concrete slab it sat on. It was truly a sad sight. When you're in Hilo next. Visit The Pacific Tsunami Museum. It's a tiny museum but it's a storehouse of information on the science of tsunamis and earthquakes. It's worth a long visit. There's an *olelo*, Hawaiian saying, I want you to remember. A short one, *'Iliki ke kai I ka 'ope'ope la, lilo; i lilo no he hawawa*. A person who fails to watch out often loses. Never turn your back on the sea.'"

"We shall do that. Thanks for suggesting it, Papa."

"We live on a fascinating island. It's an interesting place to do science. Western science. Astronomy on Mauna Kea. Volcanology in Hawaii Volcanoes National Park. Oceanography through the University of Hawaii. Hawaiian forest bird recovery on Keauhou Ranch. Alternative energy research at the Keahole Natural Energy lab. Hawaiian science. Lots of folks doing good work on food sustainability and living green. One more thing I must mention. As a family, several weeks before the Kapoho eruption, we got to frolic in Queen's Bath. It was a favorite spot for folks to go to and soak in in the warm water pool which was thermally heated. We got to see Kapoho town also before it was covered over. Our Uncle Joe had access to the eruption site as he worked for the government. We got to see the eruption up close a few days before it consumed the town."

"You sure saw and did a lot, Papa."

"Sure, did and it all is so fresh in my 'mind's eye.' So fresh. Like it all happened just yesterday. But it happened sixty years ago. Now that I have this opportunity to visit with you both and gab about it all. You know I never had this opportunity before. Don't think I'll ever have it again. You know boys. Age sneaks up on you like a robber. That is how I feel in this moment. I was young and healthy and active. I was under the mistaken notion it was going to be that way forever. I was going to be forever young. Now, my legs and arms and hands don't work like they used to. My eyes don't see as far as they once could. My mind still functions but it's going to dim at some point. So what's my advice to you both. About seven years ago. This is a true story. I was catching the last flight home from Honolulu to Kona. I was late. The security people were kind enough to give me a real quick pat down. Heck, I was flying every week at the time, so they knew me. The TSA agent tells me to make a run for my gate. I didn't have anything to carry on. Just my wallet, car keys and glasses which fit in my pocket. I make a mad dash for my gate. The terminal was a ghost town. There was me and an old man pushing a lady in a wheelchair walking towards me. They both looked as old as Methuselah. I can see my gate. I'm about two hundred feet away. The door to the jet way is still open. A voice on the intercom says, 'Gate A16 is now closed.' I hear a voice yell out behind me. 'Young man. Stop, I need to talk to you.' I know it's me he wants to talk to. In my mind I say,' k!"

"So what did you do, Papa."

"I had only two choices. Stop or be rude and run for the gate."

ΩΩΩΩΩΩΩ

"Kimo sabe did the right thing. He stopped."

ΩΩΩΩΩΩΩ

"That was Kimo."

"That was butt head Kimo and the bastard just took all the 'thunder out of my fire.' Yes, I stopped."

"And missed your flight."

"No, the gate agent saw me and waited for me. I was the last one on the plane and I did not get a warm reception because I kept everyone waiting. I had the last seat on a full flight. If I had missed it, I would have had to spend the night at the airport hotel."

"But you didn't have a change of clothes?"

"No, I did not. I would have just rented a room, woke up in the morning, turned my underwear inside out, wash my face, pat my hair down and not talk to anyone until after I brushed my teeth when I got home."

"So, what did Methuselah have to tell you that was so important?"

"Young man. Don't ever get old. Getting old sucks. And you know what?"

"What?"

"It sure does suck. So, boys, don't ever get old!"

"How are we not going to do that?"

"You're smart dudes. Go figure. You've got a lot of time in front of you to find the Fountain of Youth. Don't waste it. Seize the chance.' Do everything to moderation. Be active. Exercise. Eat well. Sleep well. Live joyfully. Find the best in everyone. Be positive. Stay far away from the Kimo's of the world. Laugh a lot. Have a sense of humor. Do crossword puzzles. Read good books. Keep an open mind about all things. Help others. Be kind to others. Live by the Golden Rule and the teachings of Tsao Ju. Have friends who lift you up when you are down. And, return the favor. That's just for starters. Well, back to my story."

"No more questions from here."

"Works for me, if it works for you."

D) There's Pele, an everyday woman attired in a red palaka shirt and red kerchief round her neck, browsing in Kress Store on Kamehameha Avenue, sucking on a red lollipop. Pele is a 'known quantity,' she clearly does not want to be bothered. As locals, we know the rule, a guiding principle we learned very early in life. "If ever you see Pele, stay away from her."

   Pele had been seen earlier meandering through several other stores on the Avenue. Koehnen's, Men's Shop, Zale's Jeweler's, National Dollar Store, Ah Mai, Y.Hata & Company. Hilo's 'coconut wireless' instantly out out a 'red alert.' She even stopped for a double vanilla cone at the Dairy Queen on Waianuenue Avenue then she walked across the street and sat on a bench under the banyan tree at Kalakaua Park. After she was done slurping on the cone, she walked up Waianuenue to the public library, stood on the Naha stone, looked up at the baby blue sky and began chanting and gesturing wildly at the sky. Folks who were in the vicinity couldn't make out what she was saying. Parents kept their kids close. When she was done, she jumped off the big rock which legend claims Kamehameha, unifier of the islands allegedly lifted all by his lonesome when he was fourteen without getting a hernia. The last people saw of Pele in her bright red palaka shirt shortly before noon, she was headed south towards St. Joseph's Catholic Church on Haili Street. Folks who saw her, swore it was Pele and they had proof. She left a sulfur scent in her wake. Several days later the Kapoho eruption occurred.

   E) There's Pele, an old hag meandering along the edge of a crater grumbling to herself in Hawaii Volcanoes National Park prior to an eruption, before setting the park on fire and without warning as to time and place. The park is the most visited place on the Big Island. It is both a local and national treasure. Like Yosemite, Grand Canyon, Yellowstone and all the other natural monuments. Halemaumau Crater, is Pele's chief residence. Her home since she started building our island a half million or so years ago. It's said even the Nene (the endangered Hawaiian goose) move out of her way when they see her approaching on a trail as they forage for ohelo berries to munch on, a small pond to bathe in or a place to spend the night with their goslings. It's their way of showing respect for and honoring the Lady of the Manor. It's said also by locals, natives, if when watching one of her spectacular eruptions she sprinkles you with her hair you are very, very special.

F) There's Pele, an earthquake spooking us at all hours of the day or night. For those of us 'Big Islanders' living on a fault zone, Pele sounds like a rumbling, runaway train coming down the track at high speed. We hear her approaching before we feel her shaking. In April 2006 we had a big shaker at around 8 am. in North Hawai'i. It was a 6.7 quake on the Richter, so strong the fault must have collapsed. We no longer can hear her coming as we lost along with a few precious ceramic pieces, and wine glasses our early warning system. But she still 'sneak attacks' us at all hours. A reminder to us, her constituents, she's alive and well. Always present and close by.

G) There's the face of a woman, Pele captured on canvas and in photos with long, streaming salt and pepper hair embedded in a flaming fountain hovering over Halemaumau Crater. The first time I met our beloved and renowned artist Herb Kane, he was amid painting a dramatic portrait of the Fire Goddess which was on display at the Jagger Museum, Hawai'i Volcanoes National Park, until 2018. The museum was severely damaged by an eruption and Herb's priceless painting had to be placed in storage for safe keeping. From time-to-time amateur photographers, post photos with Pele's face in them. Her personal revelation to them. To you skeptics out there who claim these are photo shopped, manipulated images. Fiction. Mythology. Made up. Hell no! To see is to believe. I'm a believer. For me. It's fact and reality.

"Well gentlemen that's it."
"Ah, I wish there was more, Papa."
"There is but we got to get to those questions you have for me. That's a bunch of questions. I'm sure Samuel and Lala are going to be here soon to run off to Paniau."

# 7

"So, why did you want to meet here on Hoku'ula this morning? It would have been easier to meet at your house, Papa. In a more comfortable setting. Drinking hot cocoa and munching on Tutu's chocolate chip cookies."

"It would have been, but I love this place. We could have met at our house and sat on the porch, but I thought this was a better place to meet. We would have distractions to contend with. Here on Hoku'ula, it's just the three of us, on top of the world. I get to have the two of you all to myself. We get to see all of Waimea from here. This place that I love."

"How'd you get up here, Papa?"

"I hiked it."

"You did?"

"I sure did with the help of my horsey."

"Your horse?"

"Yep."

"I don't see your horse. Where is your horse?"

"Right here. And right here. My two-legged horse."

"Papa, my dad is right. You are a clown. So, you walked up Hoku'ula."

"Had to start at dawn. The ground was covered in *uhiwai* still. Had an early start. My legs are not what they used to be. Now, I must whip them to get them to move."

"*Uhiwai?*"

"The morning dew that collects on the grass. That thin white layer that hangs over portions of Waimea in the morning until the sun warms up the land."

"There's a song about it."

"'E Ku'u Morning Dew.' Co-Written by a cousin of ours. Dr. Larry Lindsey Kimura."

"You know him?"

"Yes, I do."

"How do you know him?"

"We were in school together. He's two years older than me. I know him well. Larry is a professor at the University of Hawai'i. And he's recognized as the one who saved the Hawaiian language from going extinct. Started a movement through a radio show. He's just a quiet, no drama guy who does good work quietly. Works in the shadows. Has no need for awards and plaques and all that."

"I'd like to meet him someday. Along with Kimo."

"I can arrange that. He's a just a phone call away. So, getting back to your question, Elliot. Why are we here on the summit of Hoku'ula? I wanted you and Kui to see our beautiful town on this gorgeous day from a distance. And a wide expanse of our island from here as well. Which obviously you will never see from our deck. Forgive me for being redundant but I wanted to talk with you alone in the great outdoors uninterrupted. Away from it all. These days we spend too much time, indoors. Watching TV and playing with our gadgets. iPhones. iPads. Tablets. PC's. We've lost touch with our Earth Mother. I wanted you to be close to the *'aina* (land). Feel the good earth. Feel Waimea pulsating through us. I wanted you to hear the wind whistling through the trees. I wanted you to see the clouds rolling across the plains. I wanted you to hear the the meadow larks singing in the sky high above us. I wanted you to see the beauty of the island we live on. I wanted you to see Waimea I Ka La'i from a distance. That's why. Have you both been up here before?"

"No, we wanted to but..."

"Ah, that nasty sign. Ignore. Just ignore that ...... sign."

"But it says we'll be cited and prosecuted for trespass. For climbing over that gate. Do you have permission for us to be up here today, Papa?"

"No, I don't. We don't need permission."

"Why not?"

"I'm *keiki o ka 'aina* (child of) to Waimea. So are you, Elliot. And you, Kui."

"What does that mean? We hear so much these days about being *keiki o ka 'aina*. Because of the protest the Thirty Meter Telescope."

"The 'seed' from which you came was planted here. When I see you in a year and I have a chance to finish the 'suck face' piece of my Creation Story you will quickly connect the dots. Understand what it means. My seed was planted here. As was Uncle Ben's and Keola's. And both of your dad's. We are sure footed, not foot loose. This is our *'aina*. Waimea will always be our *'aina*. Waimea is our home. It will always be home. We may leave but in leaving we leave knowing we will always be able to come home to our *'aina hanau* (birth land). And should we never return to Waimea, Waimea will always be in our *pu'uwai* (heart). My 'seed' was planted here and when I come to die my ashes will be scattered in this special place. We are not immigrants. Nor settlers. We are not pilgrims. We are rooted in this land because we were conceived and born here."

"What's wrong Papa? Why are you covering your ears? Is something wrong?"

"Hold on. I must get rid of this ……. It's Kimo interrupting us again."

ΩΩΩΩΩΩΩ

"Kimo Sabe, you are being a hypocrite. You are taking these two boys down a primrose path."

"No, I am not!"

"Oh yes. Yes, you are. Royally and totally."

"No, I'm not."

"Wait until the guard who patrols the area shows up. You are going to be ah, embarrassed to put it mildly. Your 'keiki o ka 'aina' BS is going to crash and burn in front of these boys."

"You're supposed to be my advisor!"

"I am, Kimo Sabe. I am. It's simple 'Rule of Law' stuff. But I know my role."

ΩΩΩΩΩΩΩ

"What did Kimo have to say this time, Papa.?"

"Ah, his same old rubbish. Same old bull ….! Overreaching again. Now, he's a lawyer. Stepping into my *ahupua'a* (territory)."

"How?"

"Telling me, we are not supposed to be up here."

"Well, shouldn't we leave?"

"Hell no. We have a right to be here."

"We don't ever want to get in trouble with the ranch."

"Come on. Don't be a bunch of panties …....?

ΩΩΩΩΩΩΩ

"Kimo Sabe. You're being a poor example. A very bad example. Well call me, when you need me."

"Go back to your zen garden and stay there, Kimo. Sayonara!"

"It will be soon, Kimo Sabe. Very, very soon. 'When the cherry blossoms bloom.' See you in about two hours."

ΩΩΩΩΩΩΩ

"Guys let's hunker down to business. Waimea is truly a special place. There is a spirit here that just draws one in. Draws us in, brings us home."

"It's so quiet. And the views all around us are stunningly spectacular. So, we are sitting here on *Hoku'ula*. What does it translate into English?"

"'Red Star.' So, this is the first time for both of you. You've never been up here before?"

"No, never!"

"Aren't you in Scouts?"

"Yes."

"Haven't you earned a hiking merit badge?"

"Yes."

"We hiked different parts of the island to qualify for our hiking merit badge."

"And Maui. But not up here."

"I see. Guess things change. Well, I'm glad I suggested we meet here. You boys are in great physical shape. You made the climb up here look easy."

"It was. But are we supposed to be here?"

"Why do you keep asking?"

"The sign on the gate we climbed over sure has some nasty language on it."

"Eh, just ignore that sign. The next time I come up here I'm going to yank that sign off the ……. gate and burn it. I just said it and I will say it again. We're *keiki o ka 'aina*. We have a right to be here. Plus, we're related to Kamehameha. We're royalty. You bet your bottom dollar; we have a right to be here."

"We do?"

"Hell yes, so to hell with that ……. sign. And pull out our genealogy book when you have a chance. We're in the book. The first Lindsey who came here married one of Kamehameha's granddaughters. So, we're related to the Big Dog himself. Don't let that sign stop you!"

"You're joshing, Papa."

"About us having *ali' i* (royal) blood."

"No, I'm not. I swear to God. What makes you think I'm joshing?"

"My mom says sometimes you like to make up stories is why."

"Really."

"Really. In fact, you've gotten me in trouble several times."

"Where? With whom?"

"In school with some of my teachers"

"Really! How so?"

"A couple Christmas' ago you told me Redi Kilowatt invented the light bulb in 1892."

"I did?"

"Yes, you did."

"Humm. I don't remember but eh but that *was a* couple of Christmas' ago you say. These days I can't remember what I did yesterday much less what I said several years ago. So, what happened?"

"I argued with my science teacher about it. I told him, my Papa said it was Redi Kilowatt along with Ben Franklin."

"Some of these teachers think they know it all. You gotta watch some of them. Not all but some for sure. So, what he say?"
"He said Thomas Edison invented the light bulb."
"He did?"
"Yes, he did. Did you do a fact check?"
"I did."
"And?"
"He was right."
"Are you sure?"
"Yes, he was."
"Well, I'll be."
"There was another time when you told me what I took to be fact and it wasn't. I argued with my history teacher. She was not happy with me. My mom and dad were not happy with me."
"And the fact you argued about was?"
"Christopher Columbus discovered Hawaii in 1778."
"I was just kidding with you, Kui. It was Jimmy Cook on the USS Dissolution, 1772."
"Papa, you had the year right. It was Captain James Cook aboard the HMS Resolution."
"Well, I hope your teacher had a sense of humor. Was able to laugh it off."
"Not this teacher, Papa."
"She must hate men. Especially old men. Is she married?"
"Yes, she is as a matter of fact. She's really a nice person but I did really make her angry insisting that you said it was Christopher Columbus. There were a few other times, but Elliot and I know better now."
"How so?"
"We fact check whatever you tell us is fact these days to keep from embarrassing ourselves."
"Hold up guys. My 'headphone' is ringing again."
"Your 'headphone.'"
"My psychic apparatus. Give me a minute."

ΩΩΩΩΩΩΩ

"Kimo, I told you to stay in your cave."
"Yes, you did but I have to chime in."
"What now?"
"Kimo Sabe, you cannot mess around with these boys' heads. You're their Papa."
"So, what's new."
"You must be a 'shining' example to them. You can't be joking around."
"You're telling me that I need to grow up, Kimo."
"Yes. I'm just doing my job. You lifted the thought right out of my mind, Kimo Sabe. Bravo."
"Tell me! How are you doing your job?"
"Protecting you from yourself, is how. As your Ego I'm doing my job the best I know how. I'm giving you 'sound advice.' I'll go back in my cave now. I've got a letter to write to Sigmund Freud and Ben Spock."
"Go back in your cave, Kimo and write your letters. I want to proof them before you mail them out. And please stay there. If I need your help, I will ask for it."

ΩΩΩΩΩΩΩ

"Papa, Kui and I sure want to meet your friend, Kimo. Can we?"
"He sure can be irritating. You don't need to meet him? No, I don't recommend it. I will not allow it."
"But we want to."
"He's a waste of time."
"But why?"
"He's too damn negative. Kimo's such a pessimist. That's why! He will not contribute to making your life better or happier. He'll be a bad influence on both of you. You both have a good sense of humor. I don't want him to rob you of that. He can be so damn cynical."
"Cynical?"
"Yes, cynical. I don't want him to influence you. Be a bad influence on you two. That would I know really bother your parents. And I want to be sure, I'm always on their good side. What's so funny Elliot? What's that smile about anyway?"

"Nothing Papa. Well, nothing important, I should say."

"That was a quick recovery. Someone must have said something to you about me and I know what it is."

"What?"

"That I'm a bad influence! Isn't that so?"

"That's pretty, close Papa. But don't worry, Papa. You'll always be, our Papa."

"For sure?"

"For sure!"

"Alpha and Omega."

"Alpha and Omega. The beginning and the end. I'm glad I brought my favorite bottle of wine. I must toast to Alpha and Omega."

"Papa, it's only 10:30 in the morning."

"It's Happy Hour somewhere in New England. And in Dublin, our Irish relatives started Happy Hour at some pub two hours ago. They're probably listening to some Isla Grant music off the juke box. Or Don O'Donnell. I can see them doing a 'river dance.' Kicking up their feet and lifting them knees high. Guys, we got to plan a trip to Ireland, in particular County Cork, real soon before me and Tutu are overwhelmed by brain fog. Well, we gotta get back to business."

"Hey, Papa we got some trespassers to deal with. Shall we chase them away?"

"Nah, it's okay. Let's have some fun in the sun. Let's do this."

"Do what, Papa?"

"Let them climb halfway up the hill. Then we'll tell them to turn around because they're trespassing."

"That's cruel, Papa."

"It is but what the heck. Let's have some fun, first. Keep an eye on these pilgrims. When they get to the strawberry guava patch let me know. I'll deal with them."

"Will do, Papa. It's going to be a while, but we'll keep an eye on them."

"What does your surveillance show?"

"It looks like a tribe of folks, Papa."

"Think we're going to have to call in back up?"

"Not sure."

"Keep a close eye on the bunch."

"Will do. Why are you talking about reinforcements. About back up?"

"The last time I was up here I had to deal with a few young punks. These days people are not respectful like in the early days. Too many punks running about. A lot of them are useless 'crack heads.' Guys with strong backs who don't want to work or can't hold a job because they have a drug issue or crappy attitudes. I had a pocketknife pulled on me for telling these four punks who had cut school to beat it."

"Papa, you were here by yourself?"

"I was!"

"You should have known better."

"I'm not going to let a bunch of young punks keep me from doing what I want to do. Scare me off my hill. Heck no! You know, in the 'ole days. Young people respected their elders. Nowadays, they don't. Now I carry a can of mace and this in my bag."

"Papa, you are…"

"Kui, I will do what an 'ole geezer' must do."

"Papa, it's just a handful of young people. Not the majority."

"Sorry, I should be using a pointed paint brush, not a roller. I met the 'handful' the other day. I was not impressed. And I hope I never meet them again. For their sake as well as mine because the result will not be pretty."

# 8

"So where were we before I was rudely interrupted by Kimo?"
"We were going to reiterate why we want to visit with you today, Papa?"
"Well go ahead. Elliot, you're the youngest of you both right. Why don't we start with you."
"Kui is but I'll be happy to start. If it's okay with you, Kui?"
"It's okay."
"But make sure you both keep an eye on that trespassing bunch for me."
"Of course. Maybe when you have some time Papa drop by the ranch office. Suggest to the manager to use a drone to patrol the area."
"Elliot that's a great idea. You're a genius. I will. I certainly will. They've got a guard but he's useless. I caught him sleeping on the job the other day. I will do that."
"There's a girl in our class. I'm sure she'll be glad to set the system up for them. Did you know Papa, the Army uses drones in Iraq and the people operating them are sitting at computers in Florida?"
"No, I didn't."
"They are fighting a war thousands of miles away from the battlefield. And most of the computer operators are women. They find the targets and take them out using drones."
"Really? From sitting on their butts looking at computers in Florida?"
"Yep."
"Well, I'll be a 'son of a gun.'"
"It's amazing what technology can do, Papa."

"I'm sure glad I'm not in school with you boys. I'd be lost. I had a hard enough time with one plus one and 'Run Jane Run.'"

"Papa, you'd probably be finding a way to cause trouble on the computer. Online gambling. Playing solitaire. Games. Stuff like that. I'm sure you'd be a regular in the principal's office."

"Probably. I would make life real interesting for everybody. The principal. Playing 'cat and mouse' was my specialty. Anything to avoid boredom. Being fenced in. Caged in like a dog in a kennel six hours a day for thirteen years. What a waste of time. What fun is that? Any way to make learning fun and relevant and purposeful. That made school fun for me. Causing trouble without getting caught. So, what would you like to know about my past. Criminal record. Jobs held. Girlfriends like that?"

"Yes, that's it. Stuff like that. But Kui and I have been talking a bit and we sure would like before we get started to know something about your friend, Kimo."

"But I already said you don't need to know, Kimo. He's an S.O.B. Why would you want to know an S.O.B?"

"Papa, because it's clear to us he has tremendous influence on you."

"What do you have to say Elliot? You've been as quiet as a field mouse."

"You obviously have a love-hate relationship with Kimo. You despise him. He tears you up, but we can see he likes you. And, you like him. It is so obvious. We can see it. Can you just tell us how you got to meet him?"

"Just that? Nothing more."

"Just that? To start."

"Of course. Just that one question? And related questions I assume."

"Here's how I met Kimo Makanuikilakilakeawe-macadangdang manapuapizzaria Campbell. I was in my Psych 101 class at UH- Hilo. A class I was auditing."

"Auditing?"

"For extra credit. On a pass-fail basis. Wow, imagine that? That was half a century ago. We were studying Sigmund Freud. I really liked the class because I liked the professor. Dr. Dixon. He was kind of a ding a ling. He wasn't like my other professors who were boring and old as the hills. I admit there were a handful of great ones who could have been my grandpa. But Dr. Dixon was young, vibrant, interesting. He was 'with it.' I even remember his name after all these many years. He welcomed open discourse. He liked to be challenged. He didn't feel like he knew it all. You'll find this out soon enough as you enter your first year of university. By the way which universities are you attending?"

"Air Force Academy, Papa."

"Wow, Elliot. Good for you. You know your dad could have gone there."

"But he didn't."

"He had his own plan. I wanted to force him to go. But Tutu was right. He would have agreed to enroll to please me but would have found a way to get kicked out. And you, Kui?"

"Santa Clara."

"Great school also. Plan to be an engineer like your dad?"

"Not sure. Maybe. Not sure. I might just sit out a year and cruise. I'm a little tired of school."

"What has it been?"

"Thirteen years."

"Santa Clara will let you do that?"

"Don't know. My parents are okay with it. They say it's my decision to make."

"If Santa Clara doesn't?"

"I've got several other options to consider. I'm not worried about it."

"Cruising is not a bad plan. I like the idea."

"I'm glad you do.?"

"Yes. You sure you want to go to university? What do you really want to do?"

"Surf. Surf. And surf."

"You got to follow your dream. Your dream. Don't fence yourself in, Kui. You've got a whole big future in front of you. And lots of time to check things out. Well, how did I meet, this ……. named Kimo? It was in psychology class. I had four straight classes before my psych class. I was tired. Just exhausted. Dixon was lecturing about Freud."

"The guy who is his colleague is a hoax."

"That's him. My mind was drifting. I ended up daydreaming. And, in the process, in my dream state, a portal popped open…"

"Portal…"

"Yes, a window. A window swung wide open in my mind and there was Kimo…"

"He's a figment of your imagination. A fictional character?"

"Yes. I was trying to pay attention to the lecture, but I was dozing. Doing my best, struggling to stay awake. Then this application, window in my mind, opened. And there on the platform, on the stage was Kimo prancing around on his toes like a ballerina in his lepaordtard."

"You mean ballerina in a leotard."

"Ballerina. Whatever you say,"

"So, that's how you met Kimo. Through a window."

"Yep, that's how, when and where, I met Kimo."

"Kimo's been living in your head for some time."

"Ever since. Almost fifty some years."

"So, you understand each other."

"Very well. Well, very well most of the time. So, we can harass each other at will most of the time. We'll get angry with each other but are able to work through our hurts quickly. The day I met Kimo..."

"In your dream..."

"Yes, he looked so forlorn and lost. In need of a friend. I grabbed my skin rope and like Maui roped the Sun. I roped Kimo by his right ankle, pulled him out of the portal, out of his funk and made him an earthling. Made him part of my psychic apparatus. My ego. To be the bridge, the link between my superego and my id."

"He's a link between your super ego and id. I don't understand."

"Yes, when I befriended him, he asked if he could bring along his older brother and sister. He didn't want to leave them behind. I felt so sorry for him and said 'of course.' Malia, his sister, is my super ego. And Kai, his brother is my id. The three make up my psychic apparatus. They also are on my internal Board of Directors. I'm President. Kimo, CEO. Kai, Treasurer. Malia, secretary. That's the basics of Freudian psychology. Freud's theory has been challenged and refuted across time but that's what I learned way back then and I have never abandoned Freud's doctrine."

"Why not?"

"It works for me. I'm a Taurus, a Bull. I'm stubbornly loyal. Anyway, moving on. I'd like to think, I rescued Kimo from living the life of a useless vagabond. An aimless wanderer adrift on a cloud. I gave him purpose. Ninety-nine per cent of the time we get along well. There have been those few times when we've 'unfriended' each other. Threatened to file for divorce even because of 'irreconcilable differences.' We've thought at times to see a counselor. Taking a break from each other. Playing with the thought that 'absence will make the heart grow fonder.' Or employing, ho'oponopono, the ancient Hawaiian practice of conflict resolution. A few times I thought about sending him and his siblings back to where they came from. I'm sure he too has misgivings about me. But in the end, after seriously looking at all the options. I keep concluding our best alternative as stupid as it sounds is to continue as a battered duo.

"What does Tutu think?"

"About Kimo?"

"Yes. What does she say?"
"She doesn't know about him."
"Really?"
"Really."
"Why not?"
"She already thinks I'm a nut case. If she heard about Kimo, she'd have me committed to the 'nut house.' I can't afford that. I gotta finish my *opala*. I'm almost there. Almost there."
"You are funny, Papa. Papa, it's *Palapala*."
"Hold for a moment, Papa."
"Why? What's going on, Elliot?"
"Looks like we're going to have some company."
"Just what we don't need. A bunch of people bothering us. I picked today to be up here thinking we'd have the *pu'u* (hill), Hoku'ula to ourselves."
"It's big enough to handle all of us, Papa."
"That's not the point, Elliot. Keep an eye on the group. How many folks do you see?"
"About twenty."
"Holy Moly. That's more than the 'carrying capacity' of this place. They must be planning to have a convention on my hill. Kui, run down there and tell them if they're planning to come up here. They are not welcome here. To turn around."
"Papa, you can't be serious?"
"I am."
"But..."
"Let me handle this. This is my *kuleana*."
"Okay. Okay. Sorry."
"You are my guests. Hoku'ula is my living room, Kui. I decide who's welcome here and who's not. This looks like a bunch of terrorists ready to assault my hill. Okay!"
"Yes. I understand, Papa."
"So run down to the gate and tell these folks they do not have permission to be here. They do not have my permission and a right to be here."
"Papa, I shall do as you say."

"That's my boy."
"I'll go with Kui, Papa."
"Good, I need some time to review your list of questions. There's four I want to eliminate. I need some time to myself. So go see what's going on at the bottom of my hill."

ΩΩΩΩΩΩΩ

"You don't have permission to be here, Kimo Sabe."
"How do you know, Kimo?"
"Because I do. You have never ever asked permission from the Ranch to be up here. Never."
"I don't need permission. I'm a native. Native to Waimea."
"Kimo Sabe. This is not the Kingdom of Hawai'i. This is the United States of America. You live in the USA now. This is 2020. Not 1893."
"Kimo, get the …. out of here."
"Okay, okay. Just trying to do my job."

ΩΩΩΩΩΩΩ

"Back so soon. Well, how did it go?"
"Very well."
"How can you say that? I see they're all organizing. Prepping to walk up the hill."
"No, they aren't. They will be doing a permission ceremony."
"Permission ceremony? What in hell is that?"
"The Chief told me they are going to ask the ancestors of Hoku'ula for permission to enter. They already have paper permission, but they need to get permission from the spirits of the 'aina, the land. Unless they get that he will abandon his plan. They already have paper permission?"
"From whom?"
"Parker Ranch. Chief Brave Eagle gave me this to give to you. It's a Proof of Permission form. I'll give it back to them. It's signed by the Ranch Manager himself. Mr. Kamakawiwoole."

"Brave Eagle. Did he tell you where they're from and why they're here, Elliot?

"Chief Brave Eagle did. He and the people with him, represent the Menominee Indian Nation from Wisconsin. He wants to visit with you. I told him you're a native. His eyes lit up when I told him that."

"So why do they want to be up here?"

"I didn't get it exactly. He just said they are here to spread something. Kui, did you hear exactly what it is?"

"Something in a beautiful gold pot. No, they just had something in a pot. They didn't say, what was in it. Holy water, maybe. One of the lady's, an elderly woman was holding on to it, clutching it to her chest. A special pot."

"Teapot maybe?"

"No, much much bigger. And, it didn't have a pour spot. Just a beautiful gold copper colored pot with a cover. She pulled it out of a cloth bag and showed it to us. It had a name inscribed on it with some dates. I've never seen anything like it before. You'll like them, Papa. They were friendly. They said they had permission to drive up but Brave Eagle said he wanted them to hike up if they 'secure permission' is how he put it to us."

"Papa, he said 'secure permission' about five times. He didn't want them to disrespect the ancestors of the land, the spirits of the place."

"Is he a young man? He sounds like a tree hugger."

"No, Papa. He looks about your age."

"And he's going to walk up. It's going to take him all day. Plus, it's going to be hot real soon. He sounds crazy. Get permission from the ancestors."

"That's what he said. The 'ancestors of the land.' Well, he said they all were. As the Chief and the elder of the group, no one in the group disagreed. They are going to do a ceremony and the Chief said after they're done with the ceremony, he'll decide where to take things."

"And, if they don't get permission what will he do?"

"They will turn around."

"That's how it should be. The *kupuna* (elders) must call the shots. Not the young squirts. It may take them a long time to get up here if the Chief is as young as me."

"I don't think so, Papa"

"Why not?"

"He looks really fit. He looks as strong as an ox."

"We shall soon see. I have a hunch as to what's in the pot. Well let's get to some of the questions you have for me. First one, Kui?

ΩΩΩΩΩΩΩ

"Kimo Sabe, you're in big trouble."

".... I don't need your advice. I don't need it. I don't want it. Don't you get it."

"Boss man, you need it. Unless you want to be embarrassed in front of your grandsons?"

"Of course, I do not want to look stupid and be embarrassed."

"So, listen up. I want to help."

"Okay, give me whatever b... ..... you need to give me."

"Good, you will not regret it. In fact, you might kiss me on the cheek after the sun goes down this evening. You might even say a Prayer of Thanksgiving. Remember me in your will even."

"I do not think so. I will not stoop that low. Not for you. So just get to it and tell me what you have to say and go back into your lava tube."

"When the group gets up here if they get the permission they need. Welcome them with open arms. With all your charm. With aloha. Brave Eagle is a Chief."

"Injun Chief."

"Boss, please, please, do not make light of this. Yes, and a highly respected Chief. Treat him with all the respect he deserves. He's a good and gracious man. A learned man. Okay."

"Okay. Quick. Quick. What else is in your 'bird brain.'"

"When the security guard shows up. Please don't cause a scene."

"How do you know I will?"

"Kimo Sabe, I know you like I know I the ridges on my hand. Please be nice. Don't use your native rights .... cause it ain't going to work. Not with this new dude. Play with him and he will play with you. For your sake. But more especially for Elliot and Kui's. I don't want you to look stupid. Not in front of your grandsons. They think the world of their, Papa. Don't disappoint them! Please. Please. Please. Be to them, the person you truly are. Have always been, Kimo Sabe."

"And who have I been?"

"A man of Aloha. A good man. Without an ego. Who has always been pleasant and fun to be around. Always worked to bring out the best in people. In others. Sure, you are hurt. Disappointed, because of the actions of your best friend yesterday. Hurt, because of one man over a business deal gone sour."

"That SOB screwed me, Kimo. Screwed me bad. He embezzled money. Big money. You know that. You saw it all before I did. You brought it to my attention. And I doubted you. I just cannot get it out of my mind."

"I know that Kimo Sabe. Just let it go. Don't let the bad faith of one person sour you. It's done. It's time to move on. You're letting this one event bring you to your knees. Get out of your funk. Don't let this destroy a lifetime of abundance. You have much to teach your grandsons through your words but more so through your actions. Be to them the 'Servant Leader' you have been to others. They idolize and respect you. They love you. They admire you. But I have to say, their Tutu has a big edge over you. Big edge. They trust you. Leave them the values you have lived by your entire life. Along with 'inheriting the Earth.' Leave them your values. That is worth more than all the gold and silver you can leave them. Please, Kimo Sabe. Your public face needs to line up with your private face. In the twilight of your years, you cannot afford to be a phony. You must be real. Genuine. Authentic. Full of Aloha. Mindful. A bright and shining example. Bring forth the 'Fruits of the Spirit.' All nine. 'Love. Joy. Peace. Patience. Kindness. Goodness. Faithfulness. Gentleness. Self-control.'"

"I appreciate the Sermon on the Mount, Kimo. You sure you didn't graduate from Seminary School? I must say like I always say. I won't allow myself to be fenced in, Kimo. I must keep my options open. He treats me right. I'll treat him right. How the …. do you know this guard or whoever he is is going to show up, Kimo? Do you know something I don't?"

"Boss, I have a feeling. That's all it is. Trust me. Well, call me if you need me. I'll come running."

"Kimo, please go back to your zen garden and prune your bonsai trees. Work some meditation in. Say namaste a de mas. Memorize a few quotes from Tsao Zu, the Dalai Lama or Dwayne Dwyer to share with me the next time you interrupt me. To incite my mind, enlighten my soul, empower my intellect. But don't hold your bad breath. Oh, and don't forget to aerate your orchids."

"Thanks for the reminder, boss. I'll find some Gabriel Iglesias videos to bring to humor you. Just holler when you need me."

ΩΩΩΩΩΩΩ

# 10

"Kui, what's going with the intruders?"
"They are forming a circle. Here take a look through my field glasses."
"It is a big group. The guy with the long feather head dress is the boss."
"Yes, Papa. That's Chief Brave Eagle."
"He looks familiar. I think I might know him. Humm. I think they are going to do a bow wow."
"Papa, you mean pow wow."
"Isn't that what I said?"
"No, Papa. You didn't."
"What did I say?"
"Bow Wow."
"Oh boy. I'm losing it. Yes, pow wow."
"Gosh the Chief sure looks old, and he says he's going to walk up? You're right. He looks as old as me. And he thinks he can walk up Hoku'ula. I got to see this."
"That's what he told me, Papa. He said it with a smile. A big smile."
"Well just maintain surveillance and keep me updated on what's going on."
"Will do, Papa."
"So, what's your first question? I've been salivating, waiting to hear it."
"Papa, we are going to rotate the questioning. Elliot will be first."
"Go ahead, Elliot."
"Papa, do you believe in God?"
"You bet I do. Heck yes."

"Why do you believe in God? Why do you believe there's a God?"

"Here we are on this magnificent day sitting on the top of Hoku'ula. What do you see? My question to your question is to both of you."

"I see our beautiful island."

"And you, Kui."

"Like Elliot. I see our beautiful island. Our very beautiful island."

"Elliot, can you be more specific?"

"I see our mountains. I see the green Kohala hills. I see the Pacific Ocean. That big pond which separates us from the rest of the world. I see the puffy clouds rolling through the valley below us. I see the cinder cones from which poured millions of cubic yards a long time ago to build the plateau on which our town now sits."

"And you Kui?"

"Papa, I see the big blue sky above us. The telescopes on Mauna Kea's summit shining in the sunlight. I see the surf at Paniau. I see a group of folks looking to join us here on Hoku'ula. All the beauty Elliot just described. And much more. And I can feel the spirit of the land."

"Feeling?"

"Yes, a spirit tugging at me. Pulling at, pulsating through me."

"Papa, like Kui. I can feel the 'spirit of the land.'"

"What does it feel like?"

"It's a good feeling. There is a sacredness to it. It's like a… a magnet."

"Magnet?"

"Yes, a magnet. A feeling I don't ever want to leave me. A feeling that tells me this is home. I'm anchored to Waimea."

"And who do you think created all this beauty for us to enjoy, Kui? And this 'spirit' you are both feeling?"

"God."

"How about you, Elliot?"

"God."

"Elliot, at night, a clear night when you look up at the sky. What do you see?"

"I see the moon, a star filled sky, sometimes Venus. I see God."

"Why do you say God did, Elliot? That this all didn't just happen. It wasn't an accident. That God planned, designed and created our islands."

"I learned that in Sunday School, Papa, when we were studying Genesis 1:1. 'In the beginning God created the heavens and the Earth.'"

"Me too. Like you, Elliot. I learned that verse in Sunday School when I was four years old. It's embedded in my brain. It's amazing. We are truly the products of our upbringing. The three of us were raised in a Christian tradition."

"So, what's your point, Papa?"

"My point is as you progress through life, you will meet others who have their own traditions and beliefs. Just respect, learn and listen to their traditions and beliefs. There's no need to impose our traditions and beliefs on them. No need at all."

"I have a question, Papa?"

"Hope, it's not a trick question. I just hope it's one I can answer."

"Is God a man or a woman, Papa?"

"I don't know, Kui. I really don't know but, in my mind, it doesn't matter whether God is a man or a lady. What matters is, we are here witnessing and enjoying all this beauty around us that in our tradition we believe God made. The clouds rolling across the Waimea Plains from Hamakua nudged by the wind south to Waikoloa and Anaehoomalu. The beauty of the mountains. Mauna Kea. Mauna Loa. Hualalai. The big blue ocean to the west. The flowing, rolling green Kohala hills. The cattle and horses quietly grazing all around us. The sky larks singing happily above us. That brilliant rainbow over Holoholoku. That rain squall moving up from Paauhau and heading towards Mana and Po'o Kanaka. There is a 'puppeteer' pulling on strings. Who's providing all this beauty for us to enjoy? That puppeteer for me is God."

"Papa, the Bible says God is a man."

"I know it does Elliot. 'Father. Son. Holy Spirit.' All men. But my thought is this. The Bible was written by men during a time when men ruled the world. So, it's only natural the authors of the Bible would be biased in favor of men. That's how I see things anyway. That's the basis for my reasoning. But does it really matter whether God is a guy or a girl? Think on it anyway."

"I have a follow up question, Papa?"

"Go for it, Elliot."

"You're not a church going person, Papa. I didn't realize until now that you believe in God. So, I'm surprised to hear you say you do. I'm surprised ..."

"No, I'm not a regular church goer. Surprised that I don't wear God on my sleeve!"

"Yes, that's a direct way of putting it."

"No, I don't. I used to when I was younger wear God on my sleeve but as I got older, I put two and two together. And saw the world differently from my parents, my Sunday School teachers and from my church. How can God accept only Christians into the Kingdom? How can God be so biased? So prejudiced?"

"But to be accepted you must believe. You must be a believer. Accept Jesus as your savior"

ΩΩΩΩΩΩΩ

"Kimo Sabe, stay on the high road. This is your teachable moment. Here's your chance to be a leftist. A liberal. You're talking with your grandsons. Your mo'opuna. Their fields of experience. Of life is not as wide as yours. Their frontal lobes and the lymbic areas of their brain are still maturing. Have a long way to go to catch up with yours. You were where they are now a long time ago. Remember?"

"I remember. I remember."

"Well, here's your chance to show them the wise man you are. Your moment to shine. Cool your jets. The days of fun and games with your grandsons are over. You are no longer 'Bozo the clown.' You are their Papa. No need for.... "

"I got this, Kimo. I got this. I will not mess this up."

"Are you sure, boss?"

"Yes, I'm sure."

"Good. Now is your chance to give up your childish ways."

"Do not worry. I will not… I will not this up, Kimo. There's too much at stake. I now realize what you've been trying to tell me. Go back and tend your orchids and bonsai trees. I got this, Kimo. Thanks."

ΩΩΩΩΩΩΩ

"Well, the reason why I'm saying what I'm saying is there was a time when I believed there was only one pathway to God. We, as Christians had the only pathway to eternity. Through our Christian God. The God I was raised to believe in when I was a little boy. We were told that he was..."

"He was a man."

"Yes, and Jesus was our only way to heaven. 'The truth and the life.' And one day when I was around ten. Maybe eleven I said to my mom I had my doubts about that."

"So, what did she say?"

"She got angry. She asked me why I was questioning my Sunday School teacher, Mrs. Baybrook. Mrs. Baybrook told her I needed help 'believing.' That I was straying from the truth."

"How so?"

"She felt Satan was influencing me. Taking me away from God. She was concerned for me. She felt I needed to be reprogrammed. I had questions she could not answer. She answered me by quoting Bible verses. And that didn't satisfy me. I was upsetting her. I repeated what I had said to Mrs. Baybrook, my Sunday School teacher."

"What did she say?"

"I really thought by being honest she would pay me on my shoulder and give me a gold sticker. I got the lickings of my life."

"Really!"

"Yep."

"Why?"

"She did not like my reasoning. She agreed with Mrs. Baybrook. 1000%. She said it was sinful for me to question the Bible. For me, to question Mrs. Baybrook and what she was teaching us. That I had the audacity to compare the behavior of people in our church to the behavior of our Japanese neighbors. And how dare I question the teachings of our church. That that was not for me to do. Who did I think I was? I had nerve. Who was I? I was just a kid. I needed to remember that. I needed to keep my big mouth shut. And my big ears open. I just had to believe."

"You got a good whipping?"

"Yep. I got licked bad. Of all the lickings I got this was the worst ever. I will never never forget it."

"Did it help?"

"Nope. It took things the other way. God gave me eyes to see, ears to hear and an active brain. No, the beating didn't slow me down. Not at all. My sight and my hearing improved. Got better in fact. I kept going to Mrs. Baybrooks class for the rest of the year. I kept my mouth shut but, in my mind, I quietly said, 'Lady you are full of poop.'" She tolerated me. I tolerated her. I employed some risk management strategies."

"Your mom must have been really strict."

"She was, so much so I had difficulty when I had lady bosses. Even lady teachers as I got older. I would see my mom in them and sometimes I did stuff to them I seriously regret. They did not deserve it. But too late for regrets now. I pressed the 'send' button. It's gone. Gone forever into cyber space."

"What did you do to them?"

"To my teachers?"

"Yes!"

"It's my secret. Like Kimo advised me. I need to give you insights that will help, not hinder or hurt you and Elliot. I'll just say this. It was kid stuff. It will not help your future. Now where was I?"

"You were going to share with us why you got whooped by your mom."

"Oh yes. I got whooped because we had Japanese neighbors who were the sweetest, most generous, most Christian people in the world in my eyes."

"They went to the same church as you?"

"No, they didn't. They had their own church which was just two churches away from ours."

"So, what were they?"

"They were Buddhists. They believed in the teachings of Buddha. As Christians we believed in Eternal Life. Our Buddhist neighbors believed in Enlightenment."

"So why did you say to your mom they were Christian?"

"Because they lived the teachings of our church more than we did. They lived the 'Fruits of the Spirit' is why."

"I get it."

"I get it too, Papa. The people in your church were hypocritical."

"Some, not all. So, I got a good licking. Got my ... whipped.

I was told to cleanse my mind of the rubbish that I was filling it with. But I was never able to."

"Why not?"

"I could not fathom how good people…"

"Like the neighbors?"

"Yes! How could a supposedly loving God we believed in send good people to hell like our neighbors because they were not Christian. I could never get it out of my head."

"So why do you still believe in the Christian God?"

"Because that's the God I was introduced to. That's the God I grew up with. He's my God and mine alone. Who am I to impose my God and my religious beliefs on others? What I learned for myself observing what was going around me here in Waimea was this. We were surrounded by folks who were Catholic, LDS, Baptists, Seventh Day Adventists. Those who went to the Hawaiian church. There were those who didn't go to church at all. Who didn't believe in any God period. And those who only came to church once or twice a year. Special occasions; Christmas, Easter, Mother's Day. I concluded when I was twelve years old that we each have our own. Our own very personal pathway to whomever we believe is our divine, our God. If we believe in one. So does that answer your question as to why I don't wear my God on my sleeve?"

"Yes, it does, Papa."

"Who God is for each of us is a personal thing. That's what I believe. I don't believe my God wants me to pound folks on the head with the Book of Common Prayer or the Bible. I really don't. Our neighbors believed in Buddha. They were good, Godly people. I don't believe they will go to hell. If God is sending them to hell, I'm going to hell with them. I'd rather be with them. But I don't believe God will."

"Why do you believe that Papa?"

"The God I believe in is a kind and loving God. A just and fair God. Who loves us all. No matter the color of our skin, the shape of our eyes, our belief system. No matter how big or small our brain or nose is. God made us all. As the song says. 'Red or yellow. Black or white. We are precious in God's sight.' I'm sure you both know that song."

"Oh, yes, we do. And Papa, I notice you never said 'He' once."

"That's very observant of you, Elliot. Very observant. God could be a 'he' or God might be a 'she.' God might have boobs. Or …. Who knows. I think the main thing is. God gets a good night's rest and wakes up rested. Ready to get to work. Like us.

That's what I think. What do you think, Kui?"

"Papa, you're so funny."

"Kui, when you look around you on this beautiful day what more do you see from what you said earlier?"

"Well, I see the big blue sky above us. I see our beautiful town below us. I see Mauna Kea's summit covered with a thick blanket of snow shining in the sun. Mauna Loa's summit is also covered in snow. There's Hualalai smiling at us in the distance. I see all the beauty described in the songs we sing in church from time to time."

"That's real sweet. I like that"

"Like what?"

"Hualalai smiling in the distance. It's so poetic. It has a nice ring to it. I should have brought my ukulele with me. What else?"

"The rolling green hills. The daisies in the meadow. That huge quilt of gray, white clouds hanging over Hamakua."

"Your turn again. You saw what you saw twenty minutes ago, Elliot. What do you see now that you have had more time to soak up the morning and muse over our conversation?"

"I see our family's old homestead at Keanu'i'omano. I see cattle grazing on the Wai'auia slopes above Anna's Heritage Center. A band of horses galloping along the Ouli edge of Waiaka stream. I see a military convoy on Saddle Road. It looks like an artillery unit slowly working their way to PTA."

"*Keanu' i'omano*. Do you know why that place is so special to our family?"

"No, I don't?"

"That's where the first Lindsey who came to Hawai'i from England in 1847, Thomas Weston Lindsey, hitched up with Mary Kaala Fay, so here we are looking down on the old homestead on this gorgeous day which the Lord has made."

"Which is now on the National Register."

"Yep. Preserved forever in a bottle. I'm fifth generation on the Lindsey side of our family. You're both seventh. Your dad's sixth. We're 'keiki o ka 'aina.' 'Children of this land.' We're 'aina hanau.' 'Born of this land.' I want you both to know that Tutu and I were at North Hawaii Community Hospital with your parents to welcome you into the world."

"You were?"

"Sure were. We were there to witness these two miracles we were waiting for for a long time. And there you were. Our precious munchkins. And here you are. Two of four precious miracles. We were also there to welcome Samuel and Lala to our 'aina hanau.' Oh, yes, we were. So, my ask of both of you is this. Be proud of our family name. Honor and protect it always. Why? We have a duty to live up to the expectations of our ancestors who proudly carry us on their shoulders. They deserve our best. They and several other families including ours who made Waimea the place it is. The Parker's, Purdy's, Bell's, Stevens, Spencer's. Always remember that."

"Remember what Papa?"

"They were good, God-fearing people. Who worked the land. Who were loyal to Waimea. Paniolo. Cattle people. Horsemen. Good, hard-working people. Folks with good values. Who raised good families. Who loved this land and did not abuse it. Who gave back more than they took from it and as a result were blessed. They were people of honor. Who could be trusted. Honest people. There's the Okuras, Horis, Wakayamas, Inouyes, Shimonos, Asatos, Yamamotos, Nakamoto's, Nishijimas, Masakis, Haras, Aokis, Palaikas, Lekalesas, Hirayamas, Okadas, Sakatas, Otas, Nakatas, Kimuras, Haradas, Hamadas, Nakanishis, Yamaguchis, Hasegawas, Sakados, Kawanos, Ninios, Gushikens, Nishijimas, Ishiharas, Kauwe's, Forbes, Kawaihaes, Greenwells, Dois, Chocks, Hayashis. A few names I know I'm missing. People who never took advantage of others. Who earned their way. Who were too proud to accept handouts. When we gave someone our word, they could take that to the bank. Folks who were grateful for what they had. Never felt entitled to anything. Were too proud to accept handouts. What else, Kui?"

"I can feel the breeze coming off of Wai'auia on my back..."

"...*Wai'auia*, that soft, gentle breeze. It's our wind welcoming us to Hoku'ula. It sure feels good, doesn't it?"

"It does. What does it feel like to you, Papa?"

"Like when Tutu and I went went walking for the first time on our first date and she brushed her soft hand across my back."

"Accidentally?"

"Purposely. Oh yeah, that feels good."

"What else?"

"I hear that cardinal singing his heart out in that stand of loblolly trees. His whistle is loud and beautiful and cheerful. He sure is a happy bird"

"It just amazes me. He's been chirping nonstop since we got here. He's going to need a glass of water real soon."

"Why do you think he's chirping his heart out?"

"It's a *kahea* (call)."

"To whom?"

"If you were him, who would it be?"

"My girl."

"He's calling his honey. Calling his honey home to the honeycomb. He's frustrated."

"What is he frustrated about?"

"He needs her close by. He's missing her. What else do you see?"

"There's that pair of sky larks hovering over us. I love their music. And, that owl keeps staring at us."

"Where?"

"He's standing on that fence post behind you. He keeps checking us out us. Staring at us."

"The *pueo* (owl) is our land *aumakua* (guardian). He was sitting on the gatepost when I got here at sunrise. He must have followed me up the hill. Soon he'll be gliding up and down the hillside."

"It is such a beautiful bird."

"One of God's wise feathered creatures. So, gents I put the question back to you. Being here now on top of Hoku'ula near the middle of a wondrous day. Seeing all this beauty above, around, below us, do you believe there is a God?"

"I do, Papa. I always have."

"And you, Kui?"

"I do."

"I do to. Both of you are my and Tutu's greatest miracles along with Samuel and Lala and your parents. You all bless me and Tutu richly every day. Both of you along with your brothers, your mom's and your dad's. You all are for us the greatest testament that God exists. You are miracles sent to us from and by God. Along with all this beauty around us. We see God in all of you. There is a God. That I do not doubt. I do not question. And I want to share with you a text message that Uncle Keola just sent me on my iPhone. I just got this. Well, he sent it last night. I opened it up when I woke up this morning. It's so timely. Hold on! I must start deleting stuff. Hold on. Here it is. It's a message sent from space on Christmas Eve 1968. Your parents weren't born yet. You weren't on the drawing board either. The two of you. So here we are on top of this *pu'u* looking at our little slice of earth. Witnessing all this glory all around us. This is what Keola sent me. A message and a photo from Apollo 8 Commander, Astronaut Frank Borman on Christmas Eve broadcast to the entire world from space which was heard by a billion people. This was his message from the Apollo spacecraft as he and his crew saw the earth rising as they were preparing to circle the moon for the fourth time. This was the message read by Borman: 'In the beginning God created the heaven and the earth.' Sound familiar?"

"Genesis 1:1."

"Very good, Kui. Genesis 1:1."

"From space."

"Yes, Elliot from Apollo 8. They were the first humans to see the dark side of the moon. To fly around the moon."

"Wow!"

"Borman years later, in reflecting on the voyage said this:

'God has given mankind a stage upon which to perform. How the play turns out is up to us." But reaching back to 1968, this was Borman's complete message to all of us who were glued to our tv sets. "...the crew of Apollo 8 have a message that we would like to send to you. 'In the beginning God created the heaven and the earth. And the Earth was without form and void; and darkness was upon the face of the deep. And the spirit of God moved upon the face of the waters. And God said let there be light and there was light. And God saw the light. That it was good. And from the crew of Apollo 8, we close with good night, good luck, a Merry Christmas and God bless all of you, all of you on the good Earth.'"

"Now look at this image. Isn't that something?"

"What is it?"

"An image of the earth rising from 240,000 miles away."

"From the window of Apollo 8."

"Yes."

"Wow."

"An image of our beautiful *honua* (earth). Our beautiful Mother Earth. How can one not believe there is a God who created the Earth and the entire solar system."

"Papa, it's only recently that you've been attending Sunday church with Tutu. Why now? Is it because you're old. You're getting ready for 'the rainbow's end?'"

"Partially but can I do some explaining?"

"Of course."

"Many years ago, I made a horrible mistake."

"Mistake?"

"Yes. I became a smarty cat."

"A smart ass."

"Exactly. I took God out of my heart and put God in my head. And left God there for a long time. Recently, I put God back in my heart. That's what happened. I missed being part of the Body of Christ. Being part of a church community."

"Are you happy you did?"

"Yes, and I regret, I abandoned God and the church for a long time. But God is back in me."

"So do you plan now to wear God on your sleeve."

"No, I never will."

"Why not?"

"As I said earlier. Each person has his or her path to God. To the Divine. For us, it's God. For others it's Allah, it's Buddha. To each his own. What works for us, works for us. For others, it might, or it will not. It's not worth debating, arguing, fighting over religion. We've had enough crusades and religious wars. We've got greater issues to resolve now. Our Country is in debt. Our State is in debt. Our County is in debt. A virus pandemic. Global warming. Sea level rise. Nuclear proliferation. Income inequality. Race relations. Political tensions that's tearing our Country apart. We need to bring our Nation back to center as things are going crazy. The disrespect for the 'Rule of Law,' the Flag, police, courts, the military. The disrespect for all the institutions that have held us together, united us for two hundred plus years. I cringe about the future, that my generation is leaving you. Well. next question."

"I wanted to cap this part of our conversation with this comment if I may, before we go on to the next question."

"Sure, go ahead."

"I was taken by a statement at the introduction to your website."

"It's been years since I looked at it. So, what did I say? I hope it's profound?"

"Papa, it's very profound. These are your exact words. 'My Mission in life is to serve my God and be a blessing to others.' What it says to me is, you carry God as you do Tutu, in your heart. And that's a good thing."

"That's very generous of you, Elliot."

"And, I agree, Papa."

"Thank you, Kui. I appreciate it. I sincerely do."

"Next question. I hope it's not about me. Enough about me."
"Papa, we're just getting started. The questions are all about you because we want to hear your memories. About you and Tutu. About family. Your kid days. How you did in school. About your mom and dad. Waimea. We want you to take us down memory lane. Your memory lane. We want to record, document and preserve those memories. Tell us a little bit about Tutu. How you met her? When you met her? Where you met her? If we can start there. We want to hear the real stuff. Not the Wikipedia stuff."

"I'll tell you about the saintly stuff from a very high level but no more."

"Aw shucks."

"Sorry Kui."

"That will be plenty, Papa. We don't want to hear the 'suck face' stuff."

"One of my buddies invited me to this party on a Saturday night. His wife now and Tutu went to the same girls' school in San Francisco. They came to UH together and were roommates. It was a Friday evening, and I was in a quandary as what I should do as I had several other invites that evening but decided on his offer. I really don't know why I accepted his offer over the others. Dennis was from Hilo. We were friends at UH-Hilo and transferred to UH-Manoa in our junior year."

"Why did you?"

"Because UH-Hilo was just a two-year college. Our options were, go to Oahu or to the mainland if we wanted to earn a degree."

"Okay."

"I could have gone to the mainland but one of my UH-Hilo professors had set me up with a program at UH-Manoa. It was a great deal academically which would have led to a PhD which at the time I was set on pursuing. I was fortunate in that I had several scholarships, so all my expenses were covered. I did not have to work. I just had to focus on school."

"So, you chose to stay here."

"And I'm glad I did. The best decision I ever made. Getting back to your question. So, I go to this 'pizza and beer' party. We're having a great time. Around 11 o'clock this gorgeous *wahine* shows up."

"It was Tutu."

"Elliot, you're getting ahead of me. Yes! It was Tutu."

"She walks into the living room, but she doesn't join the party. She sits against a wall all by herself."

"She stayed to herself."

"Yep, all night. My eyeballs were like heat sinking missiles on an F-35 fighter plane. They locked in on the target. I launched my missiles and they hit the bull's eye."

"Tutu was the target?"

"Yep, she sure was. The sensors on the missiles sent back a message."

"What did it say?"

"My computer screen read, 'Jackpot but Mission not yet accomplished. Commander, this is your soul mate. But you've got a little more work to do. Request permission to return to our silos.' I quickly called back the missiles. She was totally aloof. I guess she was practicing 'social distancing.' She was getting ready for the corona virus."

"She didn't join the fun."

"No! Just kept to herself. I was trying to figure out, what was going on. There was a mystique about her that piqued my interest in her. Most of the girls had a *kumu* with them."

"What's a *kumu*?"

"'Boyfriend' for 'girls.' 'Girlfriend' for guys.' I called my buddy the next day to ask about the *wahine* who walked into the party late. He says to me. 'Brah, she get one *kumu* already. You too late.' I was of course disappointed. The next weekend. The same thing happened. Exact same scenario. My eyeballs went 'boinnng.' The fact she had a *kumu* was not going to stop me. It was 'goodwill hunting.' I began chasing her."

"This was about when?"

"Senior year, UH-Manoa, October 1970. And my plan worked. I had help. We began chasing each other. Exchanging roles. One time she was the cat. I was the mouse. The next time I was the cat. We finally met in 'midair.' At the end of the school year I graduated. Me and Tutu were on a plane flying home to Waimea. In May 1970. We got married. She got her degree at the end of first summer session. And the rest is history."

"What happened to her...?"

"'*Kumu*?' I don't know. It's a cruel world out there guys. Sometimes, you just got to do what you got to do. Put empathy aside. And here we are. Still together, fifty years later. Two sons, two daughters-in-law and four grandsons later. Can you imagine? Tutu left her family for this hick from the country. Left her beautiful 'City by the Bay.'"

"San Francisco?"

"San Francisco. Left her family. Left all the familiar places. Rearranged her life. Gave up her best friends to hook up with this 'storyteller.' This nutcase from the lime green hills of Waimea. Waimea I ka la'i. She's been chilling with me for half a century now. Can you believe that? This lady with a big, golden heart, a lot of brains in her bonnet and a mug filled with kindness. I know she gave up a lot to be with me. I'm a lucky guy with much to be grateful for. Yes, we've had our 'ups' and 'downs' but thank God the 'ups' have outweighed, out shone, outlasted the 'downs.' It never ceases to amaze me that she was willing to take a chance on this brown boy from the woods. She didn't leave her 'heart high on a hill in San Francisco.' She came off her hill and gave her heart unconditionally to me. And, in her profession as a teacher of young children, in fifty years has given so much to our community. Tutu was born to be a teacher. She knew since she was three years old that she wanted to be a teacher. She works magic with kids. She was born to be a mom, a grandma and a teacher. I'm amazed at all that she does getting the house ready for you all when your parents let you have time with us. It's a full-scale military operation. It is. I'm not kidding. Books, toys, puzzles, games, water play. The hours she spends thinking all that will make your time with us fun and worthwhile. We are blessed to have her in our presence and a core part of our family. She didn't leave her 'heart in San Francisco.' Not all of it anyway. She let me have and our family most of it. 99.99%."

"That is an 'Amen, Amen, Amen moment, Papa.'"

"Thank you and Amen, Elliot."

"I don't understand the 'heart in San Francisco' piece, Papa."

"Kui, I'm waxing poetic here. Stealing a piece of a line from a famous, popular song about San Francisco. She trusted to give her heart unconditionally to me. To this *kanaka maoli* (native) she met at a 'beer and pizza' party in..."

"You met at a 'beer and pizza' party at her house?"

"Yep. October 1969. We had our first boy calf in August 1971. Sometimes I wish I could put him back in the corral and have the rough riders at Pukalani Stables shape him up."

"Why?"

"He wasn't in the corral long enough. Came out *ahiu* (wild). In his old age he is still acting *ahiu*. We had two more bulls later. Your dad, Elliot. And, then your dad, Kui."

"Were they in the corral long enough?"

"Yep, tamed to utter perfection. Well, that's the *mea hou* (news), abbreviated version plus some, of how I met this golden girl with the golden hair and golden soul fifty years ago on the corner of Hunnewell and Vancouver at a *pa' ina* (party). Maybe I'll live long enough to tell you both the full version. There's plenty to tell. I left out a lot intentionally. For now at least. I don't want Kimo to pop out of his zen garden. I don't want to interrupt his meditation session and spoil his and my day any further on this gorgeous day. I need to be sensitive to his mental health. I don't want Kimo to develop hemorrhoids. He has enough mental issues now to deal with. There's one thing I think about from time to time."

"What's that?"

"How did my parent's meet? What was their story?"

"They never talked about it?"

"No, never. It's lost history. Before we go on to your next question. Tutu was the only girl I ever dated. The only girl's hand I ever held.

The only girl I fell in love with. When I saw her that Saturday evening more than half a century ago. She was like a magnet. I was drawn to her. And so, I chased after her with a vengeance. Something, I had never ever done. Something, I cannot explain. I could not get her out of my mind. What I will say is this. I'm the luckiest guy in the world. I'm a very, very lucky guy. 'In sickness and in health…till death do us part."

# 12

"You never talk much about your parents, Papa. Especially your dad. In fact, I don't remember you ever talking about him at all."

"Well, for one there's not much to talk about. He's just a blur on my horizon. He died when I was fourteen. My mom died when she was fifty-nine. I remember a lot about her. Much more about her."

"What little do you remember about your dad."

"It's been fifty-eight years since he left us. Left us too soon. He was forty-one. He was Superman. A very kind and nice man. Let me start here. I can tell you this. Uncle Ben and I were not raised in a kissy huggy family. We never exchanged "I love you's."

"Never!"

"I don't remember ever being hugged by my dad. Smiles, pat on the back and handshakes, yes. It was the same with my mom. Got soft pecks on my cheek from her after special events or when I left home for school on Oahu and came home for vacations or holidays. When I was inducted into the National Honor Society in 10$^{th}$ grade. She flew to Honolulu special to put my gold pin on me. It was one of the few times we took a photo together. She was thrilled. Pinned me. Gave me a soft peck on the cheek. That was it. Same thing when I flew to the mainland for the first time ever to represent Hawai'i at Henry Opukahai'a's Sesquicentennial in Cornwall, Connecticut. It was no big deal. That was life in our house. I don't ever being told by my mom or dad that they loved me."

"Really?"

"Really. But it didn't hurt me emotionally. The situation was what it was. I knew I was loved. I didn't need to be showered with kisses, hugged to death or told repeatedly that I was loved. Our home always had a loving feeling. A welcoming feeling. A feeling of aloha."

"How did you know you were loved?"

"I saw it through all the struggles our parents endured and the sacrifices my mom and dad made for me and Uncle Ben. We were their reason for living along with Jesus. We were not wealthy in the pocketbook so they scrimped and saved to give us the best education they could. They did not believe in government assistance and help from others."

"There were no 'free lunches.'"

"Nope. They were 'proud.' They taught us values, morals and ethics. The stuff that gives one character. Stuff that isn't emphasized today at home, in school, in society. It seems to be so anyways. Maybe I'm living in Lala Land. Respect for others, the 'Rule of Law,' family values, our Country, the flag. The need to go to church. To have empathy and compassion for others. Being kind, generous and considerate of others. To appreciate what little we had. The soft stuff which when we were growing up were important, valued, stressed. Hammered into us. If we wanted something we had to work for it. Guess, I'm just old fashioned. Seeing things through lenses that need a major overhaul. Need updating."

"Papa let's rewind a bit. Who was Henry Opukahai'a?"

"Henry was the first native Hawaiian to become a Christian.

The first Hawaiian convert. He convinced the missionaries to come to Hawai'i to spread the gospel. He was born in 1792 and raised in Ka'u."

"Really! He was Hawaiian."

"You seem so surprised, Elliot, about that."

"I am."

"Why?"

"I thought the missionaries invited themselves to Hawai'i. Imposed themselves on us."

"No, they did not. Not at all. Henry wanted to spread the gospel himself but was not able to."

"Why didn't he?"

"He died, but before he died, he begged the missionaries to do what he knew he would not be able to do. He knew he was running out of time. He contracted typhus, never recovered and died in 1818 in Cornwall. Henry was 26."

"And you got to go to the mainland to his ses...sesque..."

"...sesquicentennial. I was selected to be the 20th Century Henry."

"By whom?"

"The United Church of Christ Conference. I was selected to go to Cornwall with five others to celebrate the 150th Anniversary Year of his death. Rev. Edith Wolf, Aunty Annie Kanahele, Lehua Kawai, Ethel Andrade, Bob Black. We were Hawai'i's delegation to the event."

"How'd you get selected?"

"I think one, I was young like Henry. I was only 20. I was active in the Church. And two, I was destined to become a minister. I was being mentored and trained to become a minister."

"You were not?"

"Yes."

"What happened?"

"That's a long story. It's a story for another time. The short of it is, 'I saw the light.' Realized soon enough I did not want to be one. I had my own plan. If I stayed on that path, I would disgrace my church. Disgrace my family's honor. Ultimately, disgrace myself. For once I was able to say 'no.'"

"How would you have disgraced yourself?"

"Doing something stupid to find my way out of that commitment."

"Like what?"

"I don't know but I wasn't willing to risk it. I knew deep within me, despite what my mentors felt. I was not ready to wear a collar around my neck and a cloak on Sunday mornings at the church door. Welcoming folks to morning worship. Have a cross dangling from my neck and a Bible in my hand. To be on my knees in daily prayer. Voltaire said, 'Know thyself.' I was honored and appreciated the confidence they all had in me, but I was skeptical. Skeptical about myself. There were a lot of unanswered questions in my head. And, when I look back at that time. I was struggling, struggling and I now know why. Because I had taken God out of my heart and put him in my head. I was intellectualizing my faith. Not living my faith. Playing games in my mind. I had what monks would call a 'monkey mind.' An unsettled mind. A mind that jumps from one branch to another. I realize now that was a mistake. A terrible mistake, I blame on a lame excuse. I was stupidly young. I had a lot of questions rolling around in my head. And, no answers to many of them. A lot of disconnects. Short circuits in my brain."

"Who were you being mentored by?"

"The best in the church back then. Good, learned folks who were strong in our faith. Reverend John Mulholland from my high school. Reverend Edith Wolf from my home church. Imiola Congregational Church established by Reverend Lorenzo Lyons in 1835."

"He wrote 'Hawai'i Aloha.'"

"That's the guy. And the other mentor I had was Reverend Abraham Akaka from Kawaiahao Church."

"You were fortunate"

"I was blessed. To have all these folks as mentors. I will always appreciate and remember their confidence in and support of me. The doors they took me through. The life lessons they taught me. The experiences they gave me. The long trip to Cornwall to visit the home where Opukaha'ia lived until he died. It's a trip I will never forget. It was my first trip to North America. On Pan American Airways. I was amazed how long the flight was. Our first stop to refuel was in Los Angeles. I was amazed at this invention by the Wright brothers. How could this big plane carry so many people with all our luggage, stay afloat in the sky from Hilo to LAX? Then from LAX to Newark, New Jersey. Finally, on to Hartford, Connecticut? I was amazed at how big this country, which we were now a state of was. It was huge. I'll never forget when getting off the plane in Newark, New Jersey to stretch. Newark was a burned-out shell. Still smoldering from fires set by citizens angered over the assassination of Dr. Martin Luther King two weeks before in Memphis. Like what's going on now over the death of George Flloyd in Texas. I'll forever remember the visit to Yale University where Henry begged for a western education. The visit to his gravesite on a tiny knoll with snow falling all around us is still a vivid memory. This is where I met Congresswoman Patsy Mink for the first and only time. Our Hawai'i delegation sang Hawai'i Aloha and Aloha O'e to Henry with snow falling on us. It was a Hawaiian blessing with one big difference. It was snow not rain that fell on us but it worked and worked well. I will always remember tobogganing with kids who became for a brief time, pen pals. I will remember the side visit I took to Mystic Seaport where I met Wes Kemp. Wes was at the time a renown photographer with National Geographic. And, on this trip, I realized Aloha is a universal phenomenon. It's not just a Hawaiian value. The Ho'okipa and Aloha the people of Cornwall bestowed on us, was unbelievable. The people shared with us their abundance unconditionally. There was plenty of everything. Food. Music. Fun. Different 'kine,' yes. Food-finger sandwiches, fruit, cheese, crackers and apple cider. Music-piano and violin. Fun-tobogganing, sledding and skiing. Warm fellowship imbued with the Spirit of the Islands on us just as Henry experienced two centuries before. It was also a 'business' trip so I had to speak at about ten events. The New Englanders were amazed that I spoke English so well. But were sorely disappointed I did not speak Hawaiian at all. Yep, this will be a trip, I will remember forever. But it did not eliminate my ambivalence about a future in the ministry. I was torn. Really torn on the inside. I'm happy where I am today. I'm happy about my decision to walk the path I eventually took. I still serve God but not from a koa lectern, in a beautiful sanctuary with burning candles, a choir singing in the loft and an organist playing 'Amazing Grace' or 'How Great Thou Art.' I've come to realize that God is not housed in a building. God is all around us. God is in us. I really took us 'off the road less traveled' didn't I."

"That's great, Papa. Have you ever shared this stuff with others."

"No, no not in this detail. I did with Reverend Akaka but not in this detail. In a cowardly way."

"How do you mean?"

"I didn't have the nerve, the guts to face him. I called him with my decision not to move forward on the phone."

"How did he take it?"

"He was disappointed. Very disappointed. He wanted me to give things more thought. But I said my decision was final. I needed to put my struggle to rest once and for all. I needed to move on. And I did. Sorry guys. I was starting to talk about my mom and dad and ended up taking us to New England. Sorry about that. I'm surprised Kimo isn't butting in and interrupting us."

"Why did, how did Henry end up in New Emgland?

"Great question, Kui. There was a war between the chiefs. His entire *ohana* (family) was killed before his very eyes. An uncle in South Kona took him in. Henry was so distraught over all that happened, he just wanted to get out of here. So, with the help of a friend, Thomas Hopu, he was able to get passage and work on the Triumph, a ship commanded by Caleb Britnall. The year was 1807. Henry was just fifteen. Britnall, was from New England and took young Henry under his 'wing.' Treated Henry like family. That's the answer to your question. He was a good victim of circumstance. Henry was hard working and had a curious mind. He wanted to be educated in the teachings of the Christian faith and the word of God so he could bring the Gospel home to Hawai'i. But was not to be. The first boatload of missionaries he inspired to come to our islands arrived in?"

"1820."

"Very good, Elliot."

"Your mom and dad were active in the church?"

"Yes, they were. Our life, to use a stool as a metaphor was a stool with three legs. Home & family. God & church. School & education. Our life was not complicated. The life we lived was simple. Same ole. Same ole. Day in. Day out. Year after year. Life was slow in Waimea. The town was small. Our population was around two, three thousand. Waimea School had only one hundred eighty kids when Uncle Ben and I were students there. Every now and then it would bump up to two hundred then drop back down. Today, the school has over a thousand kids. Parker Ranch was our economic and political engine. If we had two hundred cars pass through Waimea on a weekday. Mamalahoa Highway was busy. I would not be surprised if we took a vehicle count at the intersection of Lindsey Road and Mamalahoa today, the count would be around ten thousand vehicles. Parker Ranch was our economic engine. Agriculture was our major industry."

"How do you mean?"

"The Ranch was the big employer. Most of our dads worked for Parker. The Parker Ranch Manager called the shots for everyone and everything that happened in Waimea. He was the boss whether you worked for the ranch or not. Waimea was a Republican town. Carter told our town folks who to vote for. If you didn't do as he said, you were in trouble."

"What kind of trouble?"

"If you worked for the Ranch, you lost your job. You were fired. If you were looking for a job with the Ranch. You were passed over. Today, Parker Ranch is a memory. Very little of it is left. When we were growing up, the Parker Ranch cowboy was our idol. Our hero. My grandpa worked for Parker. So did many of my uncles."

"What about your dad? Did he work for the Ranch?"

"No, he couldn't."

"Why not?"

"The story I was told was he made a derogatory comment about Mr. Carter, the Ranch Manager and so he could never get work with the Ranch. That was how much power the Manager wielded. He was god. Today. the influence the Ranch once had over the town is gone. The grip it had over Waimea is *pau* (done)."

"Is that good or bad?"

"In some ways it's good. In some ways, it's bad. I miss the old days. I miss seeing the cowboys riding their horses to and from work. They would be laughing, whistling and calling out to each other in Hawaiian. I miss seeing the dust clouds from the cattle drives as the cowboy's moved cattle from one section of the ranch to another. A thousand at a time. From Holoholoku to Keaumoku or Waikoloa to Pu'u Pa or Makahalau. They would shut down the highway. The cattle and horses owned the highway. Everyone knew that was the law. And we honored it. I miss going to the meat market. In fact, the meat market is gone. A parking lot covers the spot where it once stood. Beef was inexpensive. The sirloin steaks were an inch inch and a half thick. So were the round steaks. The beef cubes were two-inch squares. Poi was cheap. It was affordable. The butcher, Mr. Dochin, would always have a bone ready for our dog. For Monty. They had a special bond. When we drove up Monty knew the drill. He would run into the market. Collect his bone, run out, jump back on the seat of our dad's Model A and gnaw on his treat. Monty was our dad's best friend. He was everyone's friend. He was like our dad. Loved everyone. We never drove by a car without waving. We knew everyone when we went to pick up mail at the post office. No one was ever in a rush. To rush off without 'talking story' as we call it was a sign of rudeness. A no, no. Today it's rush, rush, rush. Rushing too nowhere. Too many of us are chasing our tails. I miss going with our dad on Friday nights to Chock Inn Store. The old man would chat for two sometimes three hours about local issues with Mr. Chock. Uncle Ben and I would sit on stools sipping soda out of a bottle, eating a candy bar and watch whatever was on TV. My favorite was orange soda. It's still my favorite. I think Uncle Ben liked strawberry soda. We learned what the phrase 'on the house' meant from Mr. Chock."

"What does it mean."

"He was treating us to whatever we wanted. So, we never turned down the opportunity to visit Mr. Chock. Mrs. Chock would pop out every now and then to help a customer with a purchase. A few times, Mr. Chock would tell a customer, until they paid up their bill, no more charging. Credit cards were not heard of back then, so we had to pay with cash or open a charge account."

"What's that?"

"He would let you buy stuff. He would record what you purchased in a book each time you came into his store. At the end of the month, he'd give you an envelope with all your purchases in it and the total amount of what he was owed. He usually gave folks a month to pay up."

"That was nice of him to do."

"Yes, it was. It was a system based on trust. Unfortunately, a few folks bought more than they should have for the month and so they could not pay up."

"So what happened to those folks?"

"Mr. Chock would find work around his place for them to do. Stock shelves. Wash windows. Mow his lawn. They managed to work things out. That's the Waimea I grew up in. Waimea I ka La'i. Waimea in the calm."

"And, once they paid up, they could start charging again?"

"A few. A few, not all. There were those he called 'chronics.' A handful. They were 'bad risks.' Irresponsible."

"What else do you remember?"

"Crime was non-existent. We were afraid of the cops. Whenever we saw a cop, we'd run and hide. We didn't have traffic control signals. We didn't need them. There were very few cars on the road. We didn't have DUI checkpoints. There weren't any bars. The town shut down at 4 pm. Those who bought alcohol usually drank at home. If somebody was driving drunk on the highway after a wedding reception or baby party which was a rare occurrence. The police would stop the driver. Take away his car keys and drive him home."

"Did your dad drink alcohol?"

"No, he couldn't."

"Why not?"

"Our mom did not allow it. It was a 'no, no' in our house. He knew better. She didn't know prohibition was a thing of the past."

"Really?"

"No. I'm kidding! Gosh! Now that I think of it. The cops really did not have much to do."

"So, if the police did not have much to do what did they do all day?"

"Drive around Waimea. Chat with people. Look busy. The police station closed for business at around 8 in the evening if I remember correctly. They'd wait patiently for someone so they could use their siren. It was a big deal if we heard a siren. There was a lot of 'rubber necking' during those times. And, phone calls to the telephone switchboard to find out what was going on. The police had very little to do which was a good thing because here in Waimea we lived in a bubble. As Waimeans we had several things going for us. The Ranch Manager was King. He ruled with an iron fist. The town was small. We had old fashioned values. We were raised on the mantra. 'Do not dishonor your family name.' That was hammered into our heads. If you did your family decided what your punishment was. Usually, it was a severe beating. We did not have a CPS Office or social workers we could appeal to. And, unless you died from your beating. The police would look the other way. Most everyone went to church on Sunday. In church we learned the ten commandments. And, to honor and respect our parents, our elders, our teachers. In school, it was the same. At the start of the school day, except rainy days, the entire student body stood at attention in front of our classrooms with our hands on oir hearts and faced the flagpole. Grade

6 was assigned to play the Star-Spangled Banner on a record player. The J.P.O.'s raised the flag."

"J.P.O.'s?"

"We had a Junior Police Officer program. J.P.O. is the acronym for the program. The older kids ran the program. They helped the younger kids, before and after school, cross the street at our main intersection. The J.P.O.'s helped the principal police the school and keep a lookout over the rascal kids. They had a purpose and were very helpful."

"Were you a J.P.O?"

"Yes, I was Elliot."

"I see."

"Any ways, getting back to the flag raising piece at the start of school. When flag raising was over, we all went into our classrooms and stood behind our desks. Someone was assigned to say a prayer before the start of class."

"Isn't that unconstitutional?"

"It is now, Kui. When I was in Sixth Grade, school prayer was ruled unconstitutional by the U.S. Supreme Court. That piece of our morning protocol was eliminated. Although I understand the reasoning behind it, I still think it was a big mistake. The Massey decision was a bad decision in my humble view."

"Why?"

"It helped to keep us walking a straight line. The day it was ruled unconstitutional and struck down by the high court was a tragic day. It was the beginning of the end for America."

"How so?"

"It was a huge piece that gave us as a community, structure. Those of us who were in Boy Scouts had the Scout Motto, Law and Oath to guide us. In school it was the same. Everyone was in alignment. Parents, teachers, Mr. Nakano, our principal. In Waimea, it was *kuleana* (responsibilities) to community that were emphasized alongside individual rights. What was in the best interest of the community superseded individual liberties during a crisis. I laugh during this corona virus pandemic as to the grumbles about the wearing of masks and the reopening of schools and businesses debate. You have those who are choosing their constitutional and individual liberties over harming their neighbors. Me, myself and I over my community. As kids there were rules in place that we followed to the letter. If we got out of line, we got whooped. Whooped in school, first. Whooped at home, later. Education was valued. Being smart. Being a nerd was applauded. Education was seen as the pathway to a good life for us growing up here in Waimea. We were made to understand for our democracy to work. We had to be informed. We had to be educated. When I see all that is happening across America today. I say to myself, the Founding Fathers were geniuses. They had great foresight. They must be shocked, seeing all that is going on in our country today. We are on the verge of a revolution. Our country is ripe for revolution. With folks struggling to pay bills. The widening income gaps. The disrespect for the 'Rule of Law.' I see scary times and a very, very 'muddy road ahead.'"

"So, you opened school with a flag raising ceremony. You went into class, and someone said a prayer."

"Yes, then we placed our right hand over our heart and repeated the Pledge of allegiance."

"Pledge of Allegiance? What's that?"

"We committed our allegiance, loyalty to our Flag, to our Republic, to our Country, to America. We had all these components that gave structure to our lives. Components that helped us develop the emotional intelligence we needed to manage our emotions through the storm's life threw at us as kids becoming teenagers, teenagers becoming adults."

"We've never had to say the Pledge Allegiance or whatever you call it in school. There is no flag raising ceremony. Someone from the office puts the flag up in the morning and takes it down in the afternoon. We don't have a flag raising ceremony."

"There's more. We then wrapped up our morning protocol singing a few patriotic songs."

"Like what?"

"'Battle Hymn of the Republic.' 'Hail Columbia.' 'America the Beautiful.' The way you're looking at me. I can tell you're thinking I'm from another planet."

"Papa, we never heard of those songs. Who took the flag down?"

"At the end of the school day."

"Yes."

"The J.P.O.'s. We knew the flag would be pulled down and folded around 2:30. It was a solemn ceremony. So as that was being done. We stood still wherever we were until the flag was down. Once it was down, we continued with whatever we were doing. You have never done that?"

"Nope. Never!"

"That taught us the essence, the value of respect. Respect for our community, our country, our family. Each other. Wow, we are really going to hell in a 'basket.' What has our Country come to? No prayer. No flag ceremony. No Pledge of Allegiance. No military draft. No sense of service to Country. No respect for the 'Rule of Law.' All I see is folks on TV taking a knee. I'm glad I'm in the 'winter' of life. As a Nation, we're going 'down the tubes.' I don't remember who said, 'A nation divided will fall apart! Fall flat on it's butt! On it's face!' I know I'm not saying it exact but the essence is there. All this nonsense. These tantrums we see nightly on the evening news is spawning a violent revolution. A revolution worse than this corona virus. Yes, all these protests and nonsense that is building, is providing a 'headwind' for an awful revolution. The infrastructure for utter chaos. An ignorant citizenry. Where the 'rich will only get richer. The 'poor poorer.' The 'dumb dumber.' What say you, Elliot?"

"I'm an optimist, Papa. We are a Nation of immigrants. We've made it this far. Our generation will figure it out. We must. We are a diverse Country. We just need to work through our differences and find a 'center point.'"

"Nobly said. I always knew you were an 'old soul.' Very well said. You sound like a wise sage. I've been trying to find that 'center point for a half century but have not been able to. I wish you well. Your generation, hopefully will find the 'needle in the haystack,' that 'middle ground.' I like your optimism. You're like my mom. She was an optimist even though she was a tyrant. She always gave me hope and purpose. But back to my dad."

"What was he like?"

"He was a very kind and generous man. He didn't have any enemies. He was always working. He was hardworking and always up to something. I followed him around like a puppy dog. Although he quit school when he was in 5<sup>th</sup> grade. He was smart. He was a whiz at math and loved to read. Our mom loved to read as well. We were never wanting stuff to read."

"Why was he allowed to leave school so early?"

"He hated school, a schoolmate and friend of his, Sonny Kaniho, told me. I guess for one, he could not sit still. And he was probably bored. I don't know. I'm just speculating. So, he was home schooled by his mom. His brothers, our uncles were all gifted. They were bright in their own way. Your great grandpa was interested in animals. In people. And, loved Waimea. Our dad had a way with people and with animals. He had horses, pigs, chickens, pigeons, goats, sheep. He had a bull named Ferdinand. A boar named Duke. If he could have owned an elephant or a tiger, I'm sure he would have had two of each. I remember one evening he came home with a ram. He put the ram in a pen. Filled a metal bucket with water. Got some grain out of the fifty-five-gallon metal drum where we stored our grain to protect it from the rats. He then poured it into a wooden box. His butt was facing the ram who was 'eye balling' him the entire time from thirty feet away. It was very skiddish about being in a new place. I think the ram was insulted that our dad had the audacity to face his buns towards him. It lowered it's head like a bull does when being teased by a matador. It started to run. Our poor dad was so focused on giving his woolly friend some supper. Plus, the sensors on his butt were 'sleeping at the switch.' Pops had no idea what was coming. The ram nailed him in his ass and flipped him over. We had sheep stew with poi and rice for a week. The first night, the stew cubes were hard on the molars. The entire jaw. The animal was wild, so the cubes had a wild taste. With more time over the kerosene burner, the cubes softened but the feral taste never went away. Whenever I have lamb at a restaurant, I flashback to that evening sixty years ago. To that dumb ass ram who went from 'farm' to 'table' quickly because he 'rammed the hand who was feeding him.' It seems like it all happened 'yesterday,' just 'yesterday.'"

"Monty, his dog was his best friend. They were very, very close. I'll share with you a sad story. After our dad died. His body was brought home for an overnight wake and vigil. It was really a 'tear jerking' scene to see Monty sitting at the screen door looking into the living room at the old man's casket and crying, whimpering his poor heart out. It was just spooky, creepy, weird. To see, his dog grieving. It's a scene I will never forget. Monty's drama upset our mom to the point where she had one of our uncles grab and haul him away because he was causing such a scene. Scaring, upsetting folks. When the undertaker returned the next morning to take our dad to the church. Monty ran, chased after the hearse. And, for several nights after our dad was buried, Monty would run around our house barking his happy bark. Like he usually did, when our dad drove up our driveway after work in his Model A."

"What was that all about?"

"Our dad was not ready to transition from this world to the next. He was having difficulty letting go of us. He was concerned we would not be able to make it without him. He was feeling badly about leaving us so abruptly is what I think. When he was living, Monty had a routine. Monty would just go nuts when he saw our dad coming up the drive. He was a medium sized dog with short legs and would run until he couldn't run anymore. It was Monty's happy bark reserved only for our dad. It was like old times."

"What else do you remember about him?"

"People loved him. When he died. The church was packed. Standing room only. Even the Buddhist priest asked our mom if he could pray over him. I was surprised she said it was okay."

"Why? That was a nice gesture."

"We were Christian is why. But it really was. Our Buddhist neighbors were going to hell. There was a Hawaiian practitioner who asked if she could do an oli (chant). Our mom denied her. But the Buddhist priest who was Japanese. He was allowed to do a whole mantra. That was a disconnect. I just could not connect the dots."

"Sort of a double standard."

"Yep. It really was."

"The Hawaiian lady did anyway."

"She sure did."

"How?"

"She just got up at a point during our dad's funeral service, barged forward and did her oli."

"What did your mother do?"

"Nothing. She was shocked. The lady just got up and started chanting. Our mom was not happy but I'm glad she didn't do or say anything. It would have spoiled, blemished the entire service for our dad. We were all so immersed in our grief anyways."

"Do you remember the lady?"

"Oh yes!"

"Is she still alive?"

"No, she died about five years ago."

"It would have been a sendoff our dad did not deserve. If our mom had intervened. The only one she would have embarrassed would have been herself."

"Did you ever get to meet the lady?"

"I did. Yes. I got to know her very well as I got older and developed a great respect for her. We got to be friends. Getting back to our dad. He was a good and decent man. A man of aloha (love) and grace. A kind and giving man. We loved him dearly. He was taken away from us too soon. Sadly, too soon!"

"So, the service went on."

"It went on and ended well. And our life went on."

# 13

"Did your mom talk about it?"

"You mean talk about the disruption to me?"

"Yes."

"She said she was upset because she knew it was going to be something ancient and heathen. Which she said it was. It was all in Hawaiian. Our mom, your great grandma, was pure Hawaiian. She was raised in the old ways. She spoke fluent Hawaiian. So, she understood every word of it."

"Did she tell you what the chant was about?"

"No, she did not but I was confused. She allowed the Hongwanji priest to do a mantra which was great. But denied a Hawaiian kahuna (priestess) permission to do her oli (chant)."

"Why, were you confused?"

"There were times along the way where she observed some of the ancient ways."

"How so?"

"She would call up the *akulele* (the Hawaiian 'fire ball) according to Uncle Ben. He saw her do it. I didn't. I was away at school. It was confusing because she was a fundamentalist Christian, 99,99% of the time. She believed in Jonathan Edwards 'fire and brimstone' …p 00.1% of the time she played her 'heathen' card.

She walked and lived in two worlds, where the 'twains' would never ever meet. It's like she was playing it safe. Leaving a door open just a squish. Just in case. Or maybe she couldn't unchain herself completely from the ancient ways. I remember when Apollo 11 I was looking the first moon landing. She said it would never happen."

"Why not?"

"God would never allow it to happen."

"Really!"

"Really!"

"Why?"

"Man was stepping into God's *kuleana* (territory)."

"'Yikes!'"

"'Yikes' is right! When the landing happened, we watched it on TV. I looked at her and said, 'See ma, it's right there. See!'"

"What did she say?"

"She essentially said it was 'fake news.'"

"Really!"

"Yes!"

"What did you say?"

"Nothing. I was not going to spoil my Sunday or hers."

"Sunday?"

"Yes, the landing took place on Sunday, July 21, 1969. It was time to move on. I learned from my mama when a fight was worth it and when a fight wasn't. On certain things, her mind was frozen in time and place. At times, I'm a replica of her. The mango, I will admit didn't fall from the tree. Got to hear Astronaut Neal Armstrong say as he stepped on the moon's surface, the first human ever to do so, say, "It's one small step for man. One giant leap for mankind.""

"Tell us three more things about your dad?"

"He was *kolohe*."

"He was rascal."

"Oh yeah. He sure was. Like his dad. He was smart, and funny and a rascal. I learned a few things from him. It's too bad he left us so soon. His passing contributed a lot I know to my decision not to go to seminary."

"How so?"

"I began in my mind to question if indeed God existed."

"Why?"

"After all the praying we did as a family to help him recover from his illness. Our mom. Me and Uncle Ben. Everyone in our church. Our minister, Reverend Thomen. Even our community had a prayer circle for him. The morning when we were told he died is when I became a doubting Thomas. I wobbled, meandered for years inside and outside of my faith."

"So where are you now?"

"I'm home where I belong. Home to stay. But that's a long story we should save for another time. I'll give you an example of his *koloheness*. There are several but this one is probably the funniest."

"We are all ears, Papa."

"Our dad liked to bird hunt. He had an old 12 gauge double barreled shotgun. Hunting season opened in November and closed in February at the Pohaukuloa Training Area."

"Any particular bird?"

"Any bird. Anything that had feathers and could fly. He liked to hunt in the training area up at PTA."

"Pohaukuloa Training Area."

"Yes. There weren't many game birds around. Quails. Francolins. Chukars. Turkeys. Every now and then, he'd shoot a quail."

"Was he a good shot?"

"He did okay. His youngest brother, our Uncle Keao, was the sharpshooter in the family. Anyway, the hunting process was this.

We had to sign in at the Hunter Check-in Station before going into the training area. And, you had to sign out when you left the area. You needed to show the game warden your license. Write down your vehicle license number. List the names of everyone in your party, and if you had a dog or dogs. Their names and tag numbers had to be recorded as well."

"Did Monty come along?"

"No. The ride and the day was too long. He would have loved to be included but 'no.' It would have been too much for him. When you checked out if you shot any birds, you had to show the ranger your catch. And there was a bag limit."

"Bag limit?"

"Yes. You could shoot I think it was five chukars max. Six quails. Three pheasants."

"On a given day?"

"That's correct. I might not have the numbers right but you get the idea. Our dad came up empty most of the time. This one evening, as our dad was signing out. The warden on duty poked fun at him for coming up empty again. Our mom was not with us that day, so I got to sit on the front seat with him. I told him the ranger wasn't very nice. I didn't like what the ranger said. I thought he was rude and stupid."

"Our dad looked at me and said. 'No worry. I'll show that S.O.B. next week. I'm going to poke him in his eye.'"

"S.O.B. Your daddy called him a Son of a Bitch."

"Son of a Bitch. A good ole S.O.B. So, the following week our dad got us up early on Saturday morning. He made us breakfast. It was a treat. German pancakes, vienna sausage and eggs, hot rice, coffee. He loaded up his shotgun. The four of us got in his Model A."

"Your mom, dad…"

"No. Our dad, me, Uncle Ben and Monty. We drove up the highway towards Lakeland."

"You didn't check in at the station?"

"We were still in Waimea. We drove up the highway. In a two mile stretch he shot two pheasants right from his jalopy. I got to retrieve one. Uncle Ben the other."

"Nowadays, you can't shoot a bird from your car. We learned that rule in Hunter Education."

"The rule was the same back then."

"You broke the law!"

"Don't tell anyone. Especially Tutu. We retrieved the birds. Took them home. The old man wrapped the pheasants in old newspaper."

"Pheasants are beautiful birds. I couldn't shoot them."

"Kui, all you have to do is shoot one. That will work all the butterflies out of your system. After that you will be able to shoot anything."

"Really?"

"Oh yeah. I was like you but after I bagged my first one it was easy. It was fun. A big thrill. I couldn't wait to shoot the next one. You're taking Hunter Education to get a license. What are you going to do with a license once you get? Frame it. Hang it up on your bedroom wall so you can stare at, admire it?"

"It's going to be cool to have one. I'll put it in my wallet and show it off to all my friends."

"Listen, stick with me. I'm going to put a shotgun in both of your hands and show you how to shoot. Everything from rock doves to mynah birds to pheasants. Even rice birds and dragon flies. You just must get the taste of it. Once you get the taste, you'll be on your way. I tell you, once you pull the trigger on your gun. Shoot your first pheasant. Feel the recoil in your shoulder. Smell the gunpowder. Retrieve the birdie. This sense of satisfaction is going to penetrate, pulsate through your entire body like an electrical current. From the top of your head to the bottom of your feet. You are going to enjoy this thrill. And you are going to sign up for an NRA card. Shooting your very first bird will give you this tremendous sense of satisfaction. Achievement! It's better than getting an A in school. You're going to want to shoot another one. Then another one. Trust me."

"Really Papa?"

"Bet my last dollar on it. Oh yeah. And I know you're going to call me to tell me about it. And you know what else?"

"What else?"

"You're going to beg me to take you on a safari to Africa. You're going to need a melatonin, dopamine or gabapentin prescription."

"Africa. Melatonin. Gabapentin. For what?"

"To quiet your nerves."

"I don't think so, Papa."

"We'll cross that bridge when we get to it."

"Papa, thanks but no thanks."

"Ah, you sound like me Elliot, when I was your age. I said I would never own a gun. I'd never be a hunter. I would just hunt birds with field glasses and a camera. Now, I have an armory. I said I would never hold a girl's hand. I met Tutu and never let her hand go. Been holding her hand for fifty years now. Any way we need to get back to the future. We got the birds. I held one. Uncle Ben the other. Their warm bodies felt nice in our cold hands on that cold Waimea morning. They were red breasted ring-necked pheasants. We went home. The old man put them on ice in a cooler. We went up to the training area. That evening he checked the birds out at the ranger station. The game warden was really impressed. He wanted to know where in the training area our dad shot the two birds. It was the first time in several years anyone had checked in a pheasant. I remember him saying. But two pheasants. He kept pressing our dad."

"So, what he say?"

"Our dad said he couldn't tell him. It was his secret. The next few weeks he'd shoot one pheasant. One week nothing. The final week, three."

"The limit for pheasants."

"Yep. He called it his 'Grand Finale.' And it was."

"Why?"

"He got sick, so we never hunted at PTA ever again. That was it."

"Didn't the ranger, the game warden suspect something was 'fishy' about your dad's story."

"I'm sure he did. The game warden had no basis to stand on but his gut feeling and the skepticism bouncing around in his fat head showed on his fat face. He did look at our dad sideways but what could he say. Nothing. Our dad laughed and said to the warden, 'See you next season.' When we drove off our dad laughingly said to us, 'Guess, I got the last laugh on that S.O.B.'"

"Did he ever watch you play sports?"

"He was always working. He came to watch me play one baseball game and one basketball game. That was all. Then he left us."

"What about school?"

"You mean like conferences with teachers or if we got in humbug?"

"Yes."

"No, that was our mom's *kuleana* (responsibility). But he valued education. He didn't want me or Uncle Ben getting our 'hands dirty' like him. Told us we should do well in school and get an office job. He paid attention to our report cards though. Always told us to do well in school. He and our mom were in total alignment when it came to school. The teacher was always boss. Always boss. When we crossed the line, no matter how big or how small, it was 'fire and brimstone' time at One Cheseboro Lane. If Waimea had a CPS Office way back, then I would have qualified for a 'frequent flyer' pass. Uncle Ben would have had a platinum card."

# 14

"Did you do well in school?"

"You mean academically?"

"Yes. I did. I liked school. The only thing I didn't like was being stuck at a desk for almost six hours a day. Kindergarten was a great year. Just play, play, play. But the years after that took some getting used to. My first and second grade teachers with help from my mom trained me 'to stay in the box.' Our mom and some of our teachers were like the horse trainers 'breaking' wild horses at Pukalani Stables. Once I was trained to sit still, I was on my way to the Grand Ole Opry."

"So once you were 'reigned in' you did well in school."

"Not only me, Uncle Ben. Yes, I did well academically and behaviorally. I surprised my teachers. My non-Hawaiian teachers especially."

"Why?"

"Some of them didn't feel that us Hawaiian kids had the smarts to do well. Our 'lamps' didn't burn as brightly as other kids."

"Like you and Uncle Ben."

"Yep. We just didn't have it in us to do well..."

"...academically?"

"Yes. We were born dumb. Our 'lamps' did not burn as brightly as the non-Hawaiian kids as I just mentioned a minute ago."

"Really?"

"Yes."

"So, what did you do?"

"I had a part of my mom inside me. I was going to show them up. She just told me when I complained to her about my teachers being biased, to do my best. To turn 'adversity into opportunity.' She didn't say it that way but that's what she meant. She was always there to give us hope and encouragement. To help us stand tall. It reached the point in intermediate school, today it's middle school, where we knew she couldn't help us anymore with our homework. She would encourage us to ask our teachers for help when we needed help. She gave us the strength we needed to push ahead. She helped us develop what is these days referred to as E.I."

"What's E.I?"

"Emotional Intelligence."

"And you did?"

"You, bet I did. I'll always remember my Religious Education teacher, Mrs. Baybrook. Good ole Mrs. Edith Baybrook. She took the cake. She asked us as a class when we were ninth graders what our plans were after graduating high school. I was the only one stupid enough to tell her my mind was set on going to college. Which one, she asked. I said Princeton Theological Seminary, Wheaton College or Oberlin.'"

"You were serious?"

"Of course, I was. Princeton Seminary was my first choice."

"Why Princeton?"

"We had to put covers on our textbooks at the beginning of the school year to protect them from getting beat up. The covers I used were book covers for the ivy league schools. Yale. Notre Dame. Stanford. Harvard. Princeton. I liked the way the Princeton book cover looked. That's why."

"What did she say?"

"She looked at me and laughed. She said I didn't have what was required to get into Princeton. That I would never be smart enough."

"She said that!"

"Yes."

"So, what did you say?"

"Couldn't say or do anything but 'grin and bear' it. I took the insult. I was embarrassed. But I fixed her at the end of the school year."

"You flat her tires."

"No. Her tradition at the end of the year was to have a recitation contest?"

"Recitation contest. What's that? Never heard of a recitation contest before?"

"She had a party on the final Friday for all of us in the class at the end of the school year at her home. It was a big deal. The Baybrooks had a beautiful home. Her husband was the Head Agronomist for Parker Ranch. There were six of us in the class. We all had to recite all the Bible verses we learned since the beginning of the year in her R.E. class, without making a mistake in front of the everyone. Once we made a mistake we were eliminated."

"One by one."

"Alphabetically, one by one. Once you were out. It was the next person's turn. Believe me it was so frickin boring to have to sit there."

"What was the prize?"

"For every verse we recited correctly we got a quarter. Back then, that was big money. The average prize was a dollar and twenty-five cents."

"Five verses out of how many?"

"Fifty verses."

"If you got everyone that was $15.00."

"Good one, Kui. Most kids were not serious about the contest. But I was. When it was my turn. I went on and on. She really tried to distract me. But that didn't break me. I got all fifty verses right. Not one single mistake."

"How did she try to distract you?"

"Stopping me and asking me questions or making a stupid remark about something. After she made me feel stupid earlier in the year and talking with my mom about my straying from the Gospel for which I got a whooping. I exercised a technique I learned in third grade from Mrs. Brand. She was a great teacher. I liked her because she believed in me."

"Technique?"

"Yes. Mrs. Brand had me read poetry and stories in front of the class. She taught me to stop and gather my thoughts, if I ever felt I needed to. I was going to show Mrs. Baybrook that I was no frickin dumb Hawaiian."

"And you did?"

"Yep."

"When my mom picked me up that Friday afternoon, my pockets were jingling with a ton of quarters. The jangle of all that silver in my pockets sounded so good. I couldn't believe it. Made twenty dollars on a Friday afternoon. I got the five-dollar bonus that Mrs. Baybrook promised as well. To celebrate we stopped at Fukushima Store on the way home. I treated my mom and Uncle Ben to an ice cream cone and soda. When we got home, I stacked what was left on my desk. There was a lot. I just sat there looking and salivating at my earnings. I think the Baybrooks had to have saimin for dinner that night."

"Fukushima Store which is now the Fish & Hog Restaurant."

"Yes."

"Did your mom ask you anything?"

"No."

"Did she say anything?"

"Yes. She said she was proud of me. First time ever. She also said my dad would have been proud of me. My head got 'fat.' Real 'fat.'"

"Where was he?"

"He had just died a couple of weeks before. I felt so good hearing her say, she was proud of me. And there were more times to come."

"Did she give you a hug."

"Of course not. I think I mentioned earlier we were not a huggy, kissy family. And, since I had a pocketful of quarters, I felt like Nelson Rockefeller."

"Nelson Rockefeller?"

"Nelson Rockefeller was the Jeff Bezos of my generation."

"Mrs. whatever her name was must have been bummed?"

"Baybrook. She was because that was the end of her 'put a quarter in the drum recitation program.' Unfortunately, I met a couple more folks like her along the way but that was okay. My mom taught me how to deal with those folks."

"How?"

"She told me and Uncle Ben essentially to 'dig in our heels.' gave us the coping skills we needed to get past whatever mental roadblocks they threw in front of us."

"'Dig in your heels?'"

"Turn 'adversity into opportunity.' To flip things over. To convert the storms life threw at us, a challenge, a friend."

"Got it."

"She was in her simple way helping us develop 'emotional intelligence.' How to manage, control our emotions. Helping us to be mentally strong. Use 'put downs' as barbells to benchpress. Gosh, I keep getting off the track here."

"That's okay. This is exactly what we wanted. A 'free flowing' conversation with you, Papa."

"You know what! I like this. I know very, very little about my grandparents. They were with us. And, then they were gone. I had some time with my Lindsey grandpa and some time with our mom's mom and stepfather, but we come from a time where kids were to be seen, not heard. We never got to ask them questions and have a conversation like we are having now. That was a 'no, 'no.' So, so much family history has been lost. Memories 'gone with the wind' forever,' tossed into the 'trash bin' forever. I'm glad I'm able to share some of my past with you."

"Why didn't you get to talk with them like we are with you?"

"That was how they were raised. So that's how they raised us. Put me back on the 'flight plan,' Elliot."

"Flight plan?"

"Yes, where are we on your list of questions?"

"We were asking you about school. You said you liked school. That you did well in school. Unfortunately, some of your teachers did not feel Hawaiian kids were as smart as the other kids. That you were…"

"Oh yes. I surprised them. I liked school because I did well in all areas. Academically, athletically, socially. And, as a leader. I'm happy to say, I honored my parents. I made them proud. They expected that of me and Uncle Ben."

"A leader?"

"I was Student Body President and Editor of the school paper in intermediate school. I was voted Most Studious and Most Likely to Succeed by my classmates when I graduated from ninth grade. Gosh guys, I started saying earlier I'm a recovering narcissist and now I'm bragging about myself. I'm regressing. This is not good."

"Papa, you're doing fine. Keep going. Please don't stop. Not now, we're rolling merrily along. So, you were a leader in our public school?"

"And I did okay in high school as well. In tenth grade I made it into NHS and remained in NHS through senior year. I was a new kid, first year sophomore. That was unheard of according to my advisor. In senior year because our school..."

"Kamehameha. Yes."

"Kamehameha School for Boys. It was a military school. Kamehameha was known as the West Point of the Pacific. It had a full on JROTC program. After completing OCS, Officer Candidate School, at the end of summer of my junior year. I was assigned to the Battalion staff. I was very disappointed about that."

"Why?"

"Because I had my heart set on being Company Commander of Company A. I was assigned to rifle Company A when I registered in 10th Grade and had worked so hard to be Company Commander. But the Professor of Military Science and others who made the final placement decisions after OCS felt differently. I ended up on the Battalion staff. It was a cozy assignment, a desk job, but not a challenging one. I will forever be grateful for the great foundation I got in Waimea School and at Kamehameha. Consequently, college was a breeze compared to high school. Often when I think about it, I just must chuckle. Yes, I always had an internal motivation to aspire. To do well. But I had external motivators as well who unwittingly helped me. Gave me the lift I needed to soar. Mrs. Baybrook, Mrs. Ujiki and a bunch of others who will remain nameless. Who thought I was a dumb because my skin was brown. All, who helped me, motivated me to aspire. Who made me stronger. Made me, *kulia i ka nu'u*. Lifted me up, encouraged me to 'Reach for the summit.' And of course, my dad and my mom, who were always our champions. My mom especially. All of them gave me the resilience, strength and motivation I needed to succeed in life. The push. The nudge, I needed to keep moving forward. Yes, there were times when I wanted to quit. Give up. But they appeared from out of nowhere and threw me a lifeline. Gave me the kick I needed in the butt to chase after and live out my dreams. The electric shock I needed to fulfill my purpose in life. A life of 'servant leadership' to family, the

Hawaiian Nation and our community at large, i.e. people in general. And, I must never forget, Tutu. Who has been there to help me through not only the 'best of times' but moreso the worst of times.' Preferring to stay in the shadows but she has always 'been the *makani* (wind) beneath my wings.' If there is a 'take away' I want to leave with you, it's this. In life, to be a success, you need the help of others. You cannot achieve success all by your lonely. And, and always remember those who helped you. And be grateful for the help they gave you."

"Tell us a little more about your mom?"

"She only went to 8th Grade, so she valued education and admired intelligent people. She was living a dream through me and Uncle Ben. She so wanted Uncle Ben and I to go to college and get degrees. She was thrilled to see my college diploma. And she was also thrilled that Tutu graduated from college and became a teacher. She really talked Tutu up to folks. It was cute to see her do that."

"Some people, in fact some of my teachers say it's wrong for parents to live their dreams through their kids. That we need to be what we want to be."

"I totally disagree."

"Why?"

"Not when parents sacrifice and scrimp and do everything to help their kids succeed. If you don't want to be a 'sacrificial lamb' for your parents own ambitions. Tell them so. In that case don't allow them to waste time and effort and resources and energy on you. In our situation, we were our mother's purpose. We were her only reason for living. She lost her husband. It was just her raising two rascals all by herself. We weren't rich. What little he left us in savings, she used to pay an attorney to settle his estate. She was a tyrant, but I do not despise her. And never will. I owe her my life. I mahalo (thank) her for all she did for us every time I visit her grave. She never said she loved us in words. But we felt her love and saw it in her actions. What's the adage? 'Action speaks louder than words.' I was true to the biblical teaching..."

"Which one?"

"The third of the ten commandments in Exodus. I honored my father and mother. I did what they wished upon me. Has it hurt me in any way? No! Not at all. I celebrate the memory of both as often as I can. In the end what we become. The path we take into the future ideally should be a shared decision. As parents we have one huge *kuleana* (responsibility). We are the stewards of our children. We have a duty to raise our kids to be kind, respectful, thoughtful, and helpful, law abiding, informed, good, contributing, grateful citizens. That's our job."

# 15

"Thank you for the homily, Papa. There is a question I want to ask that is not on the list. An 'off the wall' question."

"There's no 'off the wall' question."

"I overheard you and Uncle Ben talking about seeing your grandpa's ghost. This was several months ago. Was that for real? Or something you both made up? Dreamed up?"

"Yes, we were talking about that. Something we never talked about for a very long time."

"Tell us about it."

"Are you sure you want to hear a ghost story?"

"We're sure."

"You might not be able to sleep tonight."

"We'll be okay."

"Okay. Our Tutu-man died on March 9, 1963."

"You were there?"

"Oh yes. I was thirteen years old. I remember the discussion our uncles were having with the undertaker. The big question from Mr. Arruda, for our uncles was, should he put our grandpa's shoes on his feet as his body was being prepared for burial. One of our smart ale-ck uncles, Uncle Kimo, asked him why he was asking such a dumb question."

"And, his reply was?"

"Mr. Arruda replied, if a deceased, a dead person has his or her shoes on, they'll go strolling."

"'To where?' our Uncle Kimo asked. He was the eighth kid of eleven kids."

"What was your dad?"

"Number six. He was in the middle of the bunch. Anyway, Mr. Arruda didn't know. He was just sharing what folks had told him. Our uncles laughed and said to the mortician to put Grandpa's shoes on. Uncle Kimo, who was a funny guy said to all of us, Papa was too old to walk anywhere when he was alive. Not even to the newspaper box. Now, that Tutu-man was as dead as a doorknob. Papa wasn't going anywhere but six feet under a pile of dirt in our family cemetery."

"Where was the cemetery?"

"On our Tutu-man's property, which was a legacy of his and about a football field away from his house. From where we were. Uncle Kimo said Papa was going to lie right by our grandma's side in the graveyard so he would be too busy getting her caught up on all that had happened since she died with the family. And, whatever else he wanted to tell her. She died ten years before. 'The old goat ain't going anywhere. Put Papa's socks and shoes on.' The walking, strolling about piece was a bunch of malarkeys was his thought."

"No one disagreed."

"Nope. While our aunties wept. Our uncles laughed and traded jokes."

"Where was your grandpa?"

"Tutu-man was right there, lying in his bed."

"If we can stop here for a second. You use 'Tutu-man' and 'Papa' interchangeably. If you ..."

"Our uncles and aunties called our grandpa, 'Papa.' As grand kids, we called him 'Tutu-man.'"

"Okay, got it."

"If Tutu-man was alive he would have heard everything. With that issue resolved it was time to move Tutu-man. They lifted his body off the bed he had slept in for decades, put him on a gurney and took him to the meat wagon for the hour twenty-minute trip to Hilo for whatever needed to be done. I think it was called embalming."

"Why to Hilo?"

"That's where the only funeral home on the island was back then. The next time we saw 'Papa.' He was in a fancy casket. Tutu- man was dressed up in his brown suit. His Sunday best. He had on a white shirt and a striped red and black tie. He looked handsome. His snowy white hair and beard were nicely groomed. Of course, Uncle Kimo wanted to be sure the undertaker had put his shoes on. He looked in the coffin and looked up. A smile covered his face. The show moved on."

"Where was your dad?"

"He was not present when Tutu-man died. He was in the hospital but was able to come home for our grandpa's service. Tutu-man was not a church going man. Our dad was. Of Papa's nine son's, our dad was the favored one."

"How come?"

"Our Tutu-man could depend on him. Our dad would drop whatever he was doing, whenever our grandpa needed help. He was always there. Except when he got sick and ended up in the hospital. Thus, he was assigned the sad task of cobbling a service befitting our Tutu-man who had not made peace with the Good Lord who he probably did not believe in anyway."

"That's your observation, Papa."

"Yes, my observation and mine only."

"Did he believe in any kind of divine?"

"I don't know."

"So, what about the ghost part?"

"The main part of the story. I'm getting there. Bear with me. *Hoʻomanawanui* (patience). I'm getting there, Kui. Just one, no two more important pieces I must share. I wish Uncle Ben was here."

"Why?"

"He would be able to help fill in the gaps. He's got a great memory for those little details that really gives credibility to an incredible story like this. Thankfully, three of us were there to witness the ghostly scene."

"Three of you saw his ghost."

"Yes."

"Who?"

"Our mom. Uncle Ben. Me."

"What's the second piece?"

"That afternoon six of our uncles who were carrying Tutuman's coffin to the cemetery said there were two points along the way where his coffin felt like they were carrying a load of dried-up concrete. When they lifted the coffin off its carrier in the living room where he lay for viewing and his final send off. It was light. But the coffin got so heavy twice, they almost dropped it to the ground. They had to stop and brace themselves."

"What happened?"

"Our dad and Reverend Thomen, the officiating minister, had to coax our Tutu-man to cooperate."

"Coax! How?"

"Assure him that everything was going to be alright."

"Really?"

"Yep. We, who were there that sunny afternoon all saw it in 3-D. We saw and heard them talking to the coffin. Things lightened up both times and the parade went on."

"What do you think was going on?"

"Our Grandpa obviously was resisting."

"Resisting what?"

"He didn't want to commit himself to the earth. To the maggots and all the other flesh-eating critters is my guess. Those creatures who would gnaw away at his carcass. I don't know. That's my guess."

"Euuuw! Papa, you say things like it was no big deal."

"Elliot, I don't know how else to say it."

"What happened next?"

"The pallbearers finally made it to the cemetery, ending their struggle with their unruly passenger. They placed the coffin on 4 x 4 inch blocks over the open grave. We could see the relief on their faces. With a full crowd bearing witness to our grandpa's sendoff on a Waimea I Ka La'i afternoon. Reverend Thomen read the 23$^{rd}$ Psalm and committed Charles Notley Kahililani, Sr., one of Waimea's treasures to the Earth. The sun warmed our faces on a gorgeous afternoon. We sang three traditional songs: Hawai'i Aloha, Amazing Grace and Aloha 'Oe in the lee of Hoku'ula. Our Grandpa's grave is right there. From where we sit, it's right there."

"That's just maybe three quarters of a mile?"

"About that. The grave crew dumped tiny stones and dirt over the hole and created a perfectly shaped oval mound which was then draped in bouquets of flowers and several huge wreaths, all with tear jerking messages. If the old man read them, I'm sure he sneered at every single one."

"Why would he do that?"

"Our Tutu-man wasn't one to accept compliments with grace."

"He was rude."

"No, it was just how he was. We thought that would be the last we'd see of our grandpa but..."

"You were mistaken."

"After the burial, those who were up to it returned to our Tutuman's house to party. 'Breaking bread' was and still is a local tradition after funerals. Our dad had to return to Hilo to the hospital. He wanted to spend the night, but our mom was not in the mood to drive him back to the hospital the next day."

"Why?"

"She was mad with him over something. I don't know what. And I didn't dare ask. So, one of our uncles from Hilo gave him a ride instead. Our mom was not in the mood to take in the party either, so we went straight home from the cemetery."

"Why not?"

"Our mom was not light-hearted. A party type, she was not. She was close to our Tutuman. For sure, some of our uncles who weren't close to him would have said something awful."

"About him? Why?"

"Why? He was hard ass. He didn't let things go. Knowing her, she would have stepped right up and defended him. This little woman with the big voice. She would have ruined the party. Her decision was a good one for us to go straight home and have our own party."

"Then what happened?"

"This is the part you've both been patiently waiting for. We went home. Took our baths. Had dinner. We were watching television. At around 7 that evening the dogs started growling and barking. It was not a friendly bark. They were growling like they were ready to bite whoever it was they were barking at. It was very unusual for them to behave this way. Our mom turned on the flood lamp to light up the Mauna Kea edge of our house. There was no one in the driveway. The dogs who were in the driveway kept on barking. She yelled out to them, 'kuli kuli,' to quit barking but they would not stop. Suddenly there was Tutu-man. He was standing in front of the television in our living room."

"Really!"

"Really."

"So, what you do?"

"I said to our mom. 'Ma, what is 'Tutu-Man' doing in our house. Look, he's right there by the TV.'"

"What did she say?"

"I can't remember. What I remember graphically is the frightened look on her face. She went and got her Bible and started to pray. He must have been in our house for two minutes, but it seemed like two hours. He scared the crap out of me. I never was so scared in my life. To think just a few hours before, he was buried under a couple hundred pounds of dirt and rock. His grave draped in flowers. He was supposed to be in a cemetery four miles from our house. What in hell's name was he doing in our living room. Why didn't he bother the gang partying at his house? Why us?"

"What did he look like?"

"He was alive. He was dressed in his suit. He had his shoes on. His blue eyes were wide open. He had a bushy beard. I don't ever remember him without a beard. There he was. Just staring at us with a forlorn, somber, sad look."

"How many more times did you see him?"

"Two more times. He showed up the next two nights as well. Same scenario. Same time. Same place. The dogs would bark and growl. And, then there he was. Standing right in front of the TV looking at us, a sad look on his face. Staring at us."

"What did your mom do?"

"Her usual. She was strong in her faith and prayed. She asked God to help our Tutu-man be at peace and to just leave us alone. She also asked our minister, Reverend Thomen for help."

"Did that help?"

"It did. Reverend Thomen blessed our home. He even went to the cemetery to bless our Tutuman's grave. He didn't show up anymore."

"What did the minister say?"

"We weren't there when our mom spoke with him. We were in school. This is what she shared with me. Reverend Thomen told her he had had similar experiences with church members at some of his congregations on the mainland. She said it felt so good to hear him say that. She was afraid to approach him initially for fear he would think she was 'off her rocker.' That she was crazy. In a situation like ours, he said our grandpa was forewarning us."

"About what?"

"That something terrible was going to happen."

"Did it?"

"Our dad died two months later. We concluded that was what he was coming to warn us about. In death he needed, wanted our dad's company."

"But why your dad?"

"As I said earlier. Our dad was his favorite son. He was the one, our grandpa always turned to for help. The only one of nine boys he could turn to. He trusted our dad. Our dad died two months later and was buried beside him?"

"How did your mom take..."

"...take the minister's warning."

"It saddened her. She knew in her 'heart of hearts' there was no amount of praying she could do to turn things around. Stop! Prevent the inevitable. I know she was hoping things could be turned around. When I reflect on things. She kept telling us our dad was getting well. But she knew our dad was not getting well. That he was dying."

"What makes you believe, think, say that?"

"There were several mornings, early mornings when I could hear her sobbing in her bedroom before our dad died. A couple mornings she came to my room wanting to talk. I would pretend I was sleeping."

"Why?"

"I didn't want to talk to her because I knew what she wanted to tell me. I knew she wanted to tell me that our dad was not going to make it. I wasn't stupid. I was constantly putting two and two together. I knew the future was grim. I knew what was coming. I could see that every time our dad came home from the hospital for a short visit. An over nighter. He was getting thinner and looking sicker. The sicker he got, the more often the visits. The last time he was home I saw him crying quietly. I never ever saw him cry before. He didn't want to return to the hospital. He begged our mom not to take him back. She insisted it was best. Best for him. Best for us."

"Wow!"

"Later that same week I was looking out the classroom window. It was early afternoon. A Thursday. Not a Friday. I was in my best class. English. I happened to glance out the window. There was our mom driving up to the school office in our blue Plymouth. I watched her park and walk into the office. I knew something was wrong. Within minutes, Mr. Nakano, the principal, called me out of class. Uncle Ben was with our mom in the reception area at the office. Mr. Nakano wished us well as we walked away. He was a gracious man. We got in the car. Our mom's eyes were fiery red. All she told us was we had to go to Hilo earlier than usual. She was sorry we had to miss school. It was no big deal, but she gave us no clear reason for the early pick up. The signs as to why were obvious. Our dad's favorite suit was hanging on a hook with his favorite tie. Along with a starched shirt, still in the plastic laundry bag. His shoes were sitting on the back floor of the car. Her handkerchief was on her lap with her ragged Bible. We could tell she had been crying all morning. It was the longest drive we ever took to Hilo to our Uncle Joe's and Aunty Julia's. They were always so gracious. Always hosting us whenever we needed a place to stay. 486 Hinano Street. The ride was longer this day not because of all the sugar trucks and cane debris on the highway but because of the silence. No words spoken. No radio music. Just a gnawing deathly silence. No questions from her about school. No questions from us to her about our dad. Not even questions about nothing. Just a long, painful, silent ride."

"My oh my."

"Kui, Elliot, when I reflect on that period. What it was, we were all keeping the sadness and fear we were feeling for months, bottled up inside us. We were without our dad for almost seven months by this time. The doctor thought he was having a recurrence of tuberculosis and that was what he was being treated for. His diagnosis was unfortunately 'off the mark.' It was not his fault. Our dad was a smoker and chewed tobacco. He had throat and lung cancer. The good doctor did a 'course correct' but it was too late. His condition was not salvageable. When our dad died, our mom's feelings came gushing out like a breach in a dam across a swollen river. She sobbed, sobbed for months. It was agonizing to hear her cry. I couldn't stand it, but I didn't know how to handle it. Thank God, I was able to run away from all this grief."

"What about Uncle Ben? Did he try to cheer her up?"

"No. Like me, he was at a loss. A total loss as well. We did not have a hospice program or grief counseling then as we do today. We were hoping on hope by some miracle, by some magic, our dad would be healed. We were living in a dream land. Kidding ourselves. Did we cry our guts out like our mom? No, we never cried. I remember the morning we were moving our dad from our house to the church. I remember Uncle Ben asking me if everything was going to be alright. If we were going to be okay?"

"So, what did you say?"

"I said to Uncle Ben, 'No worry. We going to be okay.' We were told from a young age, not to cry. Boys didn't cry. Only girls and mahu's cried. In fact, we used to get lickings for crying. Like if we fell and had a terrible scrape on our arms or knees and we cried. We got whooped."

"What are mahu's?"

"Men who wish they are girls. Who want to be girls. But we were real men. Big men and big men did not cry. After our dad died, we declared our mom our HERO. Our dad had to leave us to take care of his dad, but he left us with our mom to pick up those 'broken family pieces' he left behind. Our dad left us in her good hands."

"Can you describe some of those 'broken pieces?'"

"Sorry. No! No, best these pieces be lost to, left in the past. The names of folks attached to these pieces are not here, one uncle, to speak to, to defend their misdeeds. No, they've been blown away into oblivion by the wind."

"Money must have been involved."

"Money and land sadly. The 'root of not all but some evil.' Some folks simply don't know how to manage their lives. But our mom rectified everything. What is upsetting for me is that our dad took care of everything while he was alive. One uncle screwed his good name on a deal he made and which he completely honored when he was living. She had to take care of it again after he died. To save this uncle from losing his land."

"Did your dad like your grandpa reveal himself?"

"You mean, did we ever see his ghost?"

"Yes!"

"No, he didn't show us his ghost, but he revealed his presence to us in other ways."

"He did? How?"

"Our dad was buried in the family cemetery next to our Tutu-man?"

"Who died two months before."

"Yes, what a memory. That night and every night thereafter he would show up at around 8 o'clock."

"How'd you know it was him?"

"By Monty's bark."

"His dogs bark?"

"Yes, it was a special bark reserved only for our dad. Monty would just go crazy and run round and round our house until he could not run anymore. He looked like a miniature huskie. Monty had short legs. Plus, our house was a decent sized house. It was his welcome home bark which he barked whenever our dad came driving up our long driveway. Uncle Ben said the barking stopped six months later. In November, when I went back to school in Honolulu."

"How else?"

"Our dad's favorite flower was pikake (jasmine). An aunt of ours. Aunty Maile, our dad's youngest of two sisters, worked for a florist at the Edgewater Hotel in Waikiki. She made a pikake rope lei which was strung around his casket. It was a beautiful lei. When she brought it out of the box it was cradled in, our home smelled so good."

"Like a perfume factory?"

"Yes! The fragrance of pikake was just overwhelming. He was buried with the lei attached to his casket. Every Sunday morning for months, as we were leaving the house for church. The entire house smelled of pikake."

"Is there more?"

"Our dad smoked white owl cigars. There were several times when we'd be working in the yard or in the corn field back of our house. It didn't matter the time of day. We'd smell cigar smoke."

"Was it strong?"

"Oh, yeah. He wanted us to know he was around. Oh, yeah. And Monty would go and sit wherever our dad was. We couldn't see him, but we knew Monty was sitting at his feet. Monty would look up and bark. We knew he was looking at our dad. And, when Monty stopped barking, we knew our dad was petting him on the head. Then he would start barking again. He wanted more petting. Just like when he was alive. I know it sounds crazy but it's true."

"Was it scary?"

"No, it wasn't. There were times, I wished he would show himself."

"Wouldn't you have been afraid?"

"No. No, because he was our dad."

"This went on for six months?"

"Yes. There's one more thing I want to add to cap this piece off."

"Go ahead."

"I remember there were nights when he and our mom talked on our porch."

"How did you know?"

"I heard her talking with him. Usually around midnight. It was always in hushed tones."

"What would they talk about?"

"He was always concerned about how we were doing. And she was always assuring him we were okay. Uncle Ben believes when I came home for Thanksgiving vacation, our dad was convinced I was okay. That he had nothing to worry about. So, he could head off to wherever his new journey was going to take him. That our mom, had the home front firmly under firm control. Uncle Ben was okay. I was okay. We could move on without him. He didn't need to worry about us anymore. He could transition to the next phase of life 'beyond the sunset.'"

"He stopped coming around."

"I'll answer you this way. Monty quit his barking the Sunday evening I left home to go back to Kamehameha."

"What about your mom?"

"I presume, you're asking If we saw her ghost or felt her presence after she died?"

"Yes."

"She assured us when she was living. Promised us, once she left us, she would be gone forever. She was a woman of her word. The last we saw of her was at the mortuary in one of Tutu's dresses before the undertaker closed her casket."

"I don't understand."

"One of our mom's three requests before she died was, she wanted to be buried in one of Tutu's dresses."

"Didn't you think that was odd, Papa?"

"No, not at all. My mom initially was skeptical about Tutu."

"Why?"

"Tutu was from the mainland and several of our aunties had married mainlanders and things for whatever reason had not worked out well is why. But in time as my mom got to know Tutu, she came to admire, Tutu. I think the symbolism of being buried in one of Tutu's dresses that my mom really admired was her way of having a piece of Tutu close to her forever. And, I think too, it was her way of quietly apologizing to Tutu about her initial feelings towards her. Well, enough of this paranormal stuff. This is a good time to move on."

"Papa, before we do, I want to close the loop on two remarks you made earlier."

"Earlier?"

"Your mom had two other requests. What were they?"

"You guys sure don't miss anything. One was, she wanted to be buried in the church cemetery. Not in our family cemetery next to our dad."

"Why?"

"She never said. And I don't want to speculate."

"And the other?"

"She wanted to have our dad's remains exhumed from our family cemetery and moved next to hers in the church cemetery."

"So, what is..."

"That's a promise I will not be keep."

"Why not?"

"I don't want to stir up the dead. They had their issues when they were living. Now, they should sleep in eternal peace."

"Another time maybe?"

"No, this piece needs to stay buried six feet under. It has no value to us. No value at all. We need to let 'sleeping dogs lie.'"

# 16

"You said you were able to run away from for want of a better word. All this 'drama.'"

"Ah, yes, I did. Come on guys, I'm a 'recovering narcissist.' Enough about me."

"Papa, this is our opportunity to talk with you about you. Your memories. About you. Your home life. Your education. Work. Family. About Waimea. Some of which you've already covered. So please bear with us. You left home and went to Kamehameha,"

"Yes. For me to get an acceptance in late summer to Kamehameha was a pleasant surprise. On my third attempt. After being denied twice. I applied for a third time to Kamehameha in February. Our Tutu Man dies in March. I turned fifteen in April. Our dad dies in May. Uncle Ben turned thirteen in mid-July. In early August we're playing with the dogs on the front lawn. My mom calls me into the house. She is smiling. First time, I'd seen her smile in weeks. She hands me this paper. It's a letter on fancy paper. I read it. I say to her we should turn the offer down. She says to me. 'No. N O.' I say to her, 'What about you and Ben?' She looks at me and says again, 'No. N O. What about me and Ben? We'll be okay. Don't you worry about us. This is what you've been waiting for. This is what we've been waiting for. Daddy, if he was sitting here would be proud. You're going. And you're going to make us proud.' We had a week to pack. A week later we were on a plane to Honolulu. Two weeks later I was fully enrolled as a cadet at Kamehameha School for Boys. In a week's time, I did all the required summer reading for tenth grade English. I learned how to iron clothes. How to set and clear a table. Studied the student handbook repeatedly. Practiced saying 'No, sir' and 'Yes, sir.'"

"Why?"

"Kamehameha then was a full time JROTC military school, is 'why.' My mom also said I would need to switch from speaking 'pidgin English' which I spoke perfectly to 'English.'"

"Did you?"

"Didn't have a choice. I did. In a jiffy."

"How?"

"I'm sure you've heard the phrase, 'When you're in Rome, you do as the Romans do.'"

"Yes!"

"That's what I did. I was surrounded by teachers and cadets who spoke the King's English. I watched and listened to them. Because I was in a college prep track and wanted to stay in it, I had to. I had no other option. I realized pidgin limited my language skills. So, the Webster dictionary, thesaurus and the school library became my best friends. We had essays, papers, book reports up the kazoo to write. Too many now, that I can rewind and reflect on it. In my old school I only got A's but starting out at Kamehameha in a few subjects I was getting D's and F's and that was pissing me off. Initially, I was disappointed with all the red scribbles on my papers in English but soon enough the F's became D's, D's became C's, C's became B's, B's became A's. In senior year, I ended up in the Honor's English group. Class. Miss Powers initially gave me F's and refused to read my papers."

"Why?"

"My handwriting was awful. It was terrible."

"So, what did you do?"

"I taught myself how to type with two fingers. I still type with two fingers."

"It must have been a hard adjustment?"

"It was but nothing was going to stop me. My honor. My dignity was at stake. And so was our family's. My mom's and my dad's especially. I was not going to let them down. By messing up academically or in any other way. Never. Never in a million years. I'd like to share with you a funny story."

"Go ahead, Papa. Of course. Therefore we wanted to visit with you. We have a set of questions, but these side roads are interesting to us. Absolutely. I hope it's a funny story."

"Elliot, funny now but it was not then. Now, I'm able to laugh about it. In August 1963, I was stunned. It's a story about my first night at dinner at Kamehameha. My formal welcome to Kapalama Heights."

"You were a boarding student?"

"I was. There we all were standing at attention at our tables. The Chaplain blessed the dinner. We all sit down. Every table had a host and a waiter. Each table sat eight. The host was always a senior who sat at the head of the table. He usually was a cadet officer or a ranking NCO. The waiter always sat to the right of the host. We all had assigned seats for the quarter. Everything was done by the numbers. Then we switched off to another table at the end pf the quarter. It was a nice way to meet cadets from other islands. And other grade levels. Some tables had a faculty member."

"Did yours?"

"Unfortunately. At my table was Mr. Berrington. He was in Company D dorm and taught business law. When we were seated, he started to stare me down. Our host, Master Sergeant Lau, for the benefit of those who were new cadets and not familiar with table etiquette, went over the rules quickly. My mom had already gone over all that with me, but it was a good refresher. I was the only new cadet, so everyone was looking at me. Everything had to be passed to our left. We had to always have our napkins in our laps. We had to take small bites and chew our food well. Blah. Blah blah blah blah. When he was done, he asked me if I had any questions. I told him, I didn't. Told him, 'No, sir.' The waiter at that point set the main course on the table and Sgt. Lau starts to put stuff on Mr. Berrington's dish. Faculty and officers got served first. The waiter got served last, which didn't make any sense to me at all."

"Why?"

"Because he had to shovel his food down to serve our table. Everything a waiter did was on the run. He didn't have much time to eat since he had to serve us."

"I get it."

"Anyway, Berrington is staring me down. Finally, he says, "Your last name is Lindsey?"

"Yes, sir."

"'Lindsey, I got a question for you?' I looked at him in anticipation."

"What's your question, sir?"

"How in hell did you get into Kamehameha? Into this school?"

"What did you say?"

"Nothing. I didn't know what to say. I was stunned. Then, he proceeds with a follow up question. 'How long are you planning to last here at Kamehameha, Lindsey?'"

"'Sir, I am going to be here until I graduate.' Sgt. Lau saved the day for me."

"How?"

"He looked at me and said, 'Lindsey, just keep your nose clean. You do that! You'll be okay. If you ever need help. Talk to your Company Commander, homeroom teacher, your counselor. Or me.'"

"So, what did you think?"

"That night after lights out as I lay in my bed, I thought of my dad and the game warden who laughed at him. And I said 'I'm going to show you, Berrington, S.O.B.'"

"You must have had a hard time sleeping that night?"

"I sure did. Not because of Berrington but because of the new kid next door to me. Before I elaborate on my tough time dozing off to sleep. This is what Berrington and Mrs. Baybrook, my Religious Ed teacher, did for me. I was an introvert in school."

"You were quiet?"

"I was but they set off a fire in me. I remained an introvert but became a high achieving introvert. An overachiever. Now back to my first night in Liholiho Dorm. My new home."

"What happened?"

"The kid next door. His name was Timmy. Timmy was homesick for his mommy. Poor baby cried all night. I mean cried. Guys were yelling at him to shut up. He was a freshman. A big baby. Crying for his mommy."

"Did he?"

"Shut up?"

"Heck no! He cried for about a week. His parents should have sent him to Kamehameha with his binky, a couple cans of formula and a few milk bottles to suck on to help him sleep."

"You got more stories?"

"Two more. At the end of the week. On Friday, I had to see my counselor, Mrs. Wiese. She met with the few of us tenth graders, who were just entering Kamehameha, to see how things were going. She asked me how I liked living in a dorm? I said I loved it. It was like staying in a hotel. How did I like the food? It was far better than what I ate at home. It was true. I liked the variety. We never had dessert at home, but we had dessert after dinner and lunch at Kamehameha. The regular brownies and blueberry cobblers were the best. How did I like JROTC? I loved it. I was in scouts in Waimea but JROTC at Kamehameha was like being in the army. Wearing a uniform. Fatigues in the morning to breakfast. Short sleeve khakis to class every day. Long sleeve khakis to church on Sundays. I had my dress blues hanging in my closet and I couldn't wait to wear it for our first Sunday parade which was coming up in two weeks. I already asked my friend Harvey to take a picture of me to send home. Shining brass was fun. I had my very own M-1 rifle for the year. I couldn't believe it. I had my own rifle stored in the armory in my own rifle rack. Rack 409. Oh, how I loved JROTC. Sgt. Hickey in military science was the best teacher. His Korean War stories were incredible. Can you imagine, he was a machine gunner and in holding a line against the enemy, he gunned down about a hundred reds? Not North Koreans. Chinese. Her look was one of disgust as I was recounting Sgt. Hickey's story. I could tell she was a peace nik. How did I like work squad and school service in the mornings before school? I loved it but I'd be glad to tell her what I really thought about work squad if she wanted to hear it. She nodded that she did. I told her work squad was a big joke. The work was too easy. Compared to what I had to do at home. School service was a breeze. She was writing like crazy. In between questions, she'd whip out these images for me to analyze. Which I did. How were my classes? I loved all of them. Was I struggling? No, so far so good. I reiterated I liked military science. English. Mr. Schuetz was my teacher and one of my dorm masters. He was a nice man and helping me a lot as I needed to catch up with my peers. I was a year behind. She already knew that. I told her I also liked my Great Ideas class. I thought Rev. Cole was a genius. He was a smart man. He sure gave me a lot to think about. I loved his lectures. And the list of 'thought leaders' we were going to hear during the school year was interesting. Social Studies. I was not sure about that class. Why? she asked. Mr. Mountain was a nut. I thought he was crazy. She felt a need to tell me Kamehameha didn't hire crazy teachers. Only the best. I mentioned I had one big problem area, but I was working hard on it. 'Which is? Tell me about it?' 'My handwriting. All my teachers are saying it's bad. But I'm working on it.' She wanted me to write something for her. I wrote the first paragraph of Lincoln's Gettysburg Address. Her feedback was not encouraging at all. I think I was wearing her out. Her final question was this. In reviewing my record, there was a notation from the school doctor, Dr. Sholv, that my dad had died in May. I confirmed it. She wanted to know if I missed home. I told her I did but not as much as my next-door mate, Timmy. She wanted me to elaborate. I told her since school started Timmy cried himself to sleep six nights in a row. He really needed help. Somebody had to do something to help this 'cry baby' out of his funk as he was annoying us. I almost said 'frickin cry baby' but bit my lip. Told her he was calling for his mommy. 'Can you believe it, a freshman, a freshman, crying for his mommy. She wasn't really interested in the cry baby.' She pressed me again. 'Did I miss home?' I said, 'Yes!' 'Was I homesick?' 'No.' My response, I guess, didn't make sense to her."

"Why?"

"How can one miss home but not be homesick? But I was telling her the truth."

"Did she ask you to..."

"...explain myself?"

"She did?"

"What did you say?"

"I told her being at Kamehameha was an honor. That it was a dream come true both for me and our family. Then she said, 'Oh, this is your third try.' I said, 'Yes.' I told her my mom said to work hard and to do my best. And that was what I was going to do. She also noticed I had been on the honor roll consistently since seventh grade, had scored high on the entrance exams the three times I applied and that I was student body president and editor of the school paper at my old school. She looked puzzled but didn't say anything. I told her about Mr. Berrington's remarks at dinner. My sneaky way of letting her know I knew what was going on. Again, she didn't say anything. She just smiled and emphasized I was transitioning from public school to Kamehameha. That I would have to shift gears. Kamehameha was not going to be a 'cake walk' because of the track I was in. And, to always remember how fortunate I was to be at Kamehameha. That many others wanted the opportunity but had been denied. I promised her I was going to do my very, very best. She finally stood up, put her hand out, shook my hand and wished me luck. And gave me a pink paper. She was setting up a follow up meeting with a psych something. My homeroom teacher, Mr. Schuetz, would follow up with me when that was set up. I shook her hand and thanked her for her time."

"So, what happened?"

"I went back to my dorm. My buddy Harvey wanted to know how things went with Mrs. Wiese. I told him 'Great.' I really liked her. She was a nice lady. I said she was even setting up an appointment for me with a doctor at Kaiser Hospital. Harvey wanted to see the paper in my hand. I gave it to him. He busted out laughing. I asked him what was so funny. He says to me. She thinks you're crazy. You must see a psychiatrist. I never knew what that was. He tells me it's a head doctor. You must get your head checked out."

"So did you?"

"Yes, I went to Kaiser Hospital-Ala Moana the following week. This doctor talked with me for a half hour. Showed me a bunch of cards. Asked me a bunch of questions. Wrote up a report. I had to see my counselor again. Mrs. Wiese told me, the doctor said I was okay."

"That was all?"

"That was it. I could have told her that. The next time I saw her was at the end of third quarter with my homeroom teacher, Mr. Schuetz."

"For what?"

"They wanted to give me 'nu oli.' Good news."

"Which was?"

"I was going to be inducted into the NHS."

"NHS?"
"The National Hockey Society?"
"Is there such a society?"
"Look it up."
"Papa, you're toying with us."
"Look it up. Remember, I'm a recovering narcissist. I got one more Kamehameha story and then we can move on to the next question. I think it's going to be your turn, Elliot?"
"Yes."
"That was my welcome to Kamehameha School for Boys in August 1963. 'How long are you going to last?' was Berrington's follow through question. I did last. I did make it with help from a bunch of folks. Especially my mom. And, the following year Uncle Ben was accepted."

# 17

"Your mom ended up being home alone?"
"She did. All alone in that big spooky house. That's why she'll always be our hero. She wanted only the best for the two of us. Her total world revolved around us. We were her purpose for living. She was willing to set us free, let us go so we could thrive. I want now to fast forward to May 1966. It's the Sunday before graduation. After church, four of us who were graduating, were invited by one of the school's trustees to have lunch with him at The Pacific Club. Honolulu's elite club for the rich and powerful of Honolulu society back then. Hawai'i's 'movers and shakers.' Mr. Lyman was a very, very nice and personable man. Along with being a trustee, he was a State Senator and from the Big Island. He was close to one of our aunties. We ate our best and really had an enjoyable time with him. I was not excited initially. I tried to find a reason to turn down the invitation but couldn't dream one up."

"You were glad you went?"

"I was. Really glad. When Mr. Lyman looked at you, his whole focus was on you. When he was talking to you. He made you feel like you were the most important person in the world. Have you both met a person like that?"

"Not yet."

"You will one day. And it will be a 'she.' Anyway to get across the finish line. For dessert little did we know he had a special cake made for us. We had cake and ice cream."

"What kind of cake?"

"Chocolate. We had chocolate cake with vanilla ice cream. At this point he went around the table and asked each of us what our post-graduation plan was. I was sitting to his immediate left. Because he looked at me, I assumed he wanted me to start but he stopped me. Said he wanted to hear from everyone else first. Which was perfectly fine with me. Everyone was going to college on the mainland which brought smiles to his face. One classmate was going to the Merchant Marine Academy. He was thrilled to know that and mentioned he had a brother who graduated from West Point and was an army general. When it came to me, this is what he said. 'So 'Boy.' He called me 'Boy.' 'Boy, you will be graduating and going back to Waimea to cowboy on Parker Ranch until the kikuyu grass grows out of your ears?'"

"Really?"

"Really!"

"You must have been bummed."

"No, I wasn't."

"That's not a nice thing to say."

"I was okay with it. In fact, I remember laughing."

"So, how'd you respond? What did you say?"

"I told him I had been accepted to three colleges on the mainland and UH but was still deciding what university I wanted to commit to. He was happy to know that and squeezed my shoulder. 'Boy, good for you. I'm glad to know that.' That was my Kamehameha farewell. Later when I worked for Kamehameha, he remembered me."

"Was he still a Trustee?"

"Yes, he was. And, he and I had long chats when I worked out of the President's office."

"The President of the School?"

"Yes. He would call me to come to his downtown office or if was home, to his home in Nu'uanu. He wanted to chat. We had a few long, interesting visits. But that's for another time."

"Papa, that's a neat story about lunch. Did your handwriting ever improve?"

"No, it never did. With time it got worse. But I did not get thrown out of school."

"What about Uncle Ben?"

"He did well too. My welcome and send off were the bookends of my Kamehameha School days. Days which I will always have fond memories of. I got a great education at Kamehameha. Mahalo to Ke Ali'i Pauahi who wanted us to be educated 'in the higher branches of the English language' and to 'become good and industrious men and women.' I had great teachers who were passionate about the subjects they taught. They were taskmasters."

"Like your mom?"

"Yep. And, because of them going to the university was a breeze. Mr. Schuetz, 10$^{th}$ Grade English. Mr. Clancy, 11$^{th}$ Grade English. Miss Powers, 12$^{th}$ Grade, Honors English. Mr. Greer, History and Research & Writing. Mr. Cole, Great Ideas. Rev. Mulholland, Religious Education. Mr. Johnson, Math. Mr. Johnston, Biology. I made friends with guys from across the state. Learned military discipline. Got the structure and discipline, one needs to succeed in life. The best training in leadership one can get. Master Sgt. Franklin, Sgt. Hickey and Captain Campbell, a few of our JROTC cadre whose names quickly come to mind. I liked wearing a starched, ironed uniform. I liked Wednesday drills and Sunday parades. Shining brass, spit polishing my shoes until I could see my face in it. 'Be strong and all ye, oh sons of Hawai'i. And proudly stand together hand in hand. Ring, ring Kalihi ring.' And I will never of course forget my public-school teachers. Mrs. Baird, English. Mr. Morikawa, Algebra, Science & Agriculture. Mr. Tanaka, History. Mr. Nishimoto, General Science. Mr. Hiraishi, Math. Miss Nonaka, English & Home Economics. They got me ready for Kamehameha. And my mom and our church family. I will never forget our mom. She gave me the mental strength, the coping skills I needed to weather the storms that came my way. Every single one. And our church family who were there to support us through prayer and spiritual relief. So, in a sense I was in a pressure cooker."

"How?"

"I was representing our family, so I needed to do my job. Do my part. I had a duty to make our family proud. In raising us, our mom helped Uncle Ben and I develop 'thick skin.' Skin so thick our spirits were difficult. Impossible to break. Poke holes through. We had a hard shield covering us. Protecting us. Tell me I couldn't do something. I would say in my head, 'Oh yeah. Let me show you what I can do!' And bam! Our mom used reverse psychology on us. And it worked very well across the years. In politics. In public service. In every avenue of my life. So, what's your question, Elliot?

# 18

"Describe in thirty words, first your dad. Then your mom. And our Lindsey great grandparents."

"My dad. A gentleman. Kind. Generous. Hardworking. *Olu'olu*. Do you know what that means?"

"No."

"Humble. That's five. Aloha Ambassador. Man of God. Honest. Trusting. Loved us. Loved people and Waimea deeply. Someone to emulate. Comic. Gave people his time. A good husband, father, son, brother. I went slightly over."

"Papa, it's okay. Thanks. Now your mom."

"Hard core Christian Woman. High standards. Proud. Valued Education. Wanted the best for us. A mama bear. Tai chi practitioner. Backyard psychologist. Would never get along with Benjamin Spock. Believed in 'tough love.'"

"Thirty-three words. She was a tai chi instructor?"

"Oh yes. When we got out of hand. A stick was always nearby. We gave her a lot of opportunity to practice her tai chi moves. We knew she needed practice, so we gave her all the practice she needed. We were always available. There was a 'silver lining,' added value to it all."

"Silver lining. 'Added value.' I don't understand. It was tactical on your part?"

"Kui, yes. The lickings helped us develop the thick skin I talked about earlier. She'd whoop us good when we needed a whooping. That was the 'upside.' She'd beat the demons out of us."

"There was a 'downside?'"

"There was. I have a difficult time being bossed around by wahines (ladies). Which is ridiculous! But I'm working on getting rid of that liability. It's not easy but I'm making progress. Slow but sure progress."

"So, what do you mean by slow progress."

"I voted for Hilary Clinton over Donnie Trump for President in 2016. And I'll vote again for her."

"You're not for the MAGA President?"

"Nope. I understand what he's trying to do but I disagree with his approach. He's right! The pendulum has swung too far left. It needs to swing back to center. And I loathe all his lies, misrepresentations and how he belittles and bullies' people."

"I think we should move on to our paternal great grandparents, Charles and…and Fannie…"

"I agree. Don't get me started on the fate of our Country, State and County. Charles and Fannie Lindsey. My grandparents and your great grandparents. Let's see. I got this letter from my cousin Reginald who lives in Graham, Washington recently. If I could read segments from it to answer your question. I really didn't know our Tutu-lady, Grandma Lindsey at all. I was about four when she died. One of the few things I remember about our Tutu-man is he was a master storyteller."

"Kind of like you."

"Elliot, my grandpa was my mentor. He could spin a 'mole hill into a mountain' with very little effort."

"Did you visit with him a lot?"

"A few times before Little League baseball practice."

"Was it fun?"

"It was. He would be sitting in his rocker on the porch watching the cars and whoever was walking by. He'd see me and in his high-piitched voice call out, 'Baby Robber, *pehea* (how are you)?'"

"He called you, Baby Robber?"

"That's what he called me. My dad was 'Big Robber.' I was 'Baby Robber.' He really meant Robert. He'd invite me to sit down on the steps. The sight of my glove and bat would set him off. Our cousin James across the street would appear every now and then. That would distract him."

"How?"

"He'd say to me. 'You see Butchie (James' nickname)? That boy *pilau* (bad). One day, I'm going catch that 'son of a bitch' and cut his lahos (testicles) off. Yea, I'm going to make him *lahaole*."

"What's *lahaole*?"

"A male pig who has been neutered. Had his testicles removed."

"Why would your grandpa want to do that?"

"James was a naughty kid. He was always up to mischief. Like Dennis the Menace. He was spoiled. Lived with his grandma who was old and had no control over him. He was a 'free spirit.' Did whatever he wanted."

"Did your grandpa ever catch him?"

"Nope. He tried but James knew he had to keep a safe distance from our grandpa. James was no fool. He was smart. Then he'd return to his story."

"What were his two biggest tales?"

"One was, when he pitched. He threw such a fast hard ball. The guys who caught for him all had to take a break after every inning."

"Why?"

"Their catching hand hurt so bad even though they had extra padding in their mitts?"

"Wow. What else did he say about his pitch?"

"It was so fast; the batter and the umpire often couldn't see the ball. When the ball landed in the catcher's mitt there was a loud echo. Even Mr. Chock, who was in his store a half a mile away could hear the echo when the ball landed in the catcher's mitt. And he only threw strikes. His catchers often asked the ump for a time out as they needed a rest break to shake the pain out of their catching hand. Six innings, eighteen batters, fifty-four pitches, game over."

"What else?"

"He only hit home runs. He was Waimea's home run king. When his bat connected with the ball, the ball would end up around Waiaka Bridge."

"That's about…"

"Three miles. That's just past the HELCO power plant."

"And you believed him."

"Initially. 'Hook, line and sinker.' Until my mom told me he was kidding around with me. Having fun at my expense."

"Is that a good thing, Papa?"

"Having fun at someone's expense? You must be discreet when you use humor. It should never be hurtful, mean spirited or deceitful. Humor is healthy. Generally, those who have a sense of humor live long. Hey, let's get back to Uncle Reggie. He, like James who was raised by his grandma, was raised by our grandparents. He was like their twelfth kid. You know what! I am going to exercise 'executive privilege' and read his letter in its entirety."

"Sure, go ahead."

"You need to remember; Uncle Reggie is writing about a Waimea that does not exist. Not anymore. It's about a very special time in Waimea I Ka La'i. This is a glimpse into a Waimea we will never see again. So, cherish it, absorb, envision it and share it with your cousins and future generations."

"This is history, real and personal:
Memories of Reginald E. Lindsey, 2019

"Tutu Lady (my paternal grandmother, your great great paternal grandmother) was a beautiful and caring person, her home was always open to family and visitors. Rocher's (Rocha) bus, which was a car/taxi, traveled from Kohala to Hilo, on a daily basis (an 80-mile trip one way), carrying passengers and items purchased to be delivered to patrons along the way. 'Pit stops' were frequently made at the Lindsey home, where coffee and snacks would be prepared by Tutu Lady.

She loved plants and flowers, keeping a vast flower garden, consisting of pansies, akulikuli, roses, dahlias, carnations, violets, and baby's breath. Uncle Robert (my dad) would frequently take her to Honokaa to purchase her desired plants. Tutu Man (my paternal grandfather, your great, great paternal grandfather) built her a split bamboo hot house, approximately 12x6 feet where she grew many varieties of maiden hair fern.

Tutu Lady kept a well-kept house. Supported her children and grandchildren. I remember discussing an item with her which I wanted to do but she was not in favor of. It was discussed with her, her response was, 'Hana me kou ike.' 'Do as you see fit.' So of course, I did not do it.

Tutu Lady prepared her mother's home on Cheesbrough Lane for Uncle Robert and Aunty Hannah (my parents) to move into taking two weeks to paint the entire interior of the home. Uncle Robert and Aunty Hannah were very helpful and supportive of Tutu Man and Tutu Lady for their entire lifetime. Always ready to assist with whatever needed to be done.

Tutu Man was 17 years of age when he became the foreman for the Paa Hau (Paauhau) section of Parker Ranch, overseeing 15 workers for that region. Due to the many Japanese ranch workers, he became fluent in the Japanese language, along with speaking both Hawaiian and English. At the age of 30 he married Tutu Lady, after building a lovely house for her.

One of Tutu Man's interests was to grow mango trees, three varieties of figs, plums, sugar cane, green grapes, peaches, of which many of the fruits would not ripen due to Waimea's cool weather. He also raised chickens for their eggs, ducks, turkeys, pigeons (squabs) which we had for our birthday special dinners, along with pigs and cows.

Tutu Man rode his horse to work, spending the week on the ranch areas, returning home on the weekend, leaving Tutu Lady in charge of the home. Later years when he was riding to work, his horse slipped on the wet, rainy road, falling on Tutu Man, breaking Tutu Man's leg. After that incident, Tutu Man retired from ranch life. After the accident, Uncle Bolo (Fred), Uncle Robert (my dad) and myself were the 'helpers.' Lots of yelling.

After retirement he enjoyed visits from his ranch friends, 'talking story' with Willie Kaniho (father of activist Sonny Kaniho), also a ranch foreman Napia Murtons (Maertans). Mr. Stevens (John), Kale's (Charles Stevens-long time Parker ranch hand) father. Kale worked under Tutu Man. Reminiscing about roping cattle (wild cattle) off Mauna Kea, showing much respect for him. These men would get into various discussions and if Tutu Man didn't agree, he would reach up into his shirt pocket and turn off his hearing aide.

Tutu Man and Tutu Lady hosted a monthly luau at their home, inviting friends and family. Tutu Man was interested in world events, faithfully reading the newspaper. He was also instrumental in obtaining the portion of the Lindsey estate, from the control of his oldest brother, William, who was Aunty Anna's father. William had not been sharing the proceeds with his siblings, which resulted with Tutu Man taking charge. The lands were sold with the proceeds divided equally among the siblings.

When I was about nine years old. Tutu Man and Tutu Lady and I traveled inter island for about four weeks, visiting Oahu, Kauai, Maui,

Molokai, and Lanai, spending 3-4 days on each island. During this trip, Tutu Man visited with A. W. Carter. He was living in Honolulu. Mr. Carter was very instrumental in developing Parker Ranch and who Tutu Man had much respect for.

I loved Waimea...the best place to be. As a boy growing up I and my friends and cousins were free to roam the hills from Waimea to Puako and from Hoku Ula to Holoholu Ku, hunting for pigs and wild goats. During the summer, beginning in $7^{th}$ grade, I began working for Aunty Anna. It was great. At first, I was a 'gate opener.' As they drove cattle through, I would open and close the gates. Then after two years I began working with Anna in the paeke (corral) separating the calves from the cows, picking out animals to be slaughtered. I thought I had arrived! We drove cattle from Anna's Ranch to Kawaihae Uka. I went on weekend trips to Anna's home in Kona and Kawaihae Uka. I was able to learn a lot about how to drive cattle and ranching.

For enjoyment we rode bikes to Kawaihae, going surfing and spear fishing, then hoping that someone would give us a ride up the steep hills to Waimea.

Christmas was a wonderful event. The Ranch (Parker Ranch) hosted a gathering where we sang Christmas carols, around a gigantic Christmas tree, each child receiving an age-appropriate gift from the ranch. On New Year's Day, the ranch hosted a luau for ranch employee's families and the neighboring farmers. $4^{th}$ of July were the annual horse races.

After World War II ended many US Marines, who had served in the Pacific, were housed in barracks in Waimea, waiting for transport back to the US mainland. Each Sunday the Marine Band would play as the troops marched to the Waimea Park. There they would receive medals in honor of their service. It was a thrilling event.

High School Graduation!!! Yippee!!!"

"So, gentleman what do you think? Isn't that an interesting letter of memories?"

"Papa, it sure is an interesting letter. I'm so glad he took the time to write it. I have a couple more questions?"

# 20

"Ask away, Elliot."

"The Parker Ranch sure was the center of life here from 1847 to about 2005. It's no longer the influence it once was. What happened?"

"I think Mr. Smart…"

"Who was he?"

"The owner. Mr. Smart made a big mistake when he brought outsiders to Waimea to manage the ranch. They were not like A.W. and Hartwell Carter. These were folks who had no connection to Waimea, to the people and the *'aina* (land). Who thought they knew it all. Applied continental thinking to our little neck of our Big Island. Who didn't look to the paniolo talent and *ike* (knowledge) that was deeply embedded in the paniolo who worked and loved the Ranch and who were loyal to the Parker's for generations. Who were of this place. There was a 'cultural clash' between the mainlanders, outsiders who had no connection to Waimea and us, who were born and raised here. Who built this institution along with A.W. Carter for the Parkers from the ground up. And the thanks we get from Mr. Smart is, we were not good enough to hold leadership positions in his ranch. We had to suck up to these mainlanders. In the end, they won as they Smart's ear. Sadly, they ran Parker Ranch into the ground. And, high tailed back to the mainland, leaving a mess behind them. Mr. Smart died in 1992. There were estate taxes to pay, lawsuits to settle and on and on and on. The Ranching component fell apart, when many of the old time *paniolo* (cowboys) were let go, after Smart died and the Ranch was placed in a

Trust. Parker Ranch, what is it now? It's a fading memory in the hearts of those of us who were born, raised and grew up here."

"Our Tutu-Man, I'm sure is rolling around in his grave. That is if he went back to his grave after showing up at our house in 1963. He, along with my Uncle Charlie, Uncle Johnny, Walter and Charlie Stevens, Ikua Purdy, Jiro and Ichiro Yamaguchi, Uncles Hogan and John Kauwe, Uncle Willy and Dan Kaniho, Donnie De Silva, Mr. Ah Fong, Mr. Kaula, Mr. Perreira, Mr. Horie, Mr. Nakanishi, Mr. Tanaka, Mr. Harada, Uncle Willy Palaika, Pakana Spencer, Frank Vierra, Jess Hannah, Hiram Lewi, Yunko Nakata, Hisa and Yoshi Kimura, Mr. Baybrook, Mr. Yaro Dochin, Mr. Parel, Alex Penavoroff and the many others not mentioned who all helped Parker Ranch become the icon and blessing it once was to Waimea. Do the folks who manage the ranch today know these folks? I think not. Do they care? I don't think so."

"Uncle Reggie was happy to graduate high school. He concludes his memory piece with a 'yipee yuy yay.' So, what did he do after high school?"

"He went to Hilo immediately after graduating from Honokaa High in 1956 to enlist in the Marine Corps. He could not wait to high tail it out of Waimea. And military service suited him fine. The Marine recruiter was a 'no show.' The Air Force recruiter was. So, he enlisted with the Air Force recruiter and made the Air Force his career instead. The best move, Uncle Reggie claims he ever made. It was a good way to serve our Country and see the world. He met a nice lady, Aunty Linda. They got married, had three beautiful daughters and raised a nice family. He completed his service, retiring as a Command Master Sargent and settled in Graham, Washington."

"They still live there?"

"Yes, with their three girls and their families. They are proud parents, grandparents and great grandparents. Tutu and I wish they lived nearby,"

"Why?"

"Because we share a lot of common values. Uncle Reggie and Aunty Linda have a strong sense of *ohana* (family), believe in family values, raising good kids. Have strong ethics and values. They believe in education. Are very generous. Believe in helping others. Hard work.

Subscribe to the 'Fruits of the Spirit.' The same values Tutu and I ascribe to. Uncle Reggie loves animals. Loves working with his hands. Like my grandpa and my dad."

"And, he liked the great outdoors. He used to come up here to Hoku'ula."

"You were paying attention, Elliot."

"Of course, Papa. I heard every single word."

"Yes, all this land around us was his playground. From where we sit, to Holoholoku which is that cinder cone in a straight line, three miles south out there on the plains, to Puako about twelve miles west on the coast and the Kohala Hills. This was his stomping grounds. Where he hunted..."

"Pigs and goats."

"You got it Kui. And I'm sure plovers and pheasants during bird season."

"Plovers?"

"Why not?"

"It's a protected bird!"

"Heck anything that intrudes in our air space is trespassing. And, therefore subject to be shot down. We got to move things back to center from left. Pretty soon, the government is going to pass a law protecting us from our shadow. From ourselves. America has the most crime, the most lawyers, the most people in prison because we have the most laws on the books. We got to press the reset button and go back to the good ole days. A simpler time."

"To Waimea I Ka La'i. Sorry Papa, I didn't mean to distract you."

"That's okay. Anyway, Uncle Reggie honed his leadership skills, right here in Waimea."

"How do you know that?"

"One of his buddies, Woody Young, has mentioned to me several times at breakfast Saturday morning..."

"...breakfast at Pukalani Stables."

"Yes, Uncle Reggie, Woody claims was the ringleader of their gang. They'd borrow horses..."

"You mean 'steal.'"

"No, I mean 'borrow' from Parker Ranch and ride the range from Waimea to Holoholoku, West Hawai'i Concrete, the Saddle Road Junction back to Waimea."

"They were 'borrowing.' They always returned what they 'borrowed' in good shape."

"After they had their fun."

"Yep. It was good, clean, harmless fun. They didn't hurt anyone. They were practicing 'servant leadership.' Bringing out the best in each other, even the horses."

"Waimea I Ka La'i was his 'oyster.'"

"Waimea was his 'oyster.' His Anuenue Playground. His Kahilu Theater. His Disney Land, Disney World."

"That's a nice way to sum it all up, Kui. I'm sure Uncle Reggie will like that. Hey, time is moving on. The sun is almost at high noon. How's that group of injun interlopers doing? They still 'bow wowing?'"

"Papa, it's 'pow wowing.' Let me see. I'll give you a quick update in a few seconds."

"What do you see through those field glasses?"

"I see a Parker Ranch security truck. And Samuel and Lala are standing and chatting with Chief Brave Eagle."

"Can I see?"

"Of course! Gosh, I hope they're not selling us out. The pot you were talking about is sitting on the top of the gate post. I know what it is?"

"Tell us!"

"It's an urn. It's got someone's ashes in it. They are planning to scatter the ashes here on Hoku'ula is why they are here."

"Humm. Why here?"

"Hoku'ula is significant, special to the person whose ashes are in the urn, is what I think."

"Why would it be? Why would someone from Wisconsin want their ashes to be scattered here on Hoku'ula? So far away from home."

"Good question. Guess, we'll find out soon enough."

"Hey, the party's over. Everyone's leaving, including the security guy. Lala and Samuel have a key to the gate. They're unlocking the lock. They don't have to hop the gate, Papa."

"I'll be damn. How did they pull that off? Let's knock off a couple more questions before they reach us?"

"Papa, we have time for three, possibly four more questions. Tough. controversial, troubling questions."

"For me, there are no tough, controversial, troubling questions. I'm live and direct because I want to sleep good at night. It's a free country. We enjoy all these freedoms. Assembly. Religion. Speech. Press. Jury and speedy trial. Protection from unlawful search and seizure, cruel and unusual punishment. I have my manao (opinion). You have yours. Others have theirs. If someone disagrees with me, nowadays. It doesn't bother me. In my younger days, it did. We'd settle things sometimes in ways that made matters worse. I've finally grown up. I've come to realize, discourse is a 'battle of wits.' Discourse should be civil, respectful, understanding, polite, thoughtful conversation with the end goal, a 'win win' not a 'win lose' outcome.' I do my best to listen, to walk in the other person's moccasins. To understand, where the person across from me is coming from before I open my big mouth. In the 'public square' these days, it's brains over brawn. Mind over Muscle. So, ask."

"Papa, what's your position on Mauna Kea?"
"Being a center for astronomy?"
"Yes."

"I am in full and total support of astronomy on Mauna Kea. Including, the Thirty Meter Telescope."

"There's so much controversy around the telescopes particularly the TMT."

"There is and that's okay. We live in a free country. That's what's neat about being American. On any issue, we are free to express ourselves. Do you think that would have happened under our *ali'i*? I don't think so. Dissenting heads would roll especially if you disagreed with the Chief. Dissenters would have had a speedy trial and the result would not have been humane. The TMT folks have gone through the entire process towards acquiring the necessary permits and approvals."

"So now, the 'protectors' are blocking the road."

"Now government, must exercise it's *kuleana*. The State of Hawai'i must enforce the law."

"But it's chosen not to do that, so things are at an impasse. What should government do?"

"Enforce the law. It needs to use the tools at it's disposal to uphold and enforce the law."

"Why do you support the TMT? It's so controversial."

"Why not? I believe in science. I've been supporting astronomy on Mauna Kea for fifty years."

"But what about culture?"

"What about culture? The world has changed. Our world has changed."

"How?"

"The world keeps shrinking. Changing faster and faster. Ironically, science and technology are the culprits in this controversy. The tar baby over something that happened in 1893. Something they had no part in. Science has shrunk the world. It started with the radio. Now, we have iPads and iPhones. We can connect with folks on the other side of the world in seconds. We can mobilize folks behind a movement today, not in days or months but in minutes. That's life everywhere on the planet, Kui and Elliot. As I described earlier in my Creation Story through the events Eve describes in her dreams. James Cook came upon us in 1778. Our culture, thus evolved, shifted from one of stone, fiber and wooden canoes into a culture of iron, muskets and gunships. We went from being a producing economy to a consuming economy. From subsistence to capitalism. Others with their own traditions and costumes have found their way here. We've become a melting pot. Science and culture must find a way to coexist on Mauna Kea. It must. Mauna Kea has morphed into a crusade for Hawaiian rights. When one looks at the world from the optics of a crusade, there will be no civil resolution."

"Or the telescope can move elsewhere."

"That's an option. Some of our folks liken Mauna Kea to Kahoolawe and the Hawaiian Renaissance of the 1970's. I chuckle to myself when I hear this."

"Why? The bombing was stopped on Kahoolawe. We got the island back."

"And, who, is 'we?'"

"Us. The people of Hawai'i. After the military gave up control of Kahoolawe, a civilian Commission was created to manage the island. As Hawaiians, we inherited a big, huge, expensive mess. What use is the island to us? It's not safe because there's 'live' ordnance left from more than half a century of bombing. Kahoolawe is a dangerous place. You can't walk freely on the island. You can't go there unaccompanied. You might step on a bomb and blow yourself to bits. Hundreds of millions of dollars have been spent to 'clean up' the island. Hundreds of millions more is needed to complete the 'clean up.' When will the 'clean up' be completed. No one knows. I think never. We have no muscle in

Congress. Our champions are gone. When our senior senators passed on, Senator Inouye and Senator Akaka, Hawai'i lost its influence in Congress. So, what benefit has Kahoolawe been to us as Hawaiians since we got it back?" No benefit at all. It was pure 'symbolism.' Our emotions got stirred up for a time. Mauna Kea should TMT be stopped will be the same thing. What I see in the orb circling in my mind when I compare Mauna Kea to Kahoolawe. At least the TMT folks have given millions to Big Island education and work force development so residents will be trained up and able to take on jobs when the TMT is completed. That to me is a major future as well as immediate benefit to all of us who call the Big Island our home."

"Aren't you concerned there's going to be this gigantic observatory sitting on top of Mauna Kea? It's going to be eighteen stories high."

"No, I'm not."

"Why not?"

"Mauna Kea is a big mountain. It can handle a telescope this big. Even bigger. Let's be real here."

"Some folks say a huge portion of Mauna Kea's sacred ground will be impacted, desecrated."

"All of Earth is sacred. That be the case, we shouldn't be building communities with schools, libraries, churches, fire houses, police stations, court facilities, airports and harbors, shopping centers. Oh, and hotels on our beaches. Any kind of structure anywhere on the planet period. We shouldn't be building homes. We should just spread lauhala mats on the ground to sleep on under the stars at night. We should be cooking our food on open fires. We shouldn't be driving cars and flying in airplanes. We should be walking from Waimea to Waikoloa or riding on horses to get from here to there. Waimea to Hilo or Ka'u. Are we willing to give up our cars and trucks? Our iPad's and iPhone's? Our TV's? Are we going to ride on a double hull canoe to San Francisco or Seattle or Portland or Miami Beach instead of flying on airplanes. Do we want to go back to living in caves? In thatched houses? To being hunters and gatherers? To the *kalo* patch? Is that what we want, most of us? I don't reckon so. Are we willing to give up hot showers, flush toilets, our gas or electric stove. Today's modern conveniences? I'm not. Our logic, if we dwell on the topic long enough can spin out of control.

Spin into the absurd. God created the Earth and put us on it to thrive and flourish. We just need to care for our Earth Mother. I admit, we are not doing a good job as a so called 'first world' country."

"Those who oppose TMT say our University has been doing a poor job of stewarding the mountain."

"That's in the past but today. That is not the case. The University is doing a better job of taking care of the *mauna* (mountain). They've learned from their mistakes and are doing their best to correct those mistakes."

"There are folks who say building the TMT will anger 'the old gods.'"

"The history is this. The 'old gods' were kicked out along with the ancient religion in 1819 by our own chiefs in the Battle of Kuamoo."

"Really!"

"Really and truly. It's documented history. I'm not making this up to amplify my argument. My bottom-line point is this. If the 'old gods' are still around and don't want this telescope on Mauna Kea. Let them come out from wherever they are and do what they need to do to make things *pono* (right). If the 'old gods' are still Omnipotent, Omniscient and Omnipresent. Let them speak for themselves. If they don't want the telescopes on Mauna Kea. Let them deal with the scopes. Speak for themselves. The observatories have been on the Mauna for half a century. No ancient god has stood on Mauna Kea's summit with a bull horn, shouting at the top of his or her lungs, 'Hear ye, hear ye, O my people. I hereby declare my anger and disgust at these unsightly observatories, intruding on my Mauna. At dawn tomorrow morning, I will remove all these 'pimples' from the summit of my Mountain.' The old religion and all the ancient gods are dead. They've been gone for two centuries. Mauna Kea is a sacred place. It is a very sacred place. It will take care of itself."

"Have you been on Mauna Kea since the telescopes were built?"

"Yes, twice. But I want to rewind, go back in time and add some context to my answer. We have a long relationship with Mauna Kea."

"When you say 'we,' you mean you and Uncle Ben?"

"Yes. Mauna Kea is a significant part of our lives. It's like a grandma to us."

"A Grandma."

"Yes. We grew up in her shadow and swore we would never abandon her. The entirety of the Mauna's north flank was our front yard. The

Mauna was always a looming presence in our lives. We looked for her every morning from our kitchen window while waiting for breakfast to see what she was up to. We stopped to look at her when pulling weeds in the cornfield. Helping our dad feed his pigs. Thinning Chinese cabbage, push hoeing or packing vegetables for Mr. Okura. Mr. Okura was our kindly neighbor and one of Waimea's biggest truck farmers when we were kids and was always good about giving me a job after school, on Saturdays or during the summer. When flying home for vacations from high school. Looking out of the airplane window and seeing the great mountain was so calming."

"How so?"

"I knew I was home. Home where I should be. After a storm, accompanied by *ua hau* (snow) rain, our mom guaranteed us the *mauna* would be dressed in white. She was never wrong. Not even once. I think it was in 1956 after a super storm. When the storm clouds moved seaward, and the sky cleared. Mauna Kea, from top to bottom, was dressed in white. It was a once in a lifetime gala event. It's never happened again. There were times, days when she hid behind a thick blanket of clouds. But we knew the curtain shielding her would lift at a time determined by her. That she would reappear and stand before us in a repeat performance as she has for centuries. In all her majesty. Most of the time, she's dressed in royal blue, from end to end. Periodically, wearing a crown of white upon her head. And there were those memorable times when we watched the color changes created by the light of the rising and setting sun that washed over her in early morning and at dusk. The beautiful light show she put on for us from one end of the Mauna to the other, was over in a flash. Over as quickly as it started. But we didn't mind. It was gratis, a free stunning spiritual cinema. And, we knew there would be many *hana hou* (repeat performances) for the rest of our days."

"Some folks who don't, unlike you, support astronomy on Mauna Kea, call the observatories, 'pimples' that mar, destroy the Mauna's beauty. What's your *manao* (thought)?"

"'Beauty is always in the eyes of the beholder.' I like seeing the observatories. Those 'pimples' have eyes peering into the depths of space and are making these awesome discoveries. In my eyes, they are beautiful.

They add beauty and character to the Mauna's beauty. I have my view. My opponents have theirs. Thank God, we live in America. Now all we need is the will, to find a way for science and culture to coexist."

"How can that happen, Papa?"

"We have to, must come together. Take time to listen to each other. 'Break bread,' spend time together and with a spirit of aloha do our utmost to find a center point. Find common ground rather than hurling rocks at each other on Facebook, via video clips, the evening news or op eds. It took me a lifetime to come to the realization there is only one race. Humanity. Yes, we are a planet of many countries, governments, ethnicities and cultures. But ultimately, we are all God's children. We are one. We all need to give up something. We need to find our humanity. The Aloha we talk about. We need to practice mindfulness. Live in the present moment. Not in the past. Not in the future. But in the present. It cannot be 'us' and 'them' anymore. We must focus on our similarities, tolerate our differences, see our humanness in each other regardless of our race, gender, beliefs, ethos. Find the 'tie that binds us.'"

"Why?"

"Because in the 21$^{st}$ Century the world is a dangerous place. In ancient times when we lived in caves, the danger was the saber-toothed tiger. We lived in our own little pods. The damage the tiger did then was minimal and confined to a small area. But now, we are a global community. The saber-toothed tiger today is 'man.' One psychotic man, one crazy maniac in Washington DC, Pyongyang, Baghdad, Tehran or Islamabad just needs to tap a key on a keyboard. And it's all over. We're cooked. We're history. The 'saber toothed tiger' is lurking on our good Earth somewhere. It will not be an asteroid gone awry, hurtling towards us from out in the galaxy somewhere that will end our civilization. It will be an unhappy, psychotic man who in seconds has the capability to destroy the world."

"Papa, I hope you're wrong!"

"Kui, I hope and pray I'm wrong, totally wrong for the sake of your generation and generations to come. I hope I'm hallucinating and that what I see in my crystal ball is just a hoax. A figment of my imagination run wild. So Elliot what's going on at the bottom of the hill?"

# 22

"Looks like the party's over. Everyone is driving off."
"Everyone's leaving?"
"Yes, they're all driving off."
"After all that bow wowing. All that drama. That was quite a workout. What about Samuel and Lala? Where are they?"
"They were chatting with the security guard over the gate. Now he's getting in his jeep. Looks like he's going to drive off as well. Samuel and Lala, are starting to run up the hill."
"I wish I was young again."
"Why Papa?"
"There's a few things I'd like to do over."
"Such as?"
"Not worth discussing."
"Why not?"
"It's a waste of time. Yesterday is gone. The only moment we have is now. Let's enjoy now."
"Papa, are you happy with the life you've lived?"
"Very, very, very happy. My cup is spilling over with joyful memories. My memory lane is paved with tons of beautiful memories. I've had a long, full, happy and superb life with Tutu. I'm a very lucky man. The luckiest man in the world. Tutu is my sunflower. And, you Kui and Elliot and Lala and Samuel and your parents are our sunshine, 'the pot of gold at the end of our rainbow.' Why are you asking?"
"Just curious is all. I've always thought that."

"Well, it never hurts to ask. How about you, Kui. Are you happy with your life?"

"I am."

"And you, Elliot?"

"Yes, very happy."

"What are you most happy about?"

"We have a nice family. I've got great parents. And the best big brother I could ask for. That's one. And I'm healthy."

"You Kui?"

"Same as Elliot. Plus we got a Tutu who makes it fun for us every time we come by your house."

"Yea, from when we were little. She was always reading to us. She had all these games for us to play. Puzzles to put together. Stuffed animals. Scooters, bikes, three-wheelers to ride. Water play. Art. Books. Blocks. A piano to pound on. Pop-sickles after nap. We always have her undivided attention."

"Well, you absolutely did."

"Oh, and one more thing Kui, we can't forget?"

"What have we forgotten, Elliot?"

"A nutty Papa who makes us laugh, shake our heads in disbelief at times and says something smart every now and then."

"Yea, we sure won't forget you, Papa. You and Tutu are the epicenter of our circle."

"Along with Lita, Jammu, Pap Pap and Nanny."

"Yes, of course, they are part of the circle. A big part of the circle as well."

"They must be. They must be. I'm very glad to hear that."

ΩΩΩΩΩΩΩ

"Well say something, Kimo Sabe."

"What should I say, Kimo?"

"Just say 'thank you' for the compliment! You deserve it. Don't let this be another missed opportunity."

"How am I doing?"

"Kimo Sabe, I'm going to nominate you for an Oscar and a Golden Globe award! See you in a bit. Gotta finish pinching some leaves off a bonsai tree I'm working on.

$$\Omega\Omega\Omega\Omega\Omega\Omega\Omega$$

"Papa, you have your outer space' look."
"Sorry, Kimo just appeared on my screen for a second."
"What did he want this time?"
"Nothing important. He was checking in is all. Hey, guys, thanks for the compliment. I really appreciate it. Don't get many kudos these days. So, I really appreciate it."

# 23

"My next question Papa is, what do you miss about the Waimea, the time you grew up in?"

"Wow that was seventy years ago. It's a long list so I'll just name fifty things. Does that work for you?"

"Yes, but at our next session you can name more."

"Works for me. So, help me keep count. Let' see, I miss................

............

-My mom and my dad. I could write volumes about them. They both were all about *ohana*. About family. I miss my dad's smile. I miss sitting at our kitchen table drinking tea with my mom. Come to think of it, the kitchen table was the center of life in our homes. Even when friends came by this is where we gathered."

"Why, do you think?"

"It was the warmest room in the house. So, everyone congregated in the kitchen. All the homes had a wood or kerosene stove. There was always a big bowl of poi in the center of the kitchen table and something to gnaw on. Dry fish, pipikaula (jerky) or a big pot of beef stew on the stove. I mean a big pot. There was always a coffee pot or a tea pot. The coffee was so black and strong. Cowboy coffee we called it. It was so strong I'm surprised the coffee didn't blow our eyes out of their sockets. We always had saloon pilot crackers."

"What else?"

-My uncles. Uncle Charlie, Joe, Bear, Keoni and David. Sadly, they've all passed on. They were fun to be around."

"Why?"

"They had a sense of humor. They liked to kid around."

-The cousins we were close to. Dennis, Norbert, Joey.

-Sitting on the steps of my Tutu-man's house listening to his tall tales.

"You never got tired of them?"

"No, I didn't. He was my grandpa. The stories grew, got better and more colorful every time he told them.

-Walter Okura. He was my best friend growing up. Walter lived across the highway from us. He's Japanese. We were best buddies, born two days apart. The Okuras treated Uncle Ben and me like family. They were Buddhists but lived the 'fruits of the Spirit.' The Okuras opened my eyes wide. Gave me a whole new perspective of the 'divine.' That's why I don't wear my religion on my sleeve. Made me realize, we all have our pathway to our 'divine.' We all have a 'belief system' to help us on our spiritual journey. Walters was Enlightenment. Mine was Eternal Life, John 3:16.

-The teachers who believed in me in Waimea School. Mrs. Brand. Miss Spencer. Mr. Morikawa. Mr. Tanaka. Mr. Nishimoto. Mrs. Baird. Miss Karimoto. When I got frustrated with a problem they said, 'Robert, you can do it. Yes, you can.' And, like my mom always told us. Never give up. 'Keep trying until you get it.' They made me believe in myself.

-Sunday church and after church we'd go on a kumukaukale.

"What's that?"

"'Kumukauhale? Home to home, house to house visits. We'd visit our Tutu-man for a couple hours first and if time allowed, with other family members. We always had time for others because we stayed close to home. Took the time to listen to the Earth, to nature, to others. We didn't have to call ahead to make an appointment. We'd just show up. That was our informal protocol. We always brought a makana (gift) of some kind. Always. Never went to anyone's *hale* (home) empty handed. We didn't just trade hellos and goodbyes. We had to stay and visit. The length of the visit. Well, it depended on what there was to talk, gossip, grouse about. Jippy got kicked in the head by his donkey. Hopefully he's smarter now as a result of that kick to the head. Matilda is fooling around with a soldier from PTA. If Pakana (her husband) ever gets wind of it, something bad is going to happen. He did. She hung herself. The

Ranch manager is planning to reduce the weekly meat allocation for employees. 'No good, SOB.' We used that acronym freely. On people, sometimes. On animals, always. A stay averaged an hour. Sometimes three. We never knew. Our mom made it clear. We had a job. Our job was to be quiet, to sit and listen and not look bored the entire time. We knew what we had to do. We did not want or need her to refresh our memory. With our dad, we knew we had 'wiggle room.' With the 'old lady.' Nope! We knew our place. We couldn't 'wiggle' her. Not even a millimeter. This was another of her teachable moments. She was teaching us patience, effective listening, mindfulness, how to sleep with our *makas* (eyes) open wide. If we needed help, the help was a pulled ear, a facial massage, verbal abuse, all three and all the embarrassment that came with it. We knew there would be a follow up session when we got home. Something, we did not look forward to. One stupid misstep. One mistake was enough to put us on the 'straight and narrow' for the rest of our lives. 'Tough Love.' She could have filled an entire shelf with books on the topic. Some would have been best sellers.

-Church outings. All the hikes and excursions, Rev. Thomen took us on. Pololu. Waipi'o Valley. Lapakahi. Cowboy Pond. Hoku'ula. Were it not for the good reverend, as teens, we would have never seen these beautiful slices of our special island. He was an avid photographer and documented those outings. His son, Willard, who now teaches voice in Chicago, sends us photos of those times. Some, we remember well, some are a blur, some lost to the past forever.

-Boy Scout meetings on Tuesdays after school at Kahilu Hall, and the hikes and camping trips we went on to Kaunaoa Bay (Mauna Kea Beach Hotel) and Spencer Park. The hikes and camp outs were so much fun. We hiked to Spencer Beach from Waimea on Friday afternoon after school. That was a ten-mile hike along Waiaka Stream. Me and some of my pals, instead of hiking all the way to Spencer, employed our cerebrum, critical thinking. We caught a ride with Mr. Masa Doi on the back of his delivery truck. We knew when he'd be coming through, so we made our way to Kawaihae Road to thumb a ride by the HELCO power plant. His family owned a store and several other businesses in Kawaihae. He'd pick us up and take us and our gear right to Spencer Beach Park. Hence, we got to Spencer well ahead of everyone else. We'd set up our tents, swim, make a fire and have smores. We'd catch o'ama (a type of fish) and grill it over an open fire. Although, we set up our tents, we didn't need them because the weather was always so nice and warm, the nights so calm and clear. Some of us would put a blanket down on the sand, talk late into the night and sleep right under the stars. I was one. If I knew Tutu way back then, I would have brought her along. She would have given me good reason to occupy the tent. In the mornings, when the tide was low, I'll will always remember the soft murmur of the waves washing over the shore when the tide was low. It was such a soothing, alluring, sensuous sound. The night sky was always raining stars. It was just covered with stars, comets and constellations. We'd look for the Big and Little Dippers, our birth constellations, Venus, asteroids and falling stars. Frequently, I tried to wish upon a falling star before it disappeared but was just too slow to complete my wish. I only had myself to blame. My mind was too scattered. Too cluttered. Instead of counting sheep, we'd count stars to fall asleep. And, we'd be up early, to do more fishing, go for a swim, cook breakfast. I don't know what it is, anything we ate at the beach tasted really, good. After breakfast, we'd clean up. The squad leaders would give us very short briefings. First aid, knot tying. I forget what else. It was more a time to let our breakfast settle. We weren't interested as we wanted to swim, climb trees, and sand board. A handful of us wanted to dive and spear fish. Then, as a troop we'd walk to Doi Store to slurp on shave ice and tease the monkeys. And, if we were up to it, which was most of the time, we'd stop by Chock Hoo Store, sit on the benches and harass Ahoon, the owner. She was ancient and nosey. She'd always ask me, the same old questions every single time we dropped in on her. 'Who you? You must be Lindsey boy, yeah.' 'You look like one, Lindsey. You guys, all get big kine heads.' 'You good boy? I hope you good boy.' 'Who your faddah?' 'He works ranch?' 'Where you go school? Waimea?' 'Study hard, so you get good job.' Most of us, if not all of us, would buy a soda and ice cream from her. She had one of those coolers with ice cold water in it. The soda was so cold, in a real Hamakua Soda glass bottle. My orange soda tasted so refreshing, particularly on a hot Saturday at high noon in Kawaihae. Then it was time to high tail it back to Spencer Park. Often, we'd take a side trip and watch the white tip sharks cruising around

Pelekane Bay below Pu'u Kohola Heiau where Kamehameha launched his successful effort to become the King of islands. There usually were about ten sharks in the pod. The older guys told us they were harmless, to jump in the murky bay and cruise with them. They really thought we were dumb enough to take their dare. They never swam with the sharks. We'd pick rocks off the ground instead and pitch them at the sharks. It really did not impact them at all. They had a course and stayed on it. Little did I know then, fifteen years hence, Pu'u Kohola would become a national historic site to preserve and honor Kamehameha's memory, under the jurisdiction of the US Department of the Interior. That I would be a Ranger wearing a Smokey Bear hat, telling folks about the place and working with a crew of ruffians to stabilize the temple's ancient walls. When I had night duty, in early evening I would stand along the edge of Pelekane Bay and watch the sharks as I did when I was a scout. Pitching rocks was not on the agenda, however. Spencer Park was never busy when we were scouts. Even on weekends. We had on many occasions, the entire park to ourselves. Joe Hui, Sr. was the live-in caretaker. He and his family were super nice. If we needed to call home for any reason, used their phone. If we needed any kind of help, which was rare, they were available. And we did, as scouts always do. We left the place spic and span. We could leave everything in place when we left camp and not worry about getting ripped off. Even our wallets. And the best part of it all. We had no adult supervision. We took care of ourselves. The older guys bossed us around. It was a continuum. We all had a turn. And we could not wait. Sunday afternoon, Sam Kimura, our Scoutmaster would show up with the Parker Ranch truck to pick us up and get us home to Waimea. The Ranch sponsored our troop. Boy Scout Troop 27. All that fun ended when I went to Kamehameha. I wanted to make Eagle but had to settle for Star and did not get to fill up my sash with merit badges. There was no troop I could transfer into near enough to Kamehameha with a convenient schedule. Scouting was good while it lasted. It really was. I still have dreams about those fun filled days and fun filled nights with our troop. As a side bar, we lived on the wet side of Waimea and Waimea was much rainier when we were kids. We didn't own a dryer and the roller on our washer did it's best to squeeze the moisture out of our clothes but it was never enough. So we'd go to Spencer, string rope between the kiawe (mesquite) tree limbs and help our mom hang mountains of laundry to air dry. It was so hot, in two hours our levis and all else were stiff as cardboard. I never dream about this female part of our time at Spencer Park. This sexist stuff is buried real deep in the galaxies of my memory.

-Playing baseball for Joe Cootey. Mr. Cootey was one of our hero's along with Mr. Hasegawa. Why? Playing baseball for him was fun. He didn't care if we won or lost a game. He was thrilled if we won but for him, we just had to focus on improving our skills. And he was fair. Everyone got to play. He was not a screamer. If we messed up, we messed up. He'd tell us what we needed to do the next time. Teamwork was something he emphasized. Unfortunately, I was a 'late bloomer.' I got his memo far later in life, when I had to manage people. 'Better late, than never.' Mr. Cootey's core 'servant leadership' principles came back quickly. Mr. Hasegawa was our Assistant Scoutmaster. He was the one who really was on scene for us. He should have been the one to get the Silver Beaver award. He took us on hikes and showed us what we needed to know to survive in the wild. He worked for Parker, was an avid outdoors man, hunter and taxidermist. On the battlefield, I would have felt safe with him, as my lieutenant. He was tough but kind. A good and decent model of a man. I would have followed him through a barrage of bullets because I know I'd make it out alive. Thank God for Mr. Cootey and Mr. Hasegawa. In my mind and heart, they will always be Community Treasures. They provided us boys, two outlets to be boys. Kept us, some of us, from the jailhouse. We had very few extracurricular options back then.

-Moving, chasing cattle on foot, from our Puukapu homestead to grandpa's house, on the main highway (the cattle had the right of way over cars). Four miles. Our job, keep the herd on the highway and out of people's yards or farms. A job, we never looked forward to as the animals never fully cooperated. I don't ever remember a time when the move, the chase went smoothly, without incident. Never! There were always the few renegades who chose to break loose and cause havoc. They did it on purpose. Waimea has grown. Too many people. Too many cars. Chasing cattle up and down the highway is a thing of the past. You can't ride a horse on the main highway nowadays. Thank God Almighty!

Where were you, God, when we needed you? We really needed you then. Well, at least you're finally here. 'Better late than never.'

-Visiting Mr. Chock every Friday night at his store. While he and our dad chatted, gossiped, and grumbled about local events and politics, Uncle Ben and I watched TV, drank our sodas, munched on chocolate bars.

-Watching the Parker Ranch cowboys hitching up their horses in front of the ranch office. As boys we idolized the Parker Ranch cowboy with the handlebar mustache, stetson crowning his head and casting a shadow over his weather-beaten face, riding high in the saddle, chewing 'tabakee' like it was gum and spitting the entrails on the ground, spurs jingling, cracking his bull whip to give us a thrill. The cracks rippled and resonated through the quiet afternoon air. A sound, I have not heard in sixty years. Mr. Vierra knew by cracking his whip in the air at full gallop on his *ho'o lilio* (horse) That single 'act of kindness' on his part gave us kids a big thrill. He polished off our day. We knew he was sipping whiskey on the job from a gray canister tucked away in his jacket pocket. He'd stop and chat with us from behind a pair of radioactive red eyes and sip from it. He told us it was cough medicine. Medicine to help him get rid of a cold. A cold he never was able to get rid of in all the time we knew him. Which was about twelve years. He'd look at us from under the brim of his floppy hat. Through slurred words, he'd ask us our names and what in 'god damn' hell were we up to. 'Going to a scout meeting at Barbara Hall.' He'd secure his whip to his saddle with a leather strap and wipe the drips off his chin with the red bandanna loosely tied around his wrinkled neck. He must have washed it once a month. We'd admire his rifle and his big jungle knife we called a 'bolo' knife because it was wide and long. We asked him what he used his rifle and knife for. To ward off bears and lions while working in the hills behind us. And, when he was not doing that, *ahiu wahines* (wild ladies). He liked wild ladies. 'The wilder the better.' We knew he was playing with us but nonetheless we enjoyed every darn minute and played right along with him. We knew he was married. Even when he was serious, he was funny. It's not only what he said, it was how he said what he said that was funny. He was a character of characters. We wanted to be like the Parker cowboy. They were for us legends not only in the mind. They were up 'close and personal.' We saw them every day. They were all around us. Ikua Purdy, was on top of the heap with Archie Kaaua and Eben Low. They went to compete in the 1908 world roping championship in Jasper, Wyoming. The Olympics of Roping. Ikua won. He beat America's best. Brought the trophy home to Waimea. Today, Ikua's legacy is properly memorialized, in a bronze statute at Parker Center. His weathered effigy stands proudly for all who pass through our town to see. Ikua, at full gallop on borrowed horse, *kau la ili* (lariat) in hand, chasing down a steer with determined look, doing its best to avoid capture. We know how the story ended. The Purdy DNA lives on in several our town's folk. And, from long distance, we had our Hollywood rhinestone cowboy idols; Paladin, Johnny Wayne, Clint Eastwood-you know, the jackass with the missing chair, Marshall Dillon, Miss Kitty and good ole Festus, Johnny Ringo and Wyatt Earp, Tombstone, Arizona.

-Going to Honolulu every summer for two weeks to visit our grandma, Nancy and step grandpa, Lorito Itejorde in Kalihi Valley. We spent a week with them. Our grandma was always sucking on Vicks cough drops. Lorito was Filipino, head gardener at the Philippine consulate in Nu'uanu, who never missed a day of work. He was a very jovial and sweet man, who gave me my first taste of global politics. I was eight. The occasion. To greet President Ramon Magasaysay of the Philippines. When Magasaysay's plane, en-route to Washington DC, landed at Hickam AFB for refueling. With tiny Philippine flags in hand, we were part of a cheering crowd, chanting 'mabuhay' to welcome the flamboyant President and his entourage to Honolulu. Lorito also introduced us to watermelon, cantaloupes and ice cream sandwiches. When he transitioned, Lorito, I'm sure was picked up by a throng of angels and soared with them to heaven. They were part of a cult. The Hilario Moncado Foundation. We'd spend the second week with Uncle John and Aunt Helen in Waikiki. That was before the place was covered over with concrete and the coconut groves were destroyed. Their home was on the corner of Lemon Street and Paokalani Avenue. His simple one-story wooden house along with its ancient plumeria tree was torn down to make way for a twenty-story concrete monstrosity.

-Bird season, hunting at the Pohaukuloa Training Area. Ben and I could not wait for lunch. Our mom made these indescribably delicious sardine omelets that went well with rice balls. We'd sprinkle shoyu over the omelets, chomp on them and wash the fish and egg combination down with hot tea from our thermoses. It was a lunch made for kings and gladiators. Sadly, the recipe rests with her in our church cemetery. When I reflect on that 'wrinkle in time,' the ancient memory though sad, makes me salivate.

-Watching western matinees at Palace Theater in Hilo with our cousin, Norbert. During our kid days, Ben and I, were close to Norbert. He was a year older than me. We clung to him like clams to a rock. Norbert was a surf bum and Honoli'i Bay was his second home. He had a long board and used his dad's open air, Model A, to strut around town in. It was at the Palace that we had buttered popcorn for the first time. He bought a bucket, drowning in butter, that we shared three ways. We were addicted immediately. That bucket was empty before the main show was half over. I have fond memories of the theater. The organ music. The thick, heavy drapes. The manager welcomed everyone to the matinee and there were chaperones with flashlights to help you to your seat. After the show, we'd jay walk across Haili Street, to Kuhio Grill for a root beer float, banana split or a bulky, juicy hamburger. That was a time when 'shoot um' up cinemas with cavalry were the only movies we wanted to watch. Before cultural, ethnic, political and gender 'appropriateness' invaded our national ethos, conscience and discourse.

-Eating family Chinese dinner at Sun Sun Lau restaurant. Sun Sun Lau, was a Hilo Landmark on Kamehameha Avenue, on front street. Our Uncle Joe would join us and Aunty Julia, if she was not working. She was a telephone operator, so her work schedule interfered many a time with our lunch or dinner plans. But good ole Uncle Joe was always available. He was best friends with our dad and a total ham. A total 'kick in the pants.' He was entertaining and livened up the table. Egg foo yong, sweet sour spare ribs and char siu, were my favorite dishes. Our dad had to have pork hash water cress which took a while to prepare. It was well worth the wait. The place was always busy. The food and service were 'par excellence.' We didn't have to wait long for a table even during busy times. Uncle Joe was a regular, a generous 'tipper' and charming. I swear, he could burgle a snake out of its venom and the poor reptile wouldn't have known it. The owner would see Uncle Joe and call out. 'Come. Come Lindsee. How you? How many? Go sit ovah deah. Pork manapua, yeh. How many, Lindsee? I see six. Wife no come.' 'Sit ovah deah." Then he'd direct the waitress to serve us. 'Take care dem.' Poor lady was already flustered to the max. The only one waiting tables with more people patiently waiting. She kept on smiling which was the only thing she could do. Uncle Joe was a picky eater. Our mom was not picky about food. She just ate whatever was in front of her and imposed that philosophy on us at home. Reminded us constantly about the starving kids in China and how lucky we were. She was not the best cook. There was one meal she made for supper which I could not stomach but was compelled to. Canned salmon and head cabbage with rice. The rice was consumed readily but the salmon and cabbage combination. Eeww! It took me two hours to clean my plate. Why? It was the yuckiest meal in the world. I must have drunk two gallons of water to expedite the process. To wash the nightmare in front of me in small gulps down to my nauseous stomach. There was no cheating because Hannah K. sat right there at the dinner table watching me like a hawk. I know she was having a sadistic moment and enjoying every single minute. She was. You see, her face was an open book. As open as the book she was reading while lording over me to make sure I ate every bit of my dinner. Yes, Sun Sun Lau was a landmark and a favorite stop. And right next door was an okazuya shop, a little Japanese diner. The shop put out the best cone sushi, maki sushi and pickled dishes. Sadly, the 1960 tsunami, decimated, washed away both places. But it hasn't decimated nor washed away my memories of egg foo yong, sweet sour spareribs, char siu, cone sushi and takuan.

-Laying on the grass on our front lawn on a cloudy day, gazing up at the sky, searching for 'castles in the sky' as the clouds rolled by, thinking and dreaming about the future. Pondering seriously about morphing into a Parker Ranch cowboy when I reached majority age. Never did I imagine, I would work instead for one of Waimea's biggest truck farmers as a <u>farm hand</u>. A job I loved. A tree <u>nursery laborer</u> doing handy work. Trimming hedges, pulling weeds, bundling hundreds of trees for ambitious landowners installing shelter belts along the perimeters of their ranches or farms. Another job, I enjoyed. I loved both jobs because at day's end, I didn't have to take any work home with me. Both jobs were totally stress free. UH-Manoa as a <u>senior tutor</u> for Dean Hormann- Sociology Department. He was prepping me, getting me ready to pursue a PhD. He was bummed when I told him I had a change of heart. He said he was okay with my decision but the look on his face gave him away. I loved the work because I loved working for Hormann, He gave me my assignments and left me alone. I was sorry to disappoint him. A probation officer with Family Court, dealing with guys who needed help finding the 'best' within themselves. I think I learned more from them than they did from me. Did this for seven years then applied for a one year sabbatical to the Chief Justice (CJ). Our Administrative Judge, Judge Kimura, who was a super nice man, called me in, told me straight out. I had to come up with a better reason. That a year's break to just 'goof off' was not going to cut it with the CJ. My reason had to be 'educational.' But I suffered from 'stuck brain' disease, was young (29) and reckless. My lymbic brain was not fully mature. I asked him to send my request 'up the flagpole' anyway. I would instead take a year off without pay as I was 'burning out.' He sighed and reluctantly signed off on my request. That was at 8:15 am. About an hour later, around 9, his secretary calls, 'Judge wants to see you in his chambers, now.' I knew the news was not going to be good. The CJ denied my request. He didn't want to set a precedent. Judge Kimura was sorry. The only thing I could do, if I still wanted a year's break was resign. He said he would work it out so I could return at year's end. He would hold my position. Which he did. I learned a lot as a PO about the rough side of life from rough guys. I learned a few enduring lessons. They too possessed 'the fruits of the Spirit.' The fruits just needed to be nudged, at times dragged out of them. They often needed second, even third chances. They sure didn't need homilies because they knew they'd… up. They needed kindness, compassion, aloha, patience. I got to know their habits and their families. I got to know them well. I had a great area to work. The police commanders and officers, prosecutors, public defenders were all very helpful. I was surprised how compassionate and thoughtful they were. They truly wanted the guys I worked with to get their 'act' together. Redeem themselves, pay off their debt to those they hurt and society. And ultimately find their way home. There were those rare times when I had to recommend sending someone to jail or to prison for 'shock' treatment. On two occasions, the defendants asked the presiding judges if I could drive them to jail. On one occasion, a dad was so embarrassed he had to come to court with his son,' he beat up the 'poor' boy right there in court. The bailiff and I had to pull dad off his son. There was another incident, again in juvenile court. The judge was giving a young man, his usual 'crime doesn't pay' sermon. The judge then asked, the teen if he had anything to say. He did. 'Judge, what you mean? Crime no pay. My faddah (father), one *pakalolo* (marijuana) dealer. He make plenny (plenty) money. He make big money. He drive one nice truck. We get one nice house. Crime pays.' All of us, minus the Judge, in court that day, had a difficult time holding our composure. The judge then gave the 'faddah' a sermon. I don't think it helped. At the end of it all the world kept turning. We went on to the next case. I still see a few folks around town. We'll talk and laugh about old times at the courthouse. What once was not funny, we can laugh about now. A precious piece that consumed seven years of my life. I resigned my position with the court but chose not to return. As for the CJ, fourteen years later, we both worked for another institution. He was my boss again (one of six). There was a welcome dinner for him which some of us staffers were required to attend. The hostess was introducing him to folks. I was hoping he would not remember me. When he saw me, he said to the hostess. 'I know this guy. He worked for me once. And, quit on me.' Thankfully he stopped there, shook my hand, gave me a hug, said he was happy to see me. And he meant it. He called me to his office from time to time, when he was wrestling with an issue, often simply to chat and ask for my thoughts on business we were dealing with, which I was more than happy to share with him. Once, after a board meeting, he signaled me to follow him to his office. He closed the door and gave me a 'dressing down.' It was more of a 'heart to heart,' father-son chat. CJ was a perceptive man. I was toying with the Chairman of the Board on a critical matter that was assigned to me. I needed the admonishment as I knew I was being disrespectful towards an elder. And the CJ didn't like it. A construction worker driving a dynapac shaping a golf course for Transcontinental

Development on the Kohala coast. Pounding crushed rock and gravel chips on 120 acres; bunkers, sand traps, water features and fairways with an 80,000-pound machine made of heavy solid iron. Did with the iron monster what ordinarily was supposed to be the work of three machines. I was the big dog, the pitt bull, doing the grunt work. I was to be followed by a German shepherd than a chihuahua. At the end of the day, my body shook and itched for an hour, sometimes two. Claude, my supervisor was a great guy. He would tell me to slow down but the dynapac had a mind all its own. Full throttle which was fine with me. A Japanese developer saw my work and wanted me to work for him. I was not interested though supposedly he paid well. Claude thought I was foolish to turn away an opportunity to earn triple pay and travel. Mission and enjoying work, not compensation is what have always mattered to, driven me. A National Park Ranger. I really enjoyed the work and was planning to stay at Puu Kohola NHS but there were just too many rules and at the onset I upset the boss, our Head Ranger & District Manager. I wrote something in one of my night logs about longstanding concerns needing attention that caught the 'eye' of one of our congressmen which resulted in his intervention. I was hoping someone in Honolulu or the regional office in San Francisco would respond. But DC. We got the outcome we needed. Resulted in a change she did not support which my colleagues had been asking for, for a long time. Air conditioning for our work spaces and shutters for the windows. We worked in a hot, arid area. Day temperatures could reach a hundred ten degrees plus. And the nights were warm. Wind and dust were also issues. I don't know how my log entry made it to Washington DC, but it did. She should have been happy, but she wasn't. I realized the *mana* (power) of the pen. There were so many neat projects I had the opportunity to work on. One was with our Pacific Archaeologist Ed Ladd, getting a work crew prepped to help Ed stabilize the rock walls of Pu'u Kohola, the main heiau (temple). The first protocol of the day was to gather the crew in a prayer circle before entering the heiau to start work. On days when I had the day shift, it was my task to bless the crew. This one morning, one of the crew did what he was not supposed to do. Entered the heiau before going through our protocol. I looked up at him and asked him to come down off the high wall and join the circle. He started to laugh and said, saying a prayer was a waste of time and 'total b.....t.' That he was not joining us. In seconds, some force grabbed him by his ankles and threw him up in the air. Eddie landed on his head in the middle of our circle. A fall of about twenty feet. We were all stunned. He was unconscious for about five minutes. I radioed the office to call the firehouse as we needed the EMS unit. He had to take the rest of the day off. Fortunately, he was okay, and his defiance did not infect anyone. Fifteen of us saw what we saw. 'Seeing is believing.' We believed. When the EMT's arrived, one of them said if they knew it was, they would have taken their time. A <u>truck farmer</u>, which was a bad, horrible, horrific mistake. My timing and judgment were bad. Fighting weather. Storm after storm after storm. Fighting bugs and fungus. Fighting the marketplace. Being undercapitalized. A <u>representative</u> in the State House. I had difficulty being in a vicious play pen and 'tapped out' after one term. But in one term, I made a lot of friends on both sides of the aisle, got a bill passed and several projects funded and completed for my district. As a freshman member, chaired a major committee, House Education. And, got through doors, were it not for my position, the butlers and gatekeepers would have slammed in my face. A Land Assets Director for Hawai'i's largest private landowner. Started as a clerk typist and climbed the ladder, bottom to near top rung. With the help of eleven folks, together we managed 265,000 acres encumbering resort, industrial, ag, conservation and residential leaseholds (1800 leases). I also was Operations VP for a large coffee farm. Learned how to 'dodge' bullets and arrows from long distance, to deal with an owner who loved to stretch the truth and a Latino crew who never ceased to amaze me because their work ethic was 'beyond' the call. And now, a <u>Trustee</u> with the Office of Hawaiian Affairs. I've served thirteen years and have done my very best to 'better conditions' for our people as a 'servant leader' with the help of two loyal and dedicated Aides. I have had the honor to be a sitting member of the Hawai'i Island Legislative caucus, a collective of all our island senators and house members. The only OHA Trustee who can say that. I think that's something to brag about. One of the big lessons I've learned since I was KID about life is. You need friends. You need to build relationships. You must work as a team. It's okay to be disagreeable and straight up with folks. BUT you need to do it honestly, kindly, thoughtfully. It's better to build bridges. Not walls. At midnight, November 3, 2021, I will turn into a pumpkin and just fade away into the night.

"One more Papa. One more memory.

-The annual Parker Ranch Christmas celebration at Barbara Hall. Singing Christmas carols around this humongous pine tree, hearing the minister's homily, receiving our goodie bag filled to the brim with hard candy, nuts, raisins, an apple and an orange. The culmination was Mr. Pacheco, who played Santa charging into the hall as the night was ending."

"Who was Mr. Pacheco?"

"He was a big, burly, jolly, friendly man. We knew him as Uncle Joe. By day, Uncle Joe was a Parker Ranch cowboy. At Christmas, he was Santa. Our Santa. When he charged into Barbara Hall with his bosonic voice booming 'ho, ho, ho.' His opu (belly) rolling in concentric circles. A huge eke (bag) draped over his right shoulder. The hall erupted, just went berserk. We'd sing 'Jingle Bells' repeatedly. The place for five minutes was psychotic. We filled the great hall with song. But all too soon, good things must end. The jolly time we patiently waited for, for an entire year was over. The minister from one of our churches closed the night with a pule (prayer). We said our good wishes and goodbyes. And, slowly walked into the cold night to our cars. It was time to go home for a hot cup of chocolate into which we shattered a cracker and chunks of butter. Then it was bedtime. At some point that night as us kids slept under a pile of blankets, 'sugar plums' rocked around in all our heads as we shifted from one dream to the next. And the wait for next Christmas started all over again. May I add one more?"

"Of course!"

"Our mom. I miss our chats over tea. While she was dealing with her cancer. I would look in on her every single day at home. Then the pain from her cancer, got so great, she finally had to be hospitalized. That is when she was placed on morphine. Two weeks later she died. Our mama never ever complained about the pain she was in. Her doctor, whom Tutu and I played tennis doubles with, on Sunday mornings. Dr. Nesting could not believe how she was able to manage the pain. Our mom was a strong woman. A strong Christian woman. A hardheaded woman. I'll never forget her sermons. Come to think of it, I'm like her. There would be times, she forewarned me, when I was in intermediate school. I would stumble and fall. 'Robert, get up! Keep going! Never give up!' I promised her I would. It's a promise I kept. When I see kids being brats. Screaming about not getting their way. Kids who have weak parents. Who just can't say 'no.' I laugh to myself. Our mom would take care of matters quickly."

"How?"

"Remember, she was a tai chi practitioner. She also had 'magic hands.' One of her back hand slaps was worth 'a thousand words.' May, I add another quick one. Last one. I promise."

"Go ahead, Papa."

"Our dad. Waiting for him to drive up in his Model A. Up our long driveway after working all day crushing rock at the quarry. Hearing Monty's bark. Watching this dog just go nuts over his best friend. I can still see those moments so clearly. So vividly, in my mind. Our dad's smile. Monty's bark. The banging and sputtering of our dad's simple jalopy engine. If he honked his horn, Monty would go even more 'nuts.'"

"Did you ever make it to the Parker Ranch Office?"

"No, I never made it to the Parker Ranch office to fill out a job application. I will say this. For every boss and organization I worked for. I gave them my best. My all. Put in a full, honest day's work. When I walked out the door. All but one, was glad to see me go. A few tried to convince me to stay, But I knew it was time to go. Best for them and best for me. I had reached my level of incompetence. The challenge and the passion were gone. The 'fire' was not there anymore. It was time. Time to chase another opportunity. Another rainbow. Another rabbit.

# 24

"How has Waimea changed?"
"Since I was kid?"
"Yes!"

"More people. More homes. More cars. The good news is, it's still a beautiful place. Some of our prime ag lands that used to grow cattle and vegetables are growing homes now. The trip to Hilo used to take three, almost four hours. Now, it's an hour fifteen minutes. The road was more of a one land road, sixty years ago. When you came to a bend in the road, you had to blast your horn to let an oncoming car know you were approaching. Car sickness was a real issue. Today's cars are comfortable. The drive to Kona on the upper road used to take about two hours. Today, forty minutes. People were friendlier back then I think because everyone knew everyone. We were more patriotic. Values, ethics, morals, decent behavior, respect for others and oneself were heavily emphasized. Most everyone went to church on Sundays. Even the weather has changed. Waimea used to be much wetter and much colder. People could tell right off, in Hilo or Kona, we were from Waimea because our cheeks were rosy red. Global warming has reached us. Traffic in the morning and in the afternoon is outrageous. I don't see rusty, beat-up jalopies around town these days. Most folks have a nice car. There are more motorcycles on the highway today. When we were kids, only John Bull had a motorcycle. A Harley. The beaches are crowded. Wall to wall people. Most of us had brown skin seventy years ago. If you had pale skin, you stuck out. Like a 'sore thumb.' We were from Waimea. Not Kamuela. Everyone had a nice yard filled with flowers. We never had big box stores back then. No Walmart, Costco, Target. Only four 'mom and pops.' Fukushima. I Oda. Hayashi. Chock In. The school had one hundred ninety kids. Only one old school bus. A WWII army bus. Today, eleven hundred kids, attend our beloved alma mater. And the school has a fleet of buses to move students around. Eighty years ago, kids walked five miles to school even on cold rainy mornings. Waimea didn't have a dentist. In our kid days, we went to Dr. Nakamaru in Kona. Other kids went to Dr. Sugiyama in Kona or Dr. Akioka in Honoka'a. There was only one doctor. The Parker Ranch doctor. Dr. Black, who took care of everyone. There was only one restaurant. The Parker Ranch Restaurant. Mrs. Makino was the cook. She made the best beef stew. There was only one hotel. Waimea Hotel right across from Waimea School. It burned to the ground in 1962. Cause unknown. There's more but I'll stop there."

"Do you like the changes?"

"Some I like. Some I don't. But as I've already said several times. Waimea I Ka La'i is still a beautiful, special place. Lucky, we live Waimea. Lucky, we live Hawai'i. Lucky, we live in America. I want to tackle this Hawaiian sovereignty question before Samuel and Lala get here. I can see they are minutes away. Will we achieve it? As a collective, I don't think we will!"

"Why, do you think that? That's so pessimistic."

"There's too much disunity, too much disagreement as with a lot of other topics and issues dividing us as a people. It's always difficult to find a common point to start the conversation. A common point to start, to work from. And, when and if we do get started, something will happen at some point, to blow things apart. Egos will surface, conflicts will flare. Then we're back to square one. We end up smearing, screaming, disagreeing, yelling at each other. We must learn how to disagree without being disagreeable. My mom had 'sovereignty' figured out."

"How so?"

"When I got involved with the Hawaiian movement in 1974 with Sonny Kaniho. In one of our 'heart to heart' conversations. This is what she told me, over tea of course at her kitchen table. 'Sovereignty' starts right here. She pointed at her heart. It starts right here. Inside you. In our family. At the time, I thought she was being selfish and shallow.

Now, I've come to realize. Fifty years later, that she was right. That's what she was teaching Uncle Ben and me, when we were growing up. When she told us to ignore Mrs. Baybrook and Mrs. Ujiki, all the folks, who thought we were just dumbos. She told us to turn 'adversity' on its head. To not feel sorry for ourselves. To not come home and complain to her. We needed to pull ourselves up by our 'bootstraps,' and find our way out of the quicksand we were mired in. If we wanted something, we needed to work for it. Like our neighbors. Who came here with nothing. Just hope. Came here on a 'wing and a prayer' to a strange place with nothing. Not knowing what they were walking into. And, lifted themselves up."

"Who was Mrs. Ujiki?"

"A high school counselor. Near the end of $9^{th}$ Grade, most of us it was assumed were going to Honoka'a School. She was the Honoka'a High counselor and spent a day with us in Waimea. She told us to lay out our course choices for $10^{th}$ Grade. When I completed my choices, I gave her my worksheet. Most of my choices were core courses. She gave it a quick look over and gave it back to me. Told me to change it because I would not be able to handle all the subjects I had chosen. It was too much of a load to carry. I looked at her and told her I was not changing anything. Thank God, I ended up at Kamehameha. Anyways, our mama told us. Crying and complaining, yelling and screaming, cussing and cursing, were not 'on ramps' to 'sovereignty.' A strong, resilient, grateful, compassionate, peaceful, mindful inner spirit was the only and best way to self-determination. If anyone had something to complain about. She sure did. Her family lost much after the 1893 Overthrow. The entire ahupua'a of Onomea, in North Hilo. Her ohana stewarded all that North Hilo 'aina for centuries. They had much to curse and complain about. To be bitter about. But like our Queen. They believed Akua would intervene but as we well know, it was not in the cards. Did she 'curse the dark?' No, she moved on."

"She was a strong, tough lady."

"Yep, she sure was. She absolutely was."

"This is a question I was going to ask earlier. In fact, Papa, it's the main question on my list. In eight words, describe Tutu?"

"Wow. You're sure putting the squeeze on me. Only eight words?"

"How about twenty words?"

"Alright, twenty, words!"

"My first and only, caring, kind, understanding, faithful, loyal, true, forever love. Super Mom. Super Tutu. Master teacher. Loves kids. She was born to be a mom. A Tutu. A teacher. That's more than thirty I think."

"It's okay. The next time we chat. We'll let you add an entire chapter."

"I'll hold you both to that commitment. I will."

"Last question. Describe you in ten words?"

I think for a minute. "A practical, clear-thinking liberal. A high risk, high achieving introvert."

# 25

Samuel and Lala showed up and played a video of the waves at Paniau. The call of the sea and surf was too much for Elliot and Kui. For all of them. I was amazed at how quickly they were able to race in their minds from Hoku'ula's summit to the shores of Puako. From sleds to surfboards. They all give me a bear hug and saunter off. Elliot and Kui had forgotten all about Kimo.

Poor Kimo came out of solitary. He wore his disappointment on his sleeve. Took a brief break from his zen garden. He didn't say anything, but I could sense he wanted to have face time with the boys. Together, we watch the four boys race their sleds down Hoku'ula's slope. Like I had done when I was their age. Left me, with Kimo and headed off to surf a northwest swell. To have some fun in the sun.

It was clear to me! Today's session was just the opener, a teaser to three or four more 'heart to heart,' open-air chats. I'm thinking, Po'o Kanaka, the next time. A hill five miles away, in a south easterly direction. It will give us another perspective of the place we live in. I look at the list of questions. I had answered only six on the list, but I know I answered them with substance and depth. It was well worth every minute of the time we spent together.

They did not get to meet, Kimo. I assure him, at a time appropriate, he will have all the time he needs to tell his story to them, unfiltered. They did ask about my favorite poems. To name two. There's many more. "Trees" by Joyce Kilmer. Why? First poem I learned and committed to memory in third grade. Just to show off. I recite the poem without missing a word. And Max Ehrman's, "Desiderata." Why? It's a poem fraught with wisdom, life lessons, moral principles. I share the first few stanzas with them. "Go placidly amid the noise and the haste and remember what peace there may be in silence...listen to others, even the dull and the ignorant...and take kindly the counsel of the years." I ask them to study it before we meet again. Whenever that is. They assure me, that they will. They ask me to name three of my favorite songs and artists. I quickly rattle off, Bruce Springsteen's "Wonderful Tonight" and Elvis' "Blue Christmas" and "The Wonder of You." He's the 'King' in my book. There are tons of songs I like, hundreds. Two books? Viktor Frankl's, Man's Search for Meaning, Walden by Henry Thoreau. Only two? I ask. Only two.

Samuel explains to me through his big, beautiful beaming smile that Chief Brave Eagle was here with his entire *ohana* from the Menominee Nation to scatter the ashes of a soldier on Hoku'ula. How about that! This old man can see things from a distance still. I assumed correctly. Generally, that is. Samuel put 'meat on the bones.' The soldier trained on Hoku'ula in late 1944 with the 5th Marine Division, in preparation for the assault on Iwo Jima Island. His last wish was to have his remains scattered in three places. His family's Wisconsin homestead. Hoku'ula. And Mt. Suribachi. Hoku'ula, because he was convinced Hoku'ula's spirit kept him safe in the bloody battle. After the war, he wanted to return to Waimea for a visit. In the short time that he trained here, in the fall and winter of '44, he felt so at home. Hoku'ula, was the hill his platoon rehearsed on for the assault on Mt. Surabachi. For reasons beyond his control, he was never able to make it back to Waimea. He came out of the bloody battle unscathed physically. His head, however, was messed up. Messed up for a time. PTSD. Nightmares. Panic attacks. The smell and stench of death stayed with him for a long time. The painful cries and screams of the wounded from both sides of the line as well. Residuals that followed him home in his cerebrum from a tiny island 6,000 miles away. He thought he was mentally ready for the impending, but he wasn't. When he left Waimea I Ka La'i with his regiment for a clandestine and secret battle station, he felt this protective shield wound tightly around him. When he got home from the war, the tribal medicine man was able to help him in time, dislodge the trauma mired in his cerebrum.

Upon hearing this, I felt badly. Badly, about the stupidity, insensitivity and childishness of my behavior. About making light of and poking fun at the pow wow. The Chief, Samuel said, wanted me. Wanted all of us to be part of the soldier's ceremony. I agreed. When it happened two days later, I was impressed, moved to tears, a few tears anyway. I was touched. It was well somewhat life changing. That someone who was here on Hoku'ula before I was born was so touched by our homeland and wanted when he came to die, a portion of his dust and ashes scattered here, embedded on Hoku'ula. Now who said, 'you can't teach an old doggie a new trick?'

ΩΩΩΩΩΩΩ

"Kimo Sabe, you did good."
"You think so, Kimo."
"I know so. You're one lucky, Papa."
"Yes, I am. Got a great wife. Two great sons. Two great daughters-in-law, And four great grandsons. I great couldn't ask for more. And Kimo, you're a great friend."
"I try my best, Kimo Sabe. To guide and give you helpful advice."
"I know you do. I know you do, Kimo. And I *mahalo* you. I know I can be hard on you at times." He laughs.

We watch the boys secure their sleds to the racks on their trucks with their surfboards and drive off. Off to catch waves in our warm, cobalt blue Pacific Pond. My mind goes into twilight mode. "Kimo, I'm sorry. My mind is going to be in the 'wild blue yonder' for about an hour. I'm pausing. Muting. Stay as long as you want."

"Boss, I need to get back to my plants, my trees. I'll catch you later. Let's watch the sunset together. With all this vog around us now, it will be a brilliant sunset."

"Now that's a brilliant idea. See you in an hour."

I start to pull stuff out of my memory box to update my memory. Something I've ignored for too long. I know my planet is Honua. My archipelago, Papahanaumokuakea. My moku, Keawe. My ahupua'a, Kohala. My ili 'aina, Pu'ukapu. My stream, Lanikepu. My mountain to the north, Kohala. My mountains to the south, Mauna Kea and

Mauna Loa. My mountain to the southeast, Kilauea. To the southwest, Hualalai. My harbor, the 'barking waters' of Kawaihae. My 'aina aumakua, the owl. My ocean guardian, the honu (turtle). My rain, kipu'upu'u. My wind, Kamakani o Kohala. My song, Hole Waimea. I drift off to sleep. Three hours later, Kimo is 'rattling my cage.'

"Wake up, boss. Five minutes to sunset. What's the password?"

"Aloha-ke-Akua."

"What's your user word?"

"Don't you have things reversed?"

"Yes. It's intentional."

"'waimeaikala'i.' All small letters."

It's 2200 hours. I flick off my bed stand lamp, lay my head on my pillow and reflect on my day with Elliot Lonokahikinaokala and Kui Ka Maoli, Grandsons 3 & 4. It was truly wonderful, spending a few hours with the duo on Hoku'ula Hill. Something I've never done with both. Just the three of us, heart to heart, eyeball to eyeball, cheek to cheek. Sitting in the sunshine. Feeling Mother Earth pulsating beneath our feet then zipping, rippling through our bodies. Feeling a light Kohala breeze sweeping down Waiaui'a's slope then ricocheting off our backs, rustling our hair and whistling through the loblolly trees. The same breeze provides a light thermal for our *aumakua*, the *pueo*, to soar, glide, dance on. Feeling the sun's rays taking the edge off the morning chill. Rays that have traveled a long way, 93 million miles at 186 thousand miles a second, to illuminate our world and warm our faces. We sit there in solemn silence, sopping in the beauty of Waimea I Ka La'i. The majesty of the snow draped mountains in the distance, the Waimea Plains below us, the big blue sky above, the Pacific Ocean to westward. We agree, all that is 'privileged and confidential' to us, will from this day forward not be shared 'until and unless' declassified by a plurality of us. 'Mum' is our operative word. Only name, rank, serial number. We understand. Our word is gold, enough, good enough. No need to put pen to paper.

I turn the lamp back on. I reach for the clock. I forgot to set my alarm for 0430. We need to meet at the bottom of Hoku'ula at 0515 hours with Chief Brave Eagle and company to scatter ashes on Hoku'ula's summit in early morn. And, I'm a freak about being on time.

For back up, I call SIRI to enlist her help. She's not very friendly at this time of night. She's snarly. I do my utmost to cheer her up but my good cheer only brings out the worst in her. I can't blame her. I don't think I'd like working the night shift either. I jump back in bed and pull the covers up over me. Kathy is a night owl. I can hear the TV blaring. In minutes my nostrils begin to sound like a chain saw without mufflers in the hands of a logger gone crazy, tearing through the forest. My nose is fully amp-ed. And my mind is racing. It starts to rove, meander uphill and downhill. I'm a jet plane cleared for take-off by the tower. I'm the captain pushing the throttle forward. I'm speeding off into the wild blue yonder. I start to dream. Small ones and big ones. A multitude of dreams. These are the ones I remember best.

I see Buddha under the Bodhi tree in Bodh Gaya in Bihar, India. I see my best friends, Walter Okura and Alvin Wakayama, with their obasans and moms visiting the very spot where Buddha attained Enlightenment. The divine in whom they believe and celebrated at the Hongwanji at the west edge of Church Row, two churches down from ours. I grew up brainwashed with the notion, because we were Christian we were going to heaven and because they were Buddhists, they were going to hell. I challenged the notion, got flogged for it and as a result began to 'monkey' around with my Faith for a long time.

I see <u>Jesus</u> and two of his disciples (John and Peter) before he died on the Cross, hands folded, at prayer in Gethsemane. Judas Iscariot enters the garden uninvited and wants to pray with them.

Jesus shoos the traitor away. I see a cadre of heavily armed Roman soldiers hiding behind a hedge row, ready to pounce on Jesus, a man, despised, hated and falsely accused by the Sanhedrin. I see Jesus standing outside the rock cavern in which he was entombed. He's supposed to be dead, but he is smiling and holding hands with Mary Magdalene. The massive rock slab used as a door to close the tomb, pushed to the side. Word spreads like fire across the region, that 'He is Risen.'

I see the <u>Psalmist</u> walking along the gurgling waters of Waiaka stream. He's an outlier, outside, far outside his *ahupua'a* (territory). He has no *kuleana* (business) here. Why is he here? He just landed at Kona International this afternoon. I yell at him to go back to his valley. We don't need him meddling in our business. He laughs, gives me a look of disgust and trudges away. I call the cops on him. We have a virus quarantine order in place. They need to do their job.

I see Henry Thoreau. It's late evening. I'm sitting and talking with one of my heroes on his porch at the edge of Walden Pond. The sunset is delightful. As spectacular as a Hawaiian sunset. The chatter of the birds before the sun dove beneath the horizon is astonishing. We hear all this screaming and screeching. Then just an eerie silence. A golden, deafening silence broken ten minutes later by the hoots from a barn owl. I wrote Henry about a year before and said he was the last one left on my 'bucket list' of folks I wanted to visit. He responds, 'Of course. Anytime. Come spend time with me. Stay if you want.' He suggests three days in the Fall when the leaves are turning color. I agree and stay three days. It's long enough. I didn't want to overstay and 'smell like fish.' He's disappointed. I got 'to live deliberately and face(d) only the essential facts of life' with Thoreau and enjoyed his New England *ho'okipa* (hospitality) and *aloha* (warmth). A visit, I will forever remember.

I see my grandpa, my Tutu-man. I drop in on him before Little League practice. He's happy to see me but he doesn't waste any time telling me, he's going to catch that 'son of a bitch,' Butchie, James, our cousin across the street. I ask him, 'Why? What's wrong?' 'Because that little ...t broke all the eggs my chickens laid this morning. And he picked most of the figs on my trees and fed them to the ducks. That little 'son of a bitch.' After he settles down, he asks me if I want to hear him play a song on the piano. It's a good way to prepare myself for baseball practice, to calm my nerves. I want to tell him. It's he who needs to calm his nerves. But I know better when to employ my 'wise ass' self. 'Of course. Tutu- man, I didn't know you play the piano!' 'Been playing twenty years now, Robber. Getting better and better. Stand over there and keep an eye on that thief.' He gets up from his rocker. Plops himself at the piano and plays, Waltzing Matilda. 'Robber, how about The Yellow Rose of Texas?' 'Sure.' I'm ga ga eyed. I had no idea it was a roller playing the piano. He was faking it. Playing me for a fool. I see my mom and my dad. Our dad is pleading, begging her not to take him back to the hospital. She's telling him, it's best for him and best for us. God will give us a miracle, she assures, promises him. He will get better. It's not his time. He's not convinced. But she does not budge. I wake up in the middle of their bickering, perspiring and shaking from fright. I go to the bathroom, dry myself off with a towel, drink a glass of water. I look into the living room. Kathy is fast asleep in front of the TV. I turn the TV off and put a blanket over her. I return to bed and fall asleep. SIRI wakes me up at 0430, two hours later. Time to rise and shine. It's another day in Waimea I Ka La'i.